EXIT STAGE LEFT

EXIT STAGE LEFT

A Brock and Poole mystery

Graham Ison

This first world edition published 2015
in Great Britain and the USA by
SEVERN HOUSE PUBLISHERS LTD of
19 Cedar Road, Sutton, Surrey, England, SM2 5DA.
Trade paperback edition first published
in Great Britain and the USA 2015 by
SEVERN HOUSE PUBLISHERS LTD.

British Library Cataloguing in Publication Data

Ison, Graham author.
  Exit Stage Left.
  1. Brock, Harry (Fictitious character : Ison)–Fiction.
  2. Poole, Dave (Fictitious character)–Fiction.
  3. Murder–Investigation–Fiction. 4. Actors–Death–
  Fiction. 5. Police–England–London–Fiction.
  6. Detective and mystery stories.
  I. Title
  823.9'14-dc23

ISBN-13: 978-0-7278-8484-8 (cased)
ISBN-13: 978-1-84751-587-2 (trade paper)
ISBN-13: 978-1-78010-636-6 (e-book)

Typeset by Palimpsest Book Production Ltd.,
Falkirk, Stirlingshire, Scotland.
Printed digitally in the USA.

PROLOGUE

I t was half-past midnight on a Tuesday morning in February as Lancelot Foley strolled along a deserted Freshbrook Street in London's Chelsea.

Freshbrook Street was a one-way street, and every night Foley would dismiss the taxi at the end of the road and walk the short distance to the door of the house where he was now living. To be taken round the one-way system, so that he could be set down at the front door, would cost an extra one pound and fifty pence – and although he was very well off, thanks to the legacy of a wealthy father, he was parsimonious.

On this particular night, taking the short walk would prove to be an extremely unwise decision.

Lancelot Foley, elegantly attired in a brown fedora and a brown single-breasted Ulster overcoat complete with cape, swung a silver-topped walking stick in his right kid-gloved hand as he walked. His apparel, more in keeping with the Victorian age, was a misconceived affectation that he believed enhanced his image as a West End stage actor of some renown. He was widely regarded as raffish and egotistical, even by his circle of friends – which, unsurprisingly, was rather small. Now in his late thirties, regular visits to his personal trainer at the gym in Fulham ensured that he kept his tall slim figure in good shape.

Currently appearing in a revival of Oscar Wilde's *The Importance of Being Earnest* at the Clarence Theatre, Foley played the languid poseur Algernon Moncrieff, a part that closely mirrored his own character. The role required him to have a moustache, but disinclined to wear a false one – and being put to the chore of applying it for each performance and removing it afterwards – he had grown one.

Foley could easily have afforded a Rolls Royce and employed a chauffeur to take him home each night. His father had made a fortune buying goods in quantity and selling them

at a minimal profit. His view was that it was better to sell a
hundred items at a penny profit than to sell forty-nine at two
pence profit. He began his trading career with a market stall
in Huddersfield and would buy anything that was saleable. By
the end of his life, he owned a chain of shops which, when
they were sold, realized some ten million pounds, which he
bequeathed to his son.

Young Lancelot had invested wisely, and that meant that
together with his earnings as an actor he was now worth
something in the region of fifteen million pounds. Those who
knew him, though, often said that he was the sort of man who
would enjoy Charles Dickens's *A Christmas Carol* but would
be disappointed in the ending.

It had started to snow nearly two hours earlier, at about the
time Lancelot Foley was leaving the theatre, but he was
impervious to the weather; in fact, he was in the best of spirits
and was actually whistling as he approached the roadworks.
He had almost reached the apartment of his current mistress
Jane Lawless, a few yards further along the road, when the
shadowy figure of a man emerged from a darkened doorway.

The man was aged about forty, perhaps just a shade less
than six-foot tall, and was well-built, strong and fit. He had
piercing blue eyes, which gazed out at the world with deep
cynicism, and a strong cleft-chin, upon the right side of which
was a two-inch-long scar. He wore a knee-length dark coat
with a hood that effectively shielded his identity from any
casual passer-by and rubber-soled shoes that muffled any
sound. But at that hour the street was empty, apart from the
man and Foley and the snow, and the cars parked nose to tail.

Moving stealthily, unseen and unheard, the man approached
Foley from behind just as the two of them drew parallel with
the roadworks. With a skill and speed that came only from
intensive training, he gripped Foley's head, twisted it sharply
and broke his neck. Catching the body of his lifeless victim
as it was falling to the ground, the assailant effortlessly threw
it over the barrier and into the excavation. With a similarly
casual indifference to the crime he had just committed, he
picked up Foley's fedora and walking stick, tossed them after
him, and disappeared into the night. He had not uttered a

single word. One moment Foley was alive; seconds later he was dead.

His mission accomplished, the mysterious killer made his way to his house in Romford. In order that his movements, if anyone were interested, would be more difficult to trace, he used several different modes of transport to reach the street where he had parked his car. He arrived at Romford at a little after three that same morning and was admitted by one of his trusted employees, who had waited up for his boss's return.

It was still dark at ten minutes to eight the following morning, and the red lights around the excavation in Freshbrook Street were still illuminated. It was freezing cold, and the falling snow that had not ceased all night was now about six inches deep in places. A bitter wind had drifted it against walls and the parked cars of residents and into the basement areas of the houses, but the footsteps of pedestrians on their way to catch a bus, a train or to find a cab had created a dirty, slippery slush on the pavement.

Two workmen, cursing the inclement weather, began to unload pickaxes and shovels from their truck. One of the men, cold despite his windproof high-visibility jacket, removed one of the barriers, seized a shovel in his calloused hands and carefully descended into the shallow excavation. 'Better get on with it, then. With any luck we'll finish today,' he said, and began to shovel snow out of the ditch. But he hadn't shifted more than two or three inches when he scrambled quickly out of the hole that he and his mate had dug the day before.

'What's up, Griff?' asked his companion, noting the shocked expression on his colleague's white face. 'Seen a ghost?'

'There's a body down there, Frank, that's what's up.' Griff retreated a few more paces.

'It's too early in the morning for your bloody wind-ups,' said Frank, aware that his colleague had a penchant for practical jokes. 'Who'd leave a body down a hole except a gravedigger?' He stepped across and peered down into the excavation. 'Bloody hell, you're right.'

'Get on your mobile, Frank, and call the bleedin' law,' said Griff. 'I reckon someone's done for this bloke.'

A passing pedestrian had heard Griff's comment and stopped to stare into the hole. Within seconds a small crowd had gathered, gawping at the body and discussing the macabre scene with each other, but it was at least twenty minutes before a police car arrived in the street. Not wishing to endanger his vehicle or himself on the treacherous roads, the officer had driven cautiously from Chelsea police station. After all, he'd been told that it was a *dead* body, so there was no rush.

Leaving the vehicle's blue-light bar switched on, the constable ambled across to the scene of what the police call an 'incident'. He didn't bother to don his cap because these days no one cared whether he was properly dressed or not. 'Someone found a body, squire?' he asked one of the two workmen, as if such an occurrence was an everyday happening.

'Yeah, me, Officer,' said Griff, and pointed down into the excavation.

The policeman stepped forward and gazed at the outline of a clothed body. It was just visible, but the continuing snow threatened to cover it again. 'I reckon you're right. Looks like a drunk who fell down there last night.'

'I don't think so,' said Griff. 'There was barriers all round it, and we'd switched on the lamps like the law says we has to.'

'Yeah, maybe.' The PC turned back to face the two men. 'Have you guys got a tarpaulin on your truck?'

'Yeah, should have,' said Frank.

'Good. Better chuck it over the body until the CID gets here.' The PC knew all about preserving a crime scene, although he wasn't certain that throwing a tarpaulin over a dead body was the right thing to do. Come to that, he wasn't too sure it was a crime scene anyway. But, he thought, better to be on the safe side. He'd fallen foul of the local detective chief inspector before and had no desire to do so again.

'Right,' said Frank. 'Here, Griff, bring that tarp over here and give us a hand to do what the copper says.'

'What are you supposed to be doing here, anyway?' The PC burrowed inside his voluminous jacket, eventually found an incident report book and began scribbling a few notes in it.

'Sorting out a busted sewage pipe, guv,' said Griff, 'but I doubt if we'll finish it today, not now. Not with all this. If your blokes can shut the M25 for a day because of an accident, Gawd knows how long this'll take.'

'Yeah, I reckon you're right, mate. Better have your names and addresses, just for the record.' The PC took the workmen's details and returned to his car to make a call.

Fifteen minutes later the detective chief inspector from Chelsea police station arrived, together with a detective sergeant. After a brief conversation with the two workmen to determine where the barriers had been before they'd moved them, the DCI decided that the dead man could not have fallen down the hole accidentally; it was undoubtedly a suspicious death with which he was dealing. He put up a call for a pathologist and a scenes-of-crime unit. While he was awaiting their arrival, he summoned a traffic unit and directed the crew to close the road and put in diversions. The familiar blue and white tapes were strung around the excavation and across the footway while other officers erected a tent over the crime scene and the pavement.

'Like I said, this is going to take all day,' said Griff mournfully.

'And the rest, squire,' said the PC.

Linda Mitchell, a senior forensic practitioner, arrived thirty minutes later, together with her evidence recovery unit. Five minutes after that, Dr Henry Mortlock, a Home Office patholo-gist, arrived and spent a few minutes in the hole examining the corpse.

Four policemen then descended into the excavation, removed the tarpaulin and lifted the body on to a portable examination table that Linda Mitchell's team had brought with them.

Dr Mortlock conducted a further examination of the corpse, took its temperature and dictated his findings into a pocket recorder. 'This man's been murdered, Chief Inspector. His neck has been broken,' he announced to the local DCI. 'At a rough guess, I'd say that he was the victim of someone familiar with martial arts.'

'Bugger it!' said the DCI, and radioed for a detective inspector from the Homicide Investigation Team that patrolled constantly for the sole purpose of assessing situations such as this one.

The HAT DI, as he was known, weighed up the situation very quickly and decided it was a case for the Homicide and Major Crime Command.

ONE

Having spent last night with my girlfriend at her Kingston town house, I'd travelled to work by train today instead of using my car. I arrived at Waterloo railway station and was about to descend to the depths of the Underground station to catch the tube train to Victoria when my mobile vibrated in my inside pocket. 'Hello?'

'Mr Brock?'

'I can't hear you properly. Some idiot's broadcasting incomprehensible rubbish on the tannoy. Just a minute.' Pushing my way between coffee-carrying, mobile-phone-using commuters, I moved into the archway next to Costa's coffee shop. 'OK, that's better. Go ahead.'

'Mr Brock?'

'Yes?'

'It's Colin Wilberforce in the incident room, sir. I've been trying to get you for some time.'

'I was on the train, and the signal's always poor. Anyway, what is it, Colin?' I had a bad feeling about this; the only reason that I got a call from Detective Sergeant Wilberforce at this time of the morning was that somewhere there was a dead body that required my expert attention.

'Freshbrook Street, Chelsea, sir. A couple of workmen found a dead body in an excavation there. Local police are on scene, and the HAT DI has assessed it as a murder and one for us.'

The HAT DI's job is to evaluate suspicious deaths that might be too complicated or lengthy for the local CID. He'd obviously decided that this was such a case. 'Go on,' I said.

'I've alerted DI Ebdon, Dave Poole and the team, and I understand that Doctor Mortlock and an evidence recovery unit are already at the scene.'

'You've made my day, Colin,' I said sarcastically, and terminated the call. It was just my luck to get the murder of someone found in a hole on a freezing cold, snowy February morning.

Why don't I ever get a civilized murder of an elegant blonde draped decorously on the floor of the library up at a centrally-heated manor house?

There was a queue a mile long waiting for taxis at the station cab rank. Instead of joining it, I pulled up the collar of my Barbour jacket and walked out to York Road in the vain hope of finding a taxi during the morning rush hour. However, I was lucky enough to sight a police traffic car. I stepped into the road and waved it down.

'What's your problem, mate?' enquired the radio operator, opening the window just enough for us to hear each other.

'I'm Detective Chief Inspector Brock of Homicide and Major Crime Command,' I said, producing my warrant card, 'and my problem, as you put it, is a murder in Freshbrook Street.'

'Sorry, guv. Thought you were a mad member of the public who loves policemen. Hop in.'

I just managed to get the door closed before the driver accelerated away, carving his way through the traffic with wailing siren and blue lights.

Freshbrook Street was about three miles away, but despite the awful weather my intrepid driver managed it in less than five minutes. Just long enough for me to offer up a prayer beseeching the Almighty to preserve me from an instant and painful death. But as I'm not at all religious, my prayer probably went automatically into junk mail.

A miserable inspector clutching a wet clipboard announced himself as the incident officer and demanded my particulars.

'DCI Brock, HMCC Murder Investigation Team.'

'Thank you, sir,' said the inspector, blowing on his hands before making a few notes. 'The body's in the tent, and some of your people are in the mobile police station over there.' He pointed at a trailer parked near the scene of the crime. Having provided me with the requisite logistics he finally allowed me through the tapes.

'I'm DCI Harry Brock, HMCC,' I said as I approached a man dressed in a duffel coat, a scarf and a flat cap.

'Jack Noble, guv. I'm the HAT DI. Your team's here already. So is Doctor Mortlock.'

'What's the SP, Jack?' I asked, using a bit of terminology

that CID officers had appropriated from the racing fraternity. But in our case it was shorthand to discover what was known so far.

'Dr Mortlock reckons someone broke your victim's neck, after which it looks as though he was chucked in the hole.'

'Where is Dr Mortlock?' I was surprised that the deceptively lethargic pathologist had arrived so quickly, but then I remembered that he lived in Chelsea.

'With the Metropolitan Police camping club, guv,' said Noble with a grin, and pointed at the tent.

'Would be, I suppose,' I said, and crossed to the canvas structure. 'Good morning, Henry.'

'There's nothing bloody good about it, Harry,' said Mortlock, with a brief glance in my direction. 'I'll be finished in just a minute.'

In all the years that Henry Mortlock and I had conversed over dead bodies, I'd never really learned much about him. I knew he played golf and had a predilection for classical music, frequently humming excerpts from operas and, on occasion, actually singing the odd verse or two. I also knew that he was married, but had he any children? I'd never asked.

Now, with a few moments to spare, I looked at Henry the man rather than Mortlock the pathologist. He was avuncular in bearing, rather short, maybe five-six or five-seven, and rotund of stature. His old-fashioned wire-rimmed spectacles seemed to be a part of his rounded face, as did his battered homburg hat, as though he'd been born wearing them. His appearance, that of the friendly family doctor of my youth, was countered by the occasional flash of anger when those with whom he was obliged to deal failed to follow his scientific pronouncements. He also had an acerbic wit, but that perhaps was the result of dealing with cynical coppers like me. Or perhaps it was the other way round.

'What can you tell me?' I asked, when eventually Mortlock gave me his attention.

'As I told the local chap, I reckon the deceased was the victim of a martial arts expert, Harry. Probably crept up on him, twisted his head and broke his neck.' Mortlock flicked his fingers. 'Just like that.'

'Any idea of the time of death?'

'Difficult to say. I'd think that he's been in that hole for some time, and the snow and the ambient temperature throws everything to pot, but I'd guess a good nine to twelve hours,' said Mortlock, and followed it with his standard announcement: 'I'll be able to tell you more when I get him on the slab.'

'Do we know who he is?' I asked.

He looked at me with an expression of sympathy as though I'd just asked a stupid question. 'I've no idea, Harry, but that's your job. I'll tell you what killed him. The rest is up to you.'

'Thanks a bundle.' I gathered that Mortlock was in one of his curmudgeonly moods and left it at that. He wandered off humming something from Puccini's *Turandot*. At least, I think that's what it was.

'Morning, guv.' Detective Sergeant Dave Poole, my trusty bag-carrier, ambled across the road, hands in the pockets of his sheepskin coat. Dave's nonchalant attitude is deceptive, as many a villain has discovered to his cost. In reality, he is a very astute detective and one of the best I've ever had working with me. Although of Caribbean origin, he was born in the Bethnal Green area of London's East End. His grandfather had been a medical doctor, and Dave's father is a chartered accountant. Dave graduated in English from London University, and for some reason I could never understand he decided to join the Metropolitan Police, as a result of which he frequently refers to himself as the black sheep of the family, a comment that disconcerts our politically correct hierarchy.

'Do we know who this guy is, Dave?'

'Linda Mitchell went through his belongings, guv. His name's Lancelot Foley, and he's got a wallet stuffed full of credit cards and a membership card for Equity, the actors' union. There's also a hundred quid in cash.'

'So, robbery wasn't the motive,' I said.

'No, sir,' said Dave. He always calls me 'sir' whenever I make a fatuous comment. It's his way of saying that I've just stated the obvious.

'Is there any indication as to where he lives?'

'His driving licence shows an address in Farnham in Surrey.' Dave handed me the document.

'Terrific! What the hell is he doing in a hole in Freshbrook Street, then?'

'Playing dead, guv? However, given that he's got an Equity card, I suspect he might've been appearing in a play of some sort in London. Or maybe he was recording something for television.'

'I'll get Miss Ebdon to follow that up. Where is she?'

'Organizing house-to-house enquiries, not that I think she'll have much luck. With this weather I'd think all the locals were in the warm with the curtains drawn at the time of the murder.'

'Who's Miss Ebdon got with her?'

'Charlie Flynn and John Appleby, guv.'

'See if you can find her, Dave, and ask her to see me. We can leave Charlie Flynn to take over running the house-to-house.'

It took me a moment or two to recognize Kate Ebdon when she entered the trailer that was the centre of our operations. She was wearing a fur Cossack hat, a quilted jacket and knee-length boots over her jeans. Around the office she was usually attired in tight-fitting jeans and a man's white shirt, a mode of dress that somewhat alarmed our commander. But no one else complained – not the men anyway – because her outfit accentuated her five-foot nine curvaceous figure.

A flame-haired Australian, Kate had been born and brought up in Port Douglas in Queensland. She described it as an idyllic place in which to be raised, and often spoke quite without embarrassment of the times she'd spent skinny-dipping in the Coral Sea. Arriving in England at the age of seventeen she had made brief forays into advertising and hospital administration, until finally settling for a career in the Job.

As a detective, she'd served in London's East End before graduating to the Flying Squad as a sergeant. Somewhere along the way she'd acquired a black belt in judo, and I had once seen her put a six-foot muscle-bound villain on his back with what seemed little more than a flick of her wrist. Now in her early thirties and a detective inspector in Homicide and Major Crime Command, she was one of the best homicide investigators I'd ever had the privilege of working with. As an interrogator, she had the ability to charm men and terrify women. Or the other way round if the circumstances demanded it.

'Any joy with the house-to-house, Kate?'

'Exactly what you'd expect, guv. No one saw a thing. So far, anyway. There are a few more houses to check, but I don't hold out much hope.'

'That reckons,' I said. 'The victim is a Lancelot Foley, an actor, apparently, and—'

'Yes, he is,' said Kate. 'He's appearing at the Clarence Theatre in *The Importance of Being Earnest.*'

'How did you find that out so quickly, Kate?'

'I could say that it was my superior detective ability,' said Kate, smiling, 'but my date took me to see the play last week. Foley's wife Debra is in it too. She appears under the stage name of Vanessa Drummond.'

'Your date?' This was the first I'd heard about Kate having any kind of relationship. There were rumours that she'd given pleasure to a few of her male colleagues on the Flying Squad – and that was put down to canteen scuttlebutt – but never mention of any sort of a social liaison.

'Women do occasionally go out with men,' said Kate sharply. 'It's a well-documented fact, sir.'

Kate only rarely called me 'sir' – I think she'd got the idea from Dave – and I took it as a warning that I should mind my own business.

'We'd better get round to the theatre and see what we can find out,' I said.

TWO

We left our car at West End Central police station at the end of Savile Row and took a taxi into the heart of theatreland. It is a well known fact that these days villains are not above stealing police cars left carelessly in the street. To put the police logbook on the dashboard may prevent the issue of a ticket from an enthusiastic traffic warden, but it is an open invitation to any passing low-life to do a bit of opportunistic thieving. And to score one off the Old Bill into the bargain.

The Clarence Theatre had the slightly seedy appearance to be expected of a building erected in the late nineteenth century. London's grime had taken its toll on the brickwork, and there were one or two places that showed a clear need for repointing. The small windows high up on the front of the building were dirty, though you wouldn't notice this lack of care once the lights went on. It was, however, no different from the other theatres of its age. The billboards advertised Oscar Wilde's *The Importance of Being Earnest* and prominently displayed the names of Lancelot Foley and Vanessa Drummond together with their photographs.

'It looks as though Foley's understudy is about to get his big chance,' I said as Kate and I entered the theatre.

A young woman in dirty jeans and an equally dirty T-shirt was towing an industrial vacuum cleaner listlessly across the carpet of the foyer. She paused to take the cigarette out of her mouth. 'The box office ain't open till two o'clock,' she said.

'It's against the law to smoke in here,' said Kate.

'What are you lot, then, 'ealth and safety?' The woman shot Kate a surly glance.

'No, police,' said Kate. 'Where's the manager's office?'

'Up them stairs.' The woman pointed at a door, carried on smoking and returned to her vacuuming.

The manager looked up as we entered his office, his expression possibly one of pleasure at an unforeseen interruption in what must otherwise be a mundane existence. 'Ah! We have visitors,' he said, as though addressing an invisible partner.

The office was a cramped room with an air of mustiness and decay that matched the age of the theatre. Its walls were adorned with playbills of productions long gone, as though the theatre was attempting to cling to its illustrious past. Behind a desk laden with paperwork sat a portly man probably approaching sixty. His hair, despite it being unsuitable for a man of his age, hung over his collar as if he were attempting to emulate a Shakespearian actor. His loud pinstriped suit included a waistcoat that appeared ready to burst open at its straining buttons, a spotted bow tie and a white carnation in the buttonhole. Finger-marked horn-rimmed spectacles, tipped forward on his nose, completed the picture of a flamboyant theatrical character, the type of which I thought no longer existed. I wondered if, years ago, he had been an actor and now found himself with nowhere else to go but the management of an ageing theatre.

'I'm Detective Chief Inspector Harry Brock of the Murder Investigation Team at Scotland Yard, and this is Detective Inspector Ebdon. Are you the manager?' It seemed an unnecessary question seeing that his door bore a sign inscribed with the word 'Manager', but over the years I've discovered that nothing is ever as it seems.

'Yes, indeed. Sebastian Weaver at your service, my dear sir. What seems to be the trouble? Don't tell me that "a murder has been arranged",' he said, deliberately using the title of one of Emlyn Williams's best known plays. Raising his bushy eyebrows in a burlesque of the great George Robey, he made the enquiry sound like a joke as he skirted his desk and shook hands.

'It may not have been arranged,' I said, 'but it's certainly occurred, and it's one that's not likely to afford you any comfort, Mr Weaver. It concerns Lancelot Foley.'

'Lancelot Foley? He's not murdered someone, surely?' Weaver emitted a great belly laugh that developed into a smoker's cough, putting further strain on his waistcoat buttons. He waved a hand at a couple of uncomfortable chairs. 'Take a seat, my dears,' he croaked, still half coughing and wheezing.

'Lancelot Foley's the one who's been murdered, Mr Weaver.'

'Hell's bells and buckets of blood! But he's due on stage at half-past seven this evening. Thank God there's not a matinee today.' The false bonhomie vanished in an instant, and Weaver became immediately anguished. 'What the hell am I going to do now?' He returned to the sanctuary of his desk and collapsed into his chair like a hot-air balloon that had suddenly and unaccountably deflated. It was as though this disastrous event was too much for his unhealthy physique. Plucking a voluminous red handkerchief from his top pocket, he began to clean his spectacles.

'Presumably he has an understudy,' said Kate helpfully, not appreciating that Weaver's question was a rhetorical one.

'Yes, of course he has, but the man's bloody useless. Lancelot's the one who puts bums on seats. He'll never match Henry Irving or the late, much lamented Larry Olivier of course, but he does his best. Or did, I suppose I should say.' Weaver perched his spectacles back on his nose, pocketed his handkerchief and glared at me as though Foley's untimely death was my fault. 'Where did this happen?'

'Freshbrook Street in Chelsea, late last night or early this morning,' said Kate.

'How very interesting! Was he murdered in his tart's flat, then, Inspector?'

'No, he appears to have been murdered in the street. His body was found in an excavation.'

'Christ Almighty!' exclaimed Weaver. 'Trust Lancelot to go out on a high.' He started to polish his spectacles again. 'He could always be relied on for a spectacular encore, could Lancelot.'

'This woman friend you mentioned,' I said. 'From what you say, I take it she lives in Freshbrook Street.'

'Yes. That's why I asked if he'd been murdered at her place. But I don't know whereabouts in Freshbrook Street she lives.'

'Do you at least know her name?'

'Yes, it's Jane Lawless. She's in the profession too. Mind you, knowing Lancelot, he might've picked up with another bird by now.'

'Is this Jane Lawless appearing in the same play as Foley?' I asked, not having noticed her name on the billboards.

'No, she's resting at the moment.'

I knew from conversations with my girlfriend, Gail Sutton, who is also in 'the profession', that 'resting' was a euphemism for unemployed.

A sudden thought occurred to Weaver. 'Has his wife been told?'

'You're talking about Debra Foley, I presume.' Kate was making sure, as all good detectives should, but she'd told me earlier that Debra was Lancelot's wife and that her stage name was Vanessa Drummond. 'And she's playing opposite her husband, I believe.'

'That's right,' said Weaver. 'Mind you, she's grievously miscast in the role of the Honourable Gwendolen Fairfax. She's far too big a girl to play the part, and the fact that she's supposed to be Lady Bracknell's daughter is, not to put too fine a point on it, ludicrous. I know it's a comedy, but the audience isn't supposed to laugh at the actors, but rather to laugh at the lines they speak.'

'The only address we have for Lancelot Foley is in Farnham, Surrey,' I said, 'but I imagine that he and his wife have theatrical digs somewhere in London. D'you have a London address for them?'

'Hang on a second. My contacts book is here somewhere.' Weaver shifted piles of paperwork about, eventually uncovering a worn book with Post-it notes sticking out at intervals. 'Yes, here we are,' he said, thumbing through the dog-eared pages. 'They live together—' He broke off and chuckled. 'I should have said they *did* live together. Now, let me see. Ah, yes, here we are,' he repeated. 'They actually own a house in Chorley Street, but that was before the row. I don't know which of them moved out, but I suppose she's still there as Lancelot was shacked up with Jane.'

'What's the exact address, Mr Weaver?' asked Kate, taking her pocketbook from her coat pocket.

Weaver handed Kate his contacts book and pointed a podgy finger at the entry. 'I think they were only living there while this run is on,' he continued. 'When they're resting they live at the Farnham address you mentioned and let the Chorley Street house to other theatricals.'

'You said just now that the Foleys lived together until the row, Mr Weaver,' said Kate. 'D'you know what the row was about? Was this Jane Lawless the cause of it, d'you know?'

'I've no idea, but I don't think Lancelot moved in with Jane until after the bust-up with his wife.'

'When we told you that Lancelot Foley had been murdered in Freshbrook Street, you asked if it was at Jane Lawless's flat.'

'That's right,' said Weaver.

'Did you think it possible that Jane Lawless murdered him?'

'Good heavens, no,' said Weaver. 'The thought never crossed my mind.'

'I think that's all for the moment, Mr Weaver,' I said, 'but we may need to see you again at some later date.'

'Yes, I suppose you will.' Weaver spoke in a distracted sort of way, his mind obviously pondering the crisis with which he was now faced. He took out his handkerchief and began to polish his spectacles again.

We left the unhappy manager to deal with his problems, and as I closed his office door I heard him on the phone telling someone to take down the billboards. 'No, you idiot boy, not tomorrow. Right now.'

We drove out to Chorley Street, a turning off Belgrave Square where, we had been told by Weaver, Debra Foley occupied a four-storey town house. I rang the bell on the intercom and waited for quite some time. We were on the point of leaving when a sleepy voice answered.

'Who is it?'

'Mrs Foley?' I asked.

'Yes, what d'you want?'

'We're police officers, Mrs Foley.'

'Oh God! What now?' The lock buzzed. 'I'm in the sitting room on the first floor. Come on up.'

Debra Foley was standing at the top of the stairs, and when I drew level with her I realized that she was only slightly shorter than me, and I'm over six-foot tall. As Weaver had said, she was a big girl, although buxom would be a more complimentary way of describing a woman who was over-weight. Nevertheless, with her sensuous lips, long wavy blonde hair that cascaded around her shoulders, wide hips and full bosom, she possessed a compelling sexual allure. For some inexplicable reason – my knowledge of Gail, I suppose – I imagined all actresses to be slender, but this woman was adequately covered. I guessed that she had yet to celebrate her thirtieth birthday.

'You'd better come in, I suppose,' said Debra wearily, and led the way into the sitting room. It appeared that our arrival had dragged her from her bed, but being an actress, I suppose that was to be expected. Her black satin peignoir was ankle-length and revealed bare feet. 'And how can I help the police?' she asked, an enquiring expression on her face.

'I'm Detective Chief Inspector Brock, Mrs Foley,' I said, 'and this is Detective Inspector Ebdon. It might be as well if you were to sit down.'

'I hope this isn't going to take long. I've got to shower and get dressed. I've an appointment this afternoon.' The actress lowered herself elegantly into an armchair, carefully arranged the skirt of her peignoir, and vaguely waved a hand at the sofa opposite. It was all very studied, as though she were acting a part. *But let's see how you perform when you hear what I've got to say*, I thought.

'It concerns your husband, Mrs Foley,' I said tentatively as Kate and I sat down.

'Oh? What's Lancelot been up to now?'

This was the task that all police officers hate the most. No matter how the subject is broached or what words are used in an attempt to cushion it, it eventually comes down to a bald statement of fact. 'I'm sorry to have to tell you that he's been murdered.'

'Oh Christ!' exclaimed Debra. 'That'll put the kibosh on the play. His understudy's useless and is always corpsing. Personally, I'd have thought that everyone in the profession would have known *The Importance of Being Earnest* word perfect by now. The damned play's been performed often enough. It's unbelievably tiresome having to keep whispering his first lines to him,' she said airily. 'They really should give him a radio earphone so that he can be fed his lines, but the producer is unbelievably stingy. A prompt-box would be better than nothing, but we haven't even got that.'

Of all the reactions to news of the violent death of a spouse, this was the most bizarre and callous I had ever heard. I have to admit that I was lost for words, but I did wonder if she'd already learned of her husband's death and was putting on a bravura performance to cover her grief. However, her next utterance disabused me of that thought.

'Don't look so surprised, Chief Inspector.' Debra shot me a fetching actress-like smile, the sort she would flash at the rich and famous in the stalls, I imagined. 'Lancelot and I were on the point of divorce. Adultery, unreasonable behaviour and desertion. How's that for a kick-off? You can take your pick. His dying has actually saved a lot of paperwork and the outrageous legal fees that go with it.' She paused. 'On second thoughts,' she continued, 'you can discount desertion: it was me who threw *him* out.'

'We understand that he's in a relationship with a woman called Jane Lawless.' Kate Ebdon could always be relied upon to get to the point, and on this occasion I agreed with her direct approach. I'd already decided that little was to be gained by pussyfooting about with this woman, who showed all the signs of self-indulgence and clearly didn't give a tuppenny cuss about the death of her husband.

'You've been talking to that creep Sebastian Weaver,' said Debra Foley, raising her eyebrows at Kate's strong Australian accent. She leaned across to a side table and took a chocolate from a large open box of Cadbury's Milk Tray.

'We've come straight here from the theatre,' said Kate.

'And when was Lancelot murdered?'

'As far as we can tell, at just after midnight this morning. His body was discovered face down in an excavation in Freshbrook Street.'

'Hah! So he didn't quite make it to his slut's bed,' said

Debra scornfully, and glanced towards the window. 'Like a
dull actor now,' she quoted airily, and seeing Kate's puzzled
expression, added, 'Shakespeare, my dear. *Cymbeline.*'

'What can you tell us about Jane Lawless, Mrs Foley?' I
asked.

'She's an actress who has a reputation for sleeping around
but preferably with her leading men,' said Debra cuttingly.
'But she's resting at the moment. In fact, she's been resting
for so long that I did wonder if she was actually comatose.'
She added the final comment with a measure of undisguised
malice. 'And as she doesn't currently have a leading man to
screw her, I suppose she picked on Lancelot.'

'Do you happen to have this woman's exact address, Mrs
Foley?' I asked.

'You bet I have!' Debra Foley sashayed across the room to
an escritoire and spent a moment or two rummaging through
its contents before scribbling a few lines on the back of an
envelope. 'There you are,' she said, handing it to me. 'Lancelot
had the audacity to ask me to forward any mail that came for
him,' she added as she resumed her seat.

'And did any mail arrive for him?' asked Kate, hoping that
some correspondence might assist us in our investigation.

'A few bits and pieces. I shredded them, of course. I'm not
his bloody secretary.'

'D'you know of anyone who might've wanted to harm Mr
Foley?' It was a routine question, and one that rarely produced
any satisfactory answers, but it had to be asked.

'Quite a few husbands, I should imagine.' Debra leaned
across and, using a finger and thumb, delicately took another
chocolate from the half-empty box. 'He always went for
married women. I think he felt safer with them for some
inexplicable reason. I suppose that if they got pregnant there
was always the husband to carry the can.'

'Is Jane Lawless married, then?' asked Kate.

'I haven't kept up with her current marital status,' Debra
said cattily, and waved a hand in the air. 'She was once, but I've
no idea if it lasted. For all I know they might have divorced.
I seem to recall that she married a sessions drummer a few
years ago. She found him in some sleazy nightclub, but she

dumped him very quickly. Or perhaps he dumped her. If he had any sense he would've done.'

I had quickly come to the conclusion that Debra Foley, young though she was, was an embittered and cynical woman, and although she was playing the part of a wronged wife, I suspected that she, too, may have had a few affairs. She certainly displayed no emotion at the death of her husband, and that made me suspicious. But from what my thespian girlfriend Gail had told me, the acting profession tends to breed a callous disregard for the marriage vows. And as if to confirm my view that she played the field, at that moment Debra adjusted her position slightly so that the skirt of her peignoir fell away to reveal a substantial amount of thigh. She made no attempt to replace it, but just glanced at me with a smile.

'One final point, Mrs Foley,' I said. 'Do you have the details of Mr Foley's solicitor?'

'What on earth d'you want that for?'

'Solicitors are often unwitting sources of information about murder victims,' I said airily. What I didn't say was that I was interested to know who would be the beneficiary of Lancelot Foley's will. I had a vague and unwarranted suspicion that it wasn't going to be his estranged wife. But the beneficiary might just be the killer.

'He's my solicitor as well.' Crossing once more to her escritoire, Debra Foley scribbled the details on a piece of paper and handed it to me, pausing on the way back to put another chocolate in her mouth.

'Thank you, Mrs Foley,' I said as Kate and I prepared to leave. 'I'll let you know when the coroner has released Mr Foley's body for the funeral.'

'Thank you so much, Chief Inspector.' But the sarcastically offhand way in which Debra said it left me in no doubt that she wasn't in the slightest interested. It was as though Lancelot Foley was already a past chapter in her life and even the final chapter in the book.

Having had not even a cup of tea since my scratch breakfast, I decided that lunch had become a necessity.

'D'you like Italian food, Kate?'

*   *   *

We drove the short distance to my favourite Italian restaurant in Pimlico and were fortunate enough to be able to park the car right outside. I took a chance on there being no thieves about.

The owner, an amiable Neapolitan named Luigi, bustled across the room hand outstretched, solicitous to the point of being oleaginous. Slim and swarthy with long hair and carefully cultivated stubble, he had all the charm of his race, but even so managed to convey the impression of being a reformed Mafioso. He was, however, a very good restaurateur.

'Ah, *Signor* Brock, long time no see, as the Pope said to the Archbishop of Canterbury.' Luigi cast an appraising glance at Kate. 'And you have a pretty *signorina* with you today. Allow me, *Signorina*,' he added as Kate divested herself of her fur hat and quilted jacket.

'Just you be careful, Luigi. No bottom-pinching,' I said, with mock severity. 'This young lady is a detective inspector, and she'll have you in handcuffs before you can say *santa madre*.'

'Ah! It would be a pleasure to be handcuffed by one so young and so beautiful,' exclaimed Luigi, quite unimpressed that Kate was a police officer. 'You must be very talented, *Signorina*.' Without further ado, he escorted us to a discreet table in the far corner of the room.

'Well, what did you make of Debra Foley, Kate?' I asked, once we had made our selection from the menu.

'She's one callous bitch, and despite playing the innocent, I'll bet she doesn't have a chastity belt in her wardrobe,' said Kate. '*And* I noticed that she made a point of flashing her legs at you.'

'But you have to admit they were shapely, Kate.'

'She's fat.' Kate dismissed Debra's blatant attempt at seduction with a wave of the hand. 'And she obviously didn't give a damn about the death of her husband.'

'She certainly seemed to be more concerned about whether the play would survive. Perhaps she doesn't fancy the understudy.'

'She's bound to if he wears trousers,' said Kate crushingly.

'I take it you didn't like her,' I said as Luigi brought our meals.

'I think that about sums it up, guv.'

'Is she a good actress, Kate? You said you saw the play.'

'I suppose so. It's not really my sort of thing. I prefer musicals, but my date wanted to see it and I went along with it.' Kate paused and looked apologetic. 'I'm sorry if I sounded a bit sharp earlier on, but I'm not really an early morning sort of person.'

'I can't say I noticed,' I replied diplomatically. I had noticed Kate's short retort, of course, the more so because she's normally very amiable.

Kate took a sip of her mineral water. 'The guy who took me was just someone I met at the gym who asked me to dinner and the theatre. There won't be a repeat performance. Of our meeting, I mean.'

'You don't have to explain, Kate.' I wished she hadn't raised the subject. 'Your private life is nothing to do with me or the Job.'

'It was the Job that was the trouble, guv. He's in IT, and he thinks that the world begins and ends on a computer screen. Not my sort of bloke at all. In fact, he was a bloody ocker, and I finished up telling him so.'

I was slowly learning Australian, or Strian as Kate sometimes called it, but the meaning of the word ocker deluded me.

'A loudmouth, guv,' explained Kate, seeing my puzzled expression. 'He was going on the whole time about his bloody car and his golf handicap. I don't know why I ever accepted his invitation.' She hesitated. 'A copper should only go out with another copper. They understand each other.'

She had a point. There were times when my relationship with Gail was not as smooth as it should have been. She did not always understand that police duty took precedence over social arrangements, and similarly I found it hard to accept that Gail hankered for a return to her life in the theatre, with the unsocial hours that that would entail. She'd had several offers, but had turned them down, describing them as unworthy of her talents.

When I'd queried why she had been a chorus girl when I met her, she claimed that her ex-husband, out of sheer spite about the divorce, had deliberately thwarted her efforts to get a good part.

I paid the bill, declining Kate's offer to go halves, and we made our way to Freshbrook Street to interview Jane Lawless.

THREE

We drove the mile or so from Pimlico to Freshbrook Street. The police tapes had been removed, traffic was flowing and the workmen to whom I'd spoken earlier that day were busy in the hole where Lancelot Foley's body had been found. Everything appeared to be back to normal.

The apartment we were seeking was on the first floor of a house only a few yards away from the crime scene.

'Mrs Jane Lawless?' I asked when a woman answered the door.

'Yes, I'm Jane Lawless.'

'We're police officers, Mrs Lawless.'

'I rather think that you're wasting your time. I told the other policeman who called here this morning that I hadn't seen anything. He was very circumspect in his questions, so I didn't really know what he wanted. What was it all about, anyway? First thing this morning I noticed some policemen putting tapes across the road, but I've no idea what's happened.'

'I'm Detective Chief Inspector Brock, Mrs Lawless, and this is Detective Inspector Ebdon. May we come in?'

'Of course, but as I said just now, I didn't see anything.' Jane Lawless led us into a comfortably furnished sitting room, invited us to sit down and took a seat opposite. 'So I really don't know how I can help you.'

She was an attractively buxom woman, probably around thirty and not unlike Debra Foley in build, including blonde hair that was perfectly straight and long enough to cover her shoulders. In fact she was so much like Debra Foley that it seemed that only women of that stature and colouring were of interest to Lancelot Foley. She wore an emerald green dress that was clearly designed to show off her substantial cleavage, and was short enough to display her shapely legs. High heels and black tights completed the ensemble.

'Are you about to go out, Mrs Lawless?' It appeared to me that we'd caught her just as she was on the point of leaving for an appointment.

'No, not at all.' The answer was curt and dismissive, almost as if I were enquiring into a matter that was none of my business.

'We're investigating a murder that took place here in Freshbrook Street late last night or in the early hours of this morning, Mrs Lawless.'

'So that's what it was all about! I still can't tell you anything, though. The first I knew of it was when—'

'I'm sorry to have to tell you that the victim was an actor named Lancelot Foley,' I said, interrupting bluntly.

'Oh, good God, no! It can't be true.' Jane Lawless paled dramatically and stared at me in disbelief before dissolving into sobs, the tears welling up in her eyes. 'Did you say last night?' she mumbled.

'As far as we can tell. The post-mortem is yet to be carried out. I'm given to understand that you and Mr Foley were in a relationship.'

'Of course we were in a bloody relationship; it's no secret,' snapped Jane vehemently, but she immediately apologized for her outburst. 'I'm sorry, Chief Inspector, but it's come as a terrible shock.' Taking a packet of tissues from her handbag, she used one of them to dab at her eyes, but made no attempt to wipe away her smudged mascara. 'We live together. He was on his way home. I wondered why he didn't arrive. We were going to get married. Oh, it's quite awful.' The sentences were short and staccato and punctuated by further sobs, her breasts heaving with the effort of recovering her breath. 'What happened to him?'

'As far as we can tell he was attacked in the street.'

'Was it a mugging, then?' Jane looked up and stared searchingly at me.

'We don't think so. His credit cards, cash and Rolex wristwatch were still on him when he was found. It would appear that robbery was not the motive. So far we are uncertain why he was killed.'

'But this is absolutely crazy.' She shook her head in disbelief.

'Who would do such a thing? Some sort of psychopath? Why else would Lancelot have been murdered?'

'Our enquiries are at a very early stage, Mrs Lawless,' said Kate, 'but do you know of anyone who might've wanted to harm Mr Foley?'

'Quite a few, I imagine.' Jane Lawless leaned back against the cushions of the armchair, a little more composed now, although the occasional tear trickled unchecked down her face. 'Lancelot wasn't the most likeable of men, I'm afraid. He was arrogant and egotistical. And he was rude and intolerant. He certainly didn't suffer fools, gladly or otherwise. I suppose being at the top of one's profession tends to do that to an actor.' She reached for another tissue. 'But I loved him despite all his faults.'

'I'm sorry to have to ask you personal questions so soon after Mr Foley's death, Mrs Lawless, but any small detail might help,' I said. 'Just now you mentioned marriage, but I understand that Mr Foley was still married. And so are you, I've been led to believe.' I added the last remark tentatively, assuming that Debra Foley was telling the truth when she said that Jane Lawless had been married at some time in the past.

'I was divorced years ago, and Lancelot's getting a divorce,' said Jane tersely, and she paused, running her fingers through her hair. 'I should've said he *was* getting a divorce.' Another compulsive sob followed this correction. 'It was going to be an uphill battle, though. Debra would've fought tooth and nail to prevent losing him, although she'd be more worked up at the prospect of losing his money.'

'We've already spoken to Mrs Foley,' said Kate. 'We rather got the impression that she threw Mr Foley out. At least, that's what she told us.'

I could see what Kate was driving at. If Debra Foley was so worried about her husband's money, why did she throw him out? I thought it more likely that he'd walked out on her.

'Oh, the poor innocent wronged little wife,' said Jane bitterly. 'Of course she'd say that, but the truth of the matter is she led him a dog's life; so much so that he finally left her. Debra didn't give a damn about Lancelot, but she coveted his money and his standing in the profession. The fact that she

was his leading lady in *The Importance of Being Earnest* didn't
help matters either. How she got the part is a mystery, but I
imagine it to have been the old casting couch routine. It still
goes on, you know.'

'Did they often appear opposite each other?' queried Kate.

'No, my dear, not if they could avoid it,' said Jane patroniz-
ingly. 'I'm afraid that their mutual animosity tended to spill
over, even on stage. That's all right when the script calls for
it, but a disaster when it doesn't. Fortunately, the director of
the play they're appearing in at the moment is strong enough
not to put up with any artistic tantrums.'

'Who is the director?' I asked, thinking that he was someone
else I'd have to interview.

'Gerald Andrews,' said Jane.

That was all I needed. My girlfriend Gail had been married
to this very same theatre director, but the marriage had ended
when she returned home to find him in bed with a nude dancer.
I'd met Gail a year or two after her divorce while I was investigating the murder of her friend Patricia Hunter at the Granville
Theatre. Gail and the Hunter girl had been appearing in the chorus
line of a second-rate revue called *Scatterbrain*.

'D'you know where we can find him?' asked Kate, unaware
that Andrews was Gail's ex-husband. In fact, Kate knew little
if anything of my private life.

'I think he has an office in Golden Square, but I don't know
where exactly. It shouldn't be too difficult to find him, though.
You could try *Yellow Pages*, but no doubt the theatre would
have a number for him.'

'Is there anything more you can tell us about Debra Foley,
Mrs Lawless?' I asked. 'I get the impression that you don't
like her very much.'

'I detest the bloody woman,' said Jane. 'More for the way
that she treated poor Lancelot than anything else. Furthermore,
Vanessa Drummond, as she's known on the stage, is only a
very mediocre actress.'

'I thought she was quite good,' said Kate. 'I saw the play
a few nights ago.'

'Did you really?' said Jane, in tones that could only have
been interpreted as criticism of Kate's choice of play – or,

more particularly, of its cast. 'Personally, I think she was very
lucky to get the part, but I think that was more to do with
Gerald Andrews than with her thespian ability.'

'D'you think they had an affair?' asked Kate. 'Andrews and
Debra.'

I think that's very likely, Kate, I thought. *If what Gail told
me about him is true.*

'I wouldn't be at all surprised,' said Jane, lifting her head
in a very superior sort of way. 'As I implied just now, Debra
Foley has a reputation for doing anything that would advance
her career. There was even a rumour doing the rounds that
when she was resting she supplemented her income by entertaining wealthy men about town. And I'm sure you know what
I mean by "entertaining", Chief Inspector.' She glanced at me
and emitted a cynical little laugh.

'D'you know that for a fact, Mrs Lawless?' I asked.

'Of course not, Mr Brock. I've never seen her in flagrante
delicto with a "client", if that's what you're suggesting. But
the theatre is a hotbed of gossip, and it might just be spiteful
backbiting,' she added charitably.

'I believe you are an actress as well, Mrs Lawless.'

'Yes, I am, but I've not done very much of late. Out of
choice, mind you. I'm afraid that late nights at the theatre
six days a week, with matinees on Wednesdays and Saturdays,
can be extremely tiring. Apart from anything else, speaking
the same lines every night week in and week out is incredibly
boring. I'm actually lined up for a part in a television soap,
although I'm sure that Debra would look down her rather
long and pointed nose at such an idea. But at least television
avoids the monotony of rep, and I don't subscribe to the view
that unless you've done Shakespeare you can't really call
yourself an actress. In fact I'm one of those rare actresses
who actually detests the Bard's plays. If someone offered me
the part of Portia in *The Merchant of Venice*, I'd rather starve
than take it.'

'Did Mr Foley happen to leave an address book here, Mrs
Lawless?' I asked.

'Yes, I think he did, but why would you want that?'

'Surprising though it may seem, in an overwhelming number

of murder cases we find that the murderer knew the victim.
It might just be the case with Mr Foley.'

'I see.' Jane Lawless stood up. 'Bear with me for a moment.
If it's anywhere it'll be in the bedroom.' A minute or two later,
she returned and handed me a Filofax. 'That's his diary, and
there's a section with addresses in it.'

'I'll return it in due course, Mrs Lawless,' I said. 'One other
thing: did Mr Foley always arrive home at the same time each
evening?'

'More or less. He always took a taxi from the theatre, and
it dropped him at the end of the road. He always walked the
rest of the way.'

'Is there a reason for that?' asked Kate.

Jane Lawless smiled. 'I suppose you could call it one of
his little quirks, but you'll have noticed that Freshbrook Street
is a one-way street. Lancelot worked it out once that if the
cab dropped him at the door it would cost him one pound fifty
more than being dropped at the end of the road because of
the extra mileage involved going round the one-way system.
It's not that he couldn't afford it, obviously, but he just resented
it.' She paused in thought before saying, 'And it looks as
though it cost him his life.'

'I think that will be all for the moment, Mrs Lawless. But
we may have to see you again, of course.'

'Yes, I quite understand.' As she was showing us out, Jane
Lawless paused with her hand on the edge of the door to her
apartment. 'D'you think you could let me know when
Lancelot's funeral is to take place, Chief Inspector?'

'Of course.' I just hoped that the funeral would not become
an impromptu stage for Jane Lawless and Debra Foley to tear
each other's hair out. Catfights can be extremely vicious,
whereas men just try to knock each other down.

'I think Jane Lawless put her finger on it, Kate,' I said as
we left Freshbrook Street, 'when she said that Lancelot's
parsimony cost him his life. And all for the sake of an extra
one pound fifty on the taximeter.'

'Given that it wasn't a mugging,' said Kate, 'it looks as
though he was murdered by someone who'd studied his

movements and knew about him walking the last few yards to the Lawless woman's house.'

Finally, at five o'clock that evening Kate and I reached Belgravia police station where we had our offices.

A few months ago we'd been moved from Curtis Green in Whitehall to the Empress State Building in Earls Court and had made the mistake of believing that it was to be our permanent base. But we'd counted without the 'funny names and total confusion squad' at New Scotland Yard.

However, the aforementioned squad, which is staffed entirely by boy superintendents – known in the Job as the over-promoted *Wunderkinder* – decided that Belgravia was a more suitable location. With his customary cynicism Dave had advised us that we shouldn't unpack when we got there.

On the plus side Belgravia was by far a more civilized place in which to work; Empress State Building had been out of the way, difficult to get to from central London and overall a damned nuisance.

However, the second move within months had not disconcerted Detective Sergeant Colin Wilberforce, our office manager, who had set up the incident room in the new offices without a single word of complaint. He is an administrative genius and may be relied upon to have the answer to whatever query any of us may pose. But heaven help anyone who interferes with his little empire, including me and the commander. On those rare occasions, his rebuke is similar to that of a Grenadier Guards regimental sergeant major gently admonishing a newly-commissioned subaltern.

Furthermore, Colin seems to have no desire for further promotion, something about which, somewhat selfishly, I am pleased. It is said that no one is indispensable, but in his case I have my doubts. A gentle giant who plays rugby for the Metropolitan Police, and has a cauliflower ear to prove it, he is happily married to Sonia, has three children and lives in Orpington. His spare time, so I've heard, is spent tending his garden.

'All up and running, sir,' he said cheerfully, 'and the commander would like to see you. Oh, and Doctor Mortlock's

secretary rang. Post-mortem's tomorrow morning at nine
o'clock. I've left a note on your desk.'

'Thank you, Colin.' When we'd moved yet again, I knew
that the commander would come with us; he'd be unable to
resist having an office with a prestigious Belgravia address.

'Ah, Mr Brock.' The commander was seated behind a desk
covered with tidy piles of files. He loves paper and despises
computers, claiming that he prefers to see everything written
down; no doubt the pen and paper industry loves people like
him. Nevertheless, he somewhat reluctantly pushed a file to
one side and peered at me over his half-moon spectacles. 'Tell
me about this sudden death you're dealing with.' The
commander is a pedant and refuses to describe unexplained
deaths as murder, manslaughter or suicide until a jury has said
as much and the Supreme Court has confirmed that verdict.

I explained, as succinctly as possible, the circumstances
surrounding the death of Lancelot Foley, but resisted the temptation to tell him that I already suspected Debra Foley might
somehow be involved. That would be unwise because the
commander would immediately suggest a course of action,
and he's not qualified to do so. The truth of the matter is that
some genius in Human Resources – what was once called
personnel branch – arbitrarily transferred him to the CID after
a lifetime of Uniform Branch duty where, doubtless, he inter-
fered with traffic and football hooligans. Regrettably for me,
and I suspect for the Metropolitan Police in general, he now
thinks he really is a detective.

'The death of such a well-known actor as Lancelot Foley
will undoubtedly attract a lot of publicity, Mr Brock,' said the
commander, after giving the matter due consideration. 'In the
circumstances, we must be circumspect in our dealings with
the media.'

'I don't intend to have any dealings with the media at all,
if I can possibly help it, sir,' I said.

'Not altogether wise.' The commander pursed his lips and
shook his head so that his cheeks and double chin wobbled.
'We should always tell them as much as we can, not as little
as we can get away with. That was an edict laid down by
the late Sir Robert Mark when he was Commissioner, and I

have to say that I agree with him wholeheartedly.' He opened his abandoned file and adjusted his spectacles; I'm convinced they contain plain glass and are only worn to lend gravitas to his otherwise lacklustre personality. 'Keep me informed,' he said, waving a podgy hand of dismissal.

Back in the incident room, I found Dave sitting beside Wilberforce and his computer. 'Just putting the last of the statements on file, guv. The workmen who found the body, the first PC on scene, the local DCI and all the other bit-part actors.'

'Anything from the house-to-house, Dave?'

'Nothing. As usual no one saw anything or heard anything. In view of the fact that the Foleys have a house in Farnham, I've been on to the Surrey Constabulary and they're doing the usual search of local records. But I doubt if anything useful will turn up.'

It was time for a briefing. I told the team what Kate and I had learned from our interviews with the theatre manager and with Debra Foley and Jane Lawless.

'This evening,' I continued, 'Dave and I will go back to the theatre and interview the cast members of the play the Foleys were appearing in. And tomorrow we'll be attending the post-mortem and speaking to Gerald Andrews.' I glanced around. 'Liz, where are you?'

'Over here, sir,' said Detective Sergeant Liz Carpenter, raising a hand.

'Liz, I want you and Nicola Chance to put yourselves about in Chorley Street and see what you can find out about Debra Foley; with discretion, of course. Where she goes, who she sees . . . you know the sort of thing. But wrap it up as though you're enquiring about Lancelot Foley. OK?' I looked across at Dave. 'I think we'll get going now, Dave. The performance starts at seven thirty, so we should be able to catch most of the cast before it begins. DI Ebdon and I have already seen Debra Foley, but there are still the rest of the players to interview.'

FOUR

The Clarence Theatre looked much better now that it was night time and the lights were on. Despite his apparent languor, the manager had succeeded in having the billboards replaced. Or someone had. They now showed Charles Digby playing the lead opposite Vanessa Drummond.

Dave brushed aside a job's-worth decked out in a commissionaire's flashy uniform who demanded to see our tickets, and we made our way to the manager's office.

'Here you are again, Chief Inspector.' Sebastian Weaver was seated behind his desk, wearing his customary harassed expression. 'What can I do for you?'

'I need to interview the members of the cast, Mr Weaver.'

'What, now, this minute?' Weaver was clearly appalled at my request. He pulled a watch from his waistcoat pocket and stared at it for some seconds, as though a solution to this latest problem would be found there. 'But they're getting ready to go on.'

'The play doesn't start for another hour,' said Dave.

'They have to put on make-up, you know. It's not just a case of turning up and walking on. And the dressers will get upset.' Weaver tugged at one of his pendulous ear lobes and shot Dave a critical expression as though assessing his suitability to play the lead in *Othello*. 'Oh, this is all so inconvenient.'

'It won't take long, Mr Weaver,' I said. 'It's just a formal question as to how well they knew Lancelot Foley. If they knew him well or I think that they have something to add to our investigation, I'll arrange to see them at a more convenient time. Probably at their digs.'

'I suppose it'll be all right,' muttered Weaver, albeit reluctantly. 'The play is actually in three acts,' he explained. 'Some of the cast don't go on immediately, so it might be possible to interview them first, and those that go on straightaway you could perhaps talk to later. If you see what I mean.'

He shook his head. 'Oh my God! I can see disaster looming, my dears.'

'Where will we find them?' I asked.

Weaver extracted a sheet of paper from a pile on his desk and handed it me. 'That's a list of their names, together with the numbers of their dressing rooms.'

Dave and I started with Charles Digby, Lancelot Foley's understudy, who we'd found in the dressing room recently used by Foley. A small man with thinning hair, a pallid complexion and a pointed nose that lent him a hunted expression, Digby had the appearance of a man too old and physically unsuited to play the part of Algernon Moncrieff, who was supposed to be a dashing thirty-something, but greasepaint can work miracles. I noticed immediately that Digby had a nervous tic in his right eyelid, and throughout our short conversation he frequently touched it, as if to stem its involuntary twitching. At other times one of his hands played a tattoo, either on the top of his dressing table or on his knee. Overall he was an agitated individual, but perhaps he was prone to stage fright, a condition that I'd been led to believe was, paradoxically, not uncommon among actors.

I also wondered briefly if the murder of Foley had been committed by Digby, motivated by a desire to take over the lead role, but dismissed that theory as not only improbable, but fantasy. Although I'd learned from Gail that the theatre is a cut-throat, bitchy business, I doubted that it would extend to murder. And in any event, I thought it unlikely that Digby had the strength, the courage or the ability to snap a man's neck in cold blood in a London street.

'I couldn't stand the man.' Seated in front of a mirror, Digby was applying a false moustache. 'He was full of himself. Full of himself.' He touched his right eyelid.

'How well did you know him, Mr Digby?' asked Dave, glancing down at the list of prepared questions that he had on a clipboard.

'Hardly at all, but that was enough to convince me that he had a good conceit of himself.' Digby swung round on his stool so that he was facing us. 'Whenever we met, which was rarely, we just confined ourselves to shaking each other warmly by the throat – metaphorically, of course – and left it at that.'

'What about Mrs Foley?'

'Debra's a charming girl,' said Digby, without hesitation. 'Always pleasant to everyone, even down to the young tea boy. How on earth she ever hooked up with Lancelot is a mystery.'

By ten o'clock we had interviewed every member of the cast, but the results were inconclusive or, as Dave put it, bloody useless. There were nine cast members in all, and the eight we interviewed at the Clarence were equally divided in their views of Lancelot Foley. To some, he was an objectionable individual, and his wife charming. To others, the reverse was the case. And it couldn't be accounted for by the sexes. As many women disliked Lancelot as liked him, and a similar divide existed in the case of Debra. The more people we spoke to, the more apparent became the conflicting views held by them. There seemed to be no happy medium.

We moved on to the stage staff: electricians, lighting operators, scene-shifters and the other behind-the-scenes general dogsbodies that make the whole thing work. Refreshingly, they were down to earth and unequivocal in their opinion.

As the assistant stage manager succinctly put it, 'Foley was a toffee-nosed bastard full of his own piss and importance, guv'nor. And as for his missus, she was just a scrubber who couldn't act.' And he spoke for them all.

'You always get the truth at the coal face,' said Dave.

Finally, we went to see the stage-door keeper, a wizened little man secreted in a glass-sided booth. He was reading a copy of the *Sun*, but looked up and stared at me through dirty spectacles as I tapped on the window.

'Yus, guv'nor?'

'We're police officers, Mr . . .?'

'Fred Higgins, guv'nor. You come about Mr Foley getting done in?'

'Yes, we have. D'you happen to know what time he left the theatre last night, Fred?'

'Course I do.' Higgins referred to a sheet of paper attached to a clipboard. 'A quarter to eleven on the dot, like what he always does. Have to make a note of the comings and goings in case there's a fire, see. Then we knows who's inside and who ain't.'

'I don't suppose you know where he went.'

'Course I do,' said Higgins again, a sly expression on his face. He tugged at his walrus moustache. 'I called him a cab, like what I always does.'

'D'you know where it was taking him?' I was beginning to feel like a dentist attempting to extract a reluctant tooth.

'Pimlott's, guv'nor. It's some fancy French caff in Covent Garden what calls itself a bistro. He often goes there. Probably gets a discount, seeing as how he's a skinflint.'

'Was he alone, Fred?' asked Dave.

'Nah, he had that bird wiv 'im what plays Miss Prism in the play.'

'That'll be Ruth Strickland,' said Dave, glancing at his list.

'That's her, guv'nor. Quite a dish, she is. Mind you, she's made up to look like a right battleaxe in the play, but when she's tarted up, well, she's something else, I can tell you.'

'D'you want to see her again before we leave, guv?' Dave asked me.

'No, she'll be on stage now, I expect. Anyway, he was probably just giving her lift, but we'll find out soon enough if anything was going on between the two of them.'

Dave and I arrived at Henry Mortlock's carvery on the stroke of nine the next morning, but it came as no surprise that he had already finished the post-mortem. I sometimes wondered why he bothered to give me a time that he would then ignore. On the one occasion I questioned it, he merely said that he was far too busy to worry about time.

'As I said at the scene, Harry, someone broke his neck, approximately eight hours before he was found. I can give you all the medical mumbo-jumbo if you want it, but in layman's terms and from my limited knowledge of the martial arts I would say that Foley was approached from behind, and his head was seized and twisted sharply.' Mortlock peeled off his surgical gloves and tossed them towards a clinical waste bin. And missed. 'I think it's something they teach the Special

Air Service, but whoever was responsible was clearly a strong man . . . or woman.'

'Thanks for that, Henry,' I said. 'We'll dash out and grab a passing commando.'

'It may be of some help for you to know the contents of the victim's stomach,' responded Mortlock tartly, completely ignoring my lame attempt at humour. 'Not long before his death he'd had a meal that consisted of steak tartare and chips, and red wine. Not a very good choice for a man whose cholesterol count was just above eight. If he'd kept on at that rate, he'd have had a heart attack or a stroke, I shouldn't wonder.'

'That confirms he must've had a meal between leaving the theatre and when he was murdered, and we know he left the Clarence at a quarter to eleven.' I was actually speaking my thoughts aloud.

'I'll let you have my report by late afternoon,' said Mortlock.

According to Fred Higgins, the stage-door keeper, Lancelot Foley had taken a cab to Pimlott's in the Covent Garden area. I decided that we'd go straight there from the mortuary.

The bistro was a dark and cavernous place, and as it was ten to eleven in the morning, I was not surprised to see only a few customers in there, and they seemed to be drinking coffee, while messing about with iPads or talking on their mobile phones. A sound system was playing Mozart softly.

Dave and I were approached by a languid, long-haired youth wearing an apron and 'John Lennon' spectacles. I suspected that he was a university graduate working to pay off his fees until he could get a job suited to his qualifications. By the look of him he'd have a long wait.

'You're a bit early for lunch,' he drawled, in a somewhat condescending tone, as though he were doing us a great favour by deigning to talk to us at all. 'But we could do you a coffee.'

'We're not here to dine. We're police officers,' I announced sharply. 'Is the manager here?'

'Oh, yah, hang on.' The youth disappeared through a door.

A few moments later a woman of about thirty appeared. She had short blonde hair and wore jeans and a T-shirt upon which were emblazoned the words 'Pimlott's Bistro'. 'Giles tells me you're from the police.'

'That's correct,' I said, and introduced myself and Dave. 'Are you the manager?'

'I'm Jo Pimlott, the owner. Well, half owner, really. My husband and I are joint proprietors. Giles is a nephew and is helping out waiting at table. He's actually just left university. He graduated in the performing arts.'

'Well, at least he can tell his friends he's appearing at Covent Garden.' Dave was scathingly dismissive of qualifications he described as 'ersatz degrees'.

'I understand that Lancelot Foley had a meal here last night, Mrs Pimlott,' I said, guessing that she would know if she'd catered for a distinguished actor.

'Yes, he did. In fact, he was one of our regular diners. But I saw on the television this morning that he'd been murdered. It must've been not long after he left here. What a terrible thing to have happened. He was such a nice man. That's what you're here about, I suppose.'

Once again I was surprised at yet another differing view of the late actor.

'Did he dine alone?'

'No, he had a young lady with him. I think she was an actor, too. Or actress, I suppose I should say, although Giles tells me that they all call themselves actors these days.'

'What time did he leave?' asked Dave.

Jo Pimlott pursed her lips in thought. 'It must've been about a quarter to twelve, I suppose. They only had a main course. I got the impression that they were in a bit of a hurry. Well, Mr Foley was.'

'And did the young lady leave with him?' I assumed that the young lady Jo Pimlott was talking about was Ruth Strickland, who took the part of Miss Prism in the play. *And if that was the case*, I thought, *Lancelot Foley was playing the field.* I doubted Jane Lawless would be too happy about that.

'It didn't look like it. They hugged and kissed, and then Mr Foley left. The young lady gathered up her handbag and umbrella and put on her coat. Then she went to the ladies' room and left about seven or eight minutes later. It was unusual for them to leave separately; normally, they left together.'

'Did they often dine here together, Mrs Pimlott?'

'Oh yes. I suppose about twice a week, sometimes three times.'

'When did they first start coming as a couple?' I asked.

'I suppose it was not long after Christmas. I remember Mr Foley mentioning that he was just beginning a new run at the Clarence Theatre.'

'Can you tell me what Mr Foley had to eat?' asked Dave.

'What they had to eat?' Jo Pimlott glanced at me. 'But what does Mr Foley's meal have to do with his death, Chief Inspector?'

'Possibly nothing, Mrs Pimlott, but we're checking all his movements leading up to his death. My sergeant's not suggesting that his meal had anything to do with his death.'

'I see. Just a minute.' Mrs Pimlott, still puzzled by Dave's request, retreated to the bar and thumbed through a sheaf of order slips. 'Here it is,' she said. 'Mr Foley had steak tartare and chips, and the young lady had a Spanish omelette. And they shared a bottle of the house red.' She glanced up enquiringly.

'Did he speak to anyone while he was in here? Apart from the staff, of course. Or did anyone talk to him?'

'No, I don't think so. Oh, just a minute, though. There was a young lady who asked him very politely if she could have his autograph.'

'And did he give her his autograph?'

'Yes, he did. As a matter of fact he gave her a signed photograph of himself. And he smiled and wished her good luck.'

'D'you know who she was?'

'No, I don't, because it was the young man who paid, and I'm sure he paid by credit card.' Jo Pimlott referred to her order slips once more. 'Yes, here it is. She had a burger and chips, and so did the young man with her. Just bear with me for a moment.' She took some credit card printouts from the cash register and riffled through them. 'Yes, the man paid, but I can't tell you who he was. I can give you the details of the transaction, though. I suppose that'll be enough to tell you who he is if you need to find out.'

'Thank you for your assistance, Mrs Pimlott,' I said, once Dave had noted the details of the man's credit card transaction. 'You've been very helpful.'

'I hope you catch whoever did it,' said Jo Pimlott. 'Such a nice man. He gave me two free tickets for the matinee on Saturday, but it'll hardly be worth going now he'll no longer be in it.'

I didn't bother to tell her there wouldn't be a performance at all on Saturday if the theatre manager's predictions came true.

Back in the car, Dave phoned Colin Wilberforce with the credit card transaction details and asked him to get the holder's name and address. Then he phoned Sebastian Weaver at the theatre and asked for Ruth Strickland's address.

By the time he had prised those details from the disorganized Weaver, Wilberforce was back on.

'The holder of the credit card is called John Walton, and he lives in Stockwell, guv,' said Dave as he put his phone back in his pocket.

'And I'll bet he won't be home until late.'

'He might work at home,' said Dave. 'Worth a try.'

'What about Ruth Strickland?'

'Would you believe she called in sick, guv?'

'Did she indeed?' I found that interesting.

'She lives in digs in Victoria,' said Dave.

I laughed. 'Poor old Weaver's not having a lot of luck, is he? I hope for his sake that Miss Strickland has an understudy. We'll try her first, and then we'll have a go at Walton, just in case he's at home.'

When we'd interviewed the twenty-five-year-old Ruth Strickland yesterday, she was already made up for her part as Miss Prism, and she'd struck me then as being quite plain. But seeing her today, even in figure-hugging jeans and a sweater, and her attractively bobbed black hair loose, I saw no reason to change that view. Although Fred Higgins, the stage-door keeper, had described her as being 'quite a dish', I think he may have needed new glasses. Perhaps she had hidden talents, and it wasn't her acting ability that I had in mind.

'Yes?' For a moment or two, she failed to recognize us. 'Oh, it's you,' she said eventually. 'I'm sorry, do come in. We spoke yesterday when you were at the theatre.'

'I understand from the manager that you're not feeling well, Miss Strickland.'

'It's Ruth.' She waved a hand at a settee. 'Do sit down. I must admit that I wasn't feeling too good this morning, but it was the shock of hearing about Lancelot's death that rather knocked me sideways, I'm afraid. What an awful thing to have happened.' She paused and touched her nose with a tissue: more of an affectation than a necessity, I thought. 'Personally, I don't go along with all this "the show must go on" nonsense. I just know I couldn't have given of my best at this afternoon's matinee, but I'm sure that my understudy will manage to take my place.'

'It would appear that you were probably the last person to see Mr Foley alive, Ruth, apart from his killer,' said Dave. 'That's why we've come to see you again.'

'D'you mean that no one saw him after he left the theatre?' Ruth Strickland contrived an expression of innocence, but then she is an actress. 'I think I saw him talking to the woman who plays Lady Bracknell. That would have been—'

'I'm talking about you and Mr Foley having supper together at Pimlott's Bistro,' said Dave, sharply interrupting Ruth Strickland's fantasizing.

'Oh, God! How did you know about that?'

Dave smiled disarmingly. 'Because we're detectives, Ruth. You were having an affair with Lancelot, weren't you?' He could always be relied upon to go straight for the jugular, and he couched his guess in terms that made it sound like a fact.

'But I didn't think anyone knew about us.' The question clearly disconcerted Ruth, but she made a good showing of being quite coy.

'You were seen kissing and embracing at the restaurant, just before Lancelot rushed off and left you to find your own way home.' Dave was quite good at guesswork, and he was a shrewd judge of character. 'And it's not the first time you and he dined together. So, Miss Strickland, may we have the truth from now on?'

'Heavens! If Debra gets to hear of this she'll kill me.'

'I'm afraid you haven't kept up with events, Ruth,' I said. 'Lancelot had left his wife and was in a relationship with another woman. That's probably why he dashed away; he was living with her. She's the one who might want to pick a fight with you.'

'Who is she?' Ruth began to look quite distressed.

'I'm not at liberty to say.' I was not unduly concerned whether Ruth Strickland found out about Jane Lawless, but I didn't want her confronting 'the other woman' and then perhaps comparing notes. Moreover, it served my ends to keep suspects apart for as long as possible. And right now, I hadn't ruled anyone out.

'How long had this affair with Lancelot been going on?' Dave asked casually.

'Er, about five weeks, I suppose.' Ruth sniffed and dabbed her eyes again. 'Maybe a bit longer.'

'But it was just an affair, was it? Nothing more serious than that.'

'It was serious. He was going to leave his wife when the time was right and marry me,' said Ruth as the first tears began to roll down her cheeks. 'That's what he told me, but I didn't know he'd already left her for someone else! I can't believe he'd do a thing like that to me.'

'And I suppose that, on that basis, you slept with him from time to time.' Dave was quite relentless and ignored the tears, dismissing them as part of the character she had assumed for this little scene.

'Yes,' whispered Ruth, with another unconvincing sob.

'Oh dear!' Although Dave only uttered those two words, they were eloquent in their understanding of a young woman who'd been taken for a ride. Literally.

'I don't think we need to trouble you any more, Ruth,' I said, 'but as a matter of interest, d'you know if Lancelot was seeing any of the other girls in the cast?'

'I'm sure he wasn't. In fact, I didn't think he was seeing anyone else at all.' Ruth Strickland finally broke down and dissolved into real sobs.

We left her to her grief. She was just another girl who'd

been seduced by an older married man with vague promises of marriage. She wouldn't be the last.

But when the police had departed, Ruth Strickland dried her crocodile tears and smiled. *Well, Jane Lawless,* she thought, *eat your heart out, because Lancelot told me that he'd leave all his money to me if ever anything happened to him.*

Finally, she rang the theatre. 'I'm feeling much better now, Sebastian,' she said. 'I'll be all right to appear tonight.'

FIVE

etective Sergeant Lizanne Carpenter and Detective
Constable Nicola Chance were both in their thirties
and experienced CID officers. Lizanne had obtained
a copy of the electoral roll for Chorley Street and thus had
some idea of who lived where. Arriving fairly early, they had
set about the task that DCI Brock had given them: gleaning
as much information as possible about Debra Foley, by
pretending to be interested in Lancelot.

But they met with little success. Most of the people who
were at home had either not heard of Lancelot Foley or had
heard of the murder through the medium of television, newspapers, tablets or the many social networking sites. Regrettably,
nobody had anything to say that would get the police any
closer to discovering who had murdered Foley.

It was not until half-past eleven when they called at twenty-
seven Chorley Street, a house immediately opposite the one
occupied by Debra and previously by the late Lancelot Foley,
that, in Nicola's words, they struck gold. But only after an
initial misunderstanding.

The woman who answered the door of number twenty-seven
was at the very least in her mid-seventies, if not older.
Nevertheless, she was erect of stature, and her grey hair had
been dragged back severely from her face and fashioned into
a bun at the nape of her neck. She wore a rather shapeless
grey woollen dress that reached almost to her ankles. Flat
brogue shoes and wire-framed spectacles completed the picture
of a woman who appeared to have strayed into the present
day from another age.

'Miss Dixey?' asked Lizanne, looking up after referring to
the voters' list. There were two women called Dixey listed,
and this must be one of them.

'I'm *Thelma* Dixey,' said the woman. The reason for the
emphasis became clear when at that point another woman

appeared behind her. This second woman was the image of
Thelma, but a complete contrast in attire. She was stylishly
dressed, wore make-up, red nail varnish and high-heeled shoes,
and spectacles with designer frames. 'And this is my sister
Norma. We're twins,' Thelma added unnecessarily. 'But don't
waste your time, my dear. We always vote Conservative, and
we'll do so in this by-election. Just you get along and persuade
these other people to vote for that nice young Mister . . .' She
paused and turned to her sister. 'What's his name, Norma,
dear?'

'I don't remember, Thelma, dear, but I'm sure he'll make
a good MP.' Norma shook her head in despair at her failing
memory. 'I think he's in Mr Churchill's party.'

'We're police officers, Miss Dixey,' said Lizanne, hoping
to get to the point of their visit without too much delay. 'I'm
Detective Sergeant Carpenter, and this is Detective Constable
Chance. We've not come about the election.'

'Oh, good gracious!' exclaimed Thelma. 'It's such a cold
day, and you look perished. You'd better come in and have a
cup of tea. Come along, my dears.'

The two detectives followed the Dixey twins into a sitting
room full of ageing furniture, and in which bric-a-brac and
framed photographs occupied every available space. The
windows had net curtains which, Lizanne suspected and hoped,
would have been twitched frequently by the Dixey sisters.

'Do sit down, my dears, and Norma will make some tea.'
Thelma glanced at her sister. 'You'll make the tea, won't you,
Norma, dear?' She turned to Lizanne. 'We're both eighty-one,
you know, but I'm her elder sister by four minutes. So she
always does what I tell her.' She smiled impishly. 'Apart from
when I tell her to stop dressing like a tart.'

'We're investigating a murder, Miss Dixey,' Lizanne began,
once Norma had left the room.

'Oh dear, how terrible for you,' said Thelma. 'And you're
such nice young ladies, too.'

'It's the murder of Lancelot Foley,' said Nicola.

'Oh, surely not. D'you mean that nice young actor who
lives opposite?'

'Yes, that's the one.'

'And he's been murdered, you say?'

'Early yesterday morning in Chelsea.'

'Really? But Chelsea's such a nice neighbourhood. He told me once that he was in *The Importance of Being Earnest*. I love Oscar Wilde's plays; such a clever young man. A terrible shame that he died in poverty. Or was it in Paris? Oh never mind.'

Norma came into the room with a large tea tray and put it down on a coffee table.

'That was quick,' said Lizanne.

'We have one of those clever taps that dispenses boiling water,' said Norma. 'But you have to be careful otherwise you could scald yourself. Milk and sugar?'

'These two young ladies are from the police, Norma,' said Thelma.

'I know that, Thelma. They told us that at the front door.' Norma glanced at Lizanne. 'I'm afraid my sister's memory is going,' she said.

'It certainly is not,' said Thelma vehemently. 'Anyway, you couldn't remember the name of our candidate. And that nice Mr Churchill you mentioned died years ago. You'd forgotten, hadn't you? Anyway, never mind all that. This nice young lady's just told me that that nice Mr Foley has been murdered.'

'Oh dear,' said Norma as she poured the tea and handed it round. 'What a pity.'

'So far we're at a loss to know who was responsible for the murder,' said Nicola, 'and we were wondering if you could help at all, as you live opposite.'

'As matter of fact we hadn't seen him lately, and we were wondering whether perhaps he'd moved out,' said Thelma. 'But Mrs Foley is still there. She's an actress, you know.'

'Is she really?' Lizanne hoped that by feigning ignorance of Debra Foley, the Dixey twins might be more forthcoming about her. 'I didn't know that.'

'Oh yes, she's on the West End stage, just like Mr Foley was. In fact, he told me that his wife was in the same play as he was.'

'Have you ever spoken to his wife, to Mrs Foley?'

'No, she's a bit aloof, and she's not all she makes out to

be, you know,' said Norma, butting in before Thelma could answer. 'In fact, I think she's a bit above herself.'

'Really?' said Lizanne.

'Oh yes. I've seen her going out in the afternoons looking very dowdy and wearing sunglasses. But, being famous, I suppose she dresses like that because she doesn't want to be recognized in the street. We've looked them both up on the Internet,' added Norma, revealing that she and her sister were more up to date than was at first apparent. 'Or was it on our iPads, Thelma?'

'You did it on your laptop,' said Norma, shaking her head.

'How often does Mrs Foley go out dressed like that, Miss Dixey?' asked Nicola.

'Most afternoons, except Wednesdays, Saturdays and Sundays. But only when I happen to be looking out of the window.'

'Perhaps it's something connected with the theatre,' suggested Nicola, thinking that the Dixey twins probably spent most of their time looking out of the window. When they weren't looking people up on the Internet. 'Rehearsals, perhaps?'

'But I told you that she's in a play already, and you don't have to keep rehearsing once the play is on, surely,' said Norma.

'That's right,' agreed Thelma. 'You don't keep on rehearsing.'

'You don't have to repeat everything I say,' said Norma crossly. 'I'm sure these nice young ladies heard it the first time.'

'When you've seen her going out on those afternoons, Miss Dixey,' said Lizanne, addressing Norma, 'have you seen her return?'

'No, never. I've no idea where she goes, but I suppose she goes on to the theatre from wherever she's been. Mind you, on Wednesdays and Saturdays a taxi comes for her at about one o'clock, and she's all dressed up on those occasions, but I suppose that's when she's going straight to the theatre. I think they have matinees on those days. Well, they did when we were girls, but we don't go to the theatre any more.'

'Thank you, ladies,' said Lizanne. 'You've been most helpful. And thank you for the tea.'

'See the young ladies out, Norma,' said Thelma, and poured herself another cup of tea.

'Mr John Walton?' I asked when we arrived at the flat in Stockwell where he lived. It was fortunate that he was in on a weekday mid-morning, but he told us later that he worked at home for most of the time.

'Yes.' Walton appeared to be very nervous, but I suppose two men at his door, one of whom was black, would cause a degree of uncertainty, especially in an area where there is a fairly high crime rate.

'We're police officers,' I said, and Dave and I showed Walton our warrant cards.

'What's it about?' Walton did not appear to be reassured; in fact, quite the opposite.

'Perhaps we could come in rather than hold a discussion out here, Mr Walton,' said Dave.

'Oh, er, yes, of course. Please come in.'

The sitting room was not very large, and the four armchairs it contained seemed to fill it.

'Hello.' The young woman sitting in one of the armchairs was a curvaceous redhead with a low-cut blouse, which is probably why Lancelot Foley had responded so readily to her request for his autograph.

Dave and I introduced ourselves and explained that we were attached to the Murder Investigation Team.

'Murder? Good heavens,' said the young woman. She appeared to be about twenty or so, and John Walton wasn't much older.

'Oh, this is my partner, Selina Cork,' said Walton somewhat belatedly. 'But who's been murdered?'

'Lancelot Foley, the actor,' I said.

'Oh no!' Selina Cork looked aghast. 'When?'

'You hadn't heard about it?'

'No, we hadn't. We don't watch the news very much,' said Selina, who was already proving to be a stronger character than her partner. 'We only saw him the day before yesterday. As a matter of fact he was in the same restaurant as John and me – Pimlott's in Covent Garden – and I asked him for his autograph. I knew who he was, and it was a bit cheeky, really. I thought he'd bite my head off, but he was very nice and gave me a signed photograph of himself.'

'Yes, we know all that,' I said.

'You do?' Selina stared at me as though I possessed magical powers.

'Yes, but what I'm interested in is whether you left Pimlott's before or after Mr Foley.'

'It was at the same time. But what struck me as strange is that he didn't leave with the young lady he'd been dining with.'

'Would you explain what you mean by that, Miss Cork?'

'Well, I thought it was a bit odd, really. They'd been together, talking and laughing, and then when it was time to leave, Mr Foley went off on his own.'

'Can you be sure?' asked Dave. 'Is it possible that he waited for the young lady outside?'

'No, definitely not, did he, John?'

Walton gave his partner a weak smile. 'I don't know, sweetie. I don't think so, but he might have done.'

'Oh, really!' scoffed Selina. 'Sometimes I think you walk about with your eyes shut, John Walton. And to think you're in advertising!'

I got the impression that John Walton and Selina Cork would not remain partners for much longer.

'I saw Mr Foley rush off towards the Strand; almost running, he was.'

'And the young woman was not with him?'

'No, I didn't see her again. As far as I know she stayed in the bistro.'

Beyond saying what a nice man Lancelot Foley was, neither Walton nor his partner had added anything to our pitifully small pile of evidence. To sum it up, Foley had been in the company of a young woman, but they had no idea who she was. Foley and his companion had seemed to be a normal couple and were deep in conversation the whole time they were there. Foley then left by himself and was last seen hurrying towards the Strand. I assumed that it was there that he picked up the taxi that took him to the end of Freshbrook Street.

I thanked them, and Dave and I left, doubtless leaving them with a topic of conversation that would last them for weeks.

That afternoon, I decided Dave and I would pay Lancelot Foley's solicitor a visit.

The solicitor had his chambers on the first floor of an office block in Chancery Lane. The reception area was wood panelled and richly carpeted, a clear indication that this lawyer was expensive. But what lawyer isn't?

A woman was seated in a commanding position behind a large desk. 'May I help you?' she asked. There was something in her voice that indicated that she held a fairly senior position in the organization. We later learned, however, that she was the senior partner's secretary.

'I should like to see the senior partner, please.'

'Can you tell me what it's about?' The middle-aged secretary was obviously intent upon adopting the same obstructive attitude as some receptionists occasionally to be found in doctors' surgeries. Her brown hair was pulled tightly back into a ponytail – a fashion that Dave described as a Croydon facelift – and she stared imperiously at us through horn-rimmed spectacles that I was cynical enough to think were worn for effect.

'No,' said Dave firmly. 'It's a confidential matter.'

'He's very busy at the moment,' responded the secretary. 'May I make an appointment for you?' she asked. She scrolled up a page on her computer as though there were no alternative and afforded us a saccharine smile.

'No,' said Dave again, placing his hand on the woman's desk and leaning forward menacingly. 'We are police officers, and we're conducting an enquiry into the murder of one of your firm's clients. It's imperative that we see his legal representative without delay.'

'Oh!' said the secretary, rising from her desk. She glanced nervously at a waiting client who had abandoned the *Times* crossword and was taking a great interest in the conversation. 'One moment.' She went through a heavy oak door, to emerge only seconds later. 'Please come this way.' She spoke sharply, clearly disappointed that her attempt at access control had been thwarted.

'Cynthia tells me you're from the police,' said the smug, overweight man seated behind a vast desk. Unlike our beloved commander's desk, there was nothing on this one save an intercom system, a desk tidy and one or two other bits and pieces, but nothing that seemed actually to be connected with work. 'Something to do with the death of one of our clients. I presume you're talking about the unfortunate demise of Mr Foley.' He brushed at a speck on the lapel of his immaculate grey suit.

'That's correct,' I said. 'I'm Detective Chief Inspector Brock, and this is Detective Sergeant Poole.'

'Very sad,' said the solicitor smoothly, and he drew his hand across the top of his desk as though checking for dust. 'Please take a seat, gentlemen, and tell me how I may be of service to you. But you have to understand that this firm deals only with civil matters, and I'm not sure how I can assist you with anything concerning crime.' He spoke the last word as though uttering an obscenity.

That's a good sign, I thought. *I may be able to pull the wool over his eyes if he starts to get awkward.*

'It's a matter of Mr Lancelot Foley's will,' I said. 'I understand that you hold a copy of it.'

'Indeed we do, Chief Inspector, but as a matter of client confidentiality I'm sure you're aware I am not at liberty to disclose its contents without the consent of the principal beneficiary or other similarly qualified person.' The lawyer plucked a large handkerchief from his sleeve, put it to his mouth and coughed affectedly.

'And that is the problem, sir,' I said. 'I don't know who the beneficiary is until I have sight of the will. Of course, if there's likely to be some difficulty, and I'd anticipated there might be, I can go across to the Old Bailey and obtain a Section Eight warrant under the Police and Criminal Evidence Act. I could be back in half an hour.' I paused and glanced at Dave. 'You did prepare an information, just in case, didn't you, Sergeant?'

'Of course, sir,' said Dave, and patted his empty pocket.

I was fairly sure that a Crown Court judge wouldn't grant me a warrant in these particular circumstances, but I guessed that this plum-in-the-mouth solicitor was not too familiar with PACE warrants either, and his response confirmed it.

'I don't think that'll be necessary, Chief Inspector. Never let it be said that we failed to cooperate with the police. I think in this particular case I'm sure I'd be justified in helping you.' The lawyer ran his hand across the desktop again. 'I presume you're working on the theory that the beneficiary might've been responsible for this heinous crime.'

Well, he said it, I thought. 'Very perceptive of you, sir,' I murmured.

'Of course, as you undoubtedly know, if the named beneficiary is the murderer, he or she cannot inherit the estate. That's the law.' The solicitor flicked down the switch on his intercom. 'Cynthia, be so good as to bring me Lancelot Foley's last will and testament, please.'

'Of course, sir,' came Cynthia's disembodied voice. This was clearly an efficient organization, because it was less than two minutes later that she appeared in the office and placed a slim document on the lawyer's desk.

'What exactly did you want to know?' The solicitor stripped the pink ribbon from the will, and then glanced up.

'The name and address of the principal beneficiary would be quite sufficient in the circumstances, sir,' I said.

The solicitor took a pair of gold-rimmed spectacles from a smart little stand on his desk and put them on. He spent a few minutes reading the will, and then took another few minutes to scan through it again. 'There is only the one beneficiary, Chief Inspector,' he said eventually. 'Mr Foley has bequeathed his not inconsiderable estate, which I would estimate to be in excess of fifteen million pounds, give or take, to a Sally Warner with an address in Overcroft Lane, Farnham, Surrey. I've already telephoned the beneficiary and informed her of her inheritance, subject to probate, of course.' He wrote Sally Warner's details on a plain slip of paper and handed it to me.

I felt that we owed the solicitor a little token of gratitude, and as Dave and I were leaving his office, I said, 'I'm most grateful for your assistance, sir, and I assure you that no one will know where our information came from.'

'Most kind,' murmured the solicitor, and put his spectacles back in the little stand.

The secretary ignored us as we left.

'I don't think that Debra Foley or Jane Lawless will be too happy when they learn where Lancelot's money is going, Dave,' I said as we returned to the car.

'To say nothing of Ruth Strickland, guv,' said Dave, and then paused. 'It's interesting that this Sally Warner also lives in Farnham. I wonder how far she is from Lancelot Foley's house and where she fits into his life.'

'Another of his birds on the side, I suppose, but she must be someone special to cop fifteen mill under his will. Anyway, we'll soon find out.'

'Looks like a trip to darkest Surrey, then.'

'I reckon so, Dave, but first try the mobile phone number you found for Gerald Andrews and see if you can track him down. It's time we had a word with him; he might just know something.'

'Isn't Andrews the bloke who Gail—?' Dave began.

'Yes, Dave. The very same.'

SIX

I was surprised to find that Gerald Andrews was at the Clarence Theatre, but I supposed that he wanted to reassess the production now that the lead role had been taken over by Charles Digby.

'Mr Andrews, I'm Detective Chief Inspector Harry Brock, and I'm investigating Lancelot Foley's murder.'

'Ah, I thought we might meet eventually, Chief Inspector.' Andrews didn't explain why he thought that, although I was sure I knew. 'What can I do to help?' he asked as we shook hands. 'It's a very sad business, and one that could be commercially disastrous if Digby doesn't manage to pull it off. To be honest, I thought that the producer was a bit reckless to stage *Importance* in the first place.' Like everyone in the theatrical profession I'd ever met, Andrews had acquired the habit of shortening the names of plays. 'It's so well known that people would rather have something new, and preferably a musical at that. Half the audiences these days are foreigners and don't understand the language, let alone the nuances. Still, I only direct; I don't invest in productions any more, unless it's a racing certainty. Let's see if we can find somewhere quiet for a chat.'

It doesn't do to have preconceived ideas about a man of whom I had heard so much but had never met, and I found myself warming towards Andrews. He was about forty-five, and my first impression was that he was both affable and courteous. He constantly ran his hand through his full head of wavy iron-grey hair, and the suit he was wearing must have set him back at least a grand. And I'm pretty good at judging the price of a suit. The overall effect was one of a successful and wealthy theatre director.

Andrews eventually ushered Dave and me into a small office alongside the basement dressing rooms and invited us to take a seat.

'I suppose you want to know what I know about Lancelot Foley,' Andrews began. 'I certainly can't tell you who murdered him,' he said, with a diffident smile, 'but I can tell you that he had a liking for the ladies, if that's any help.'

'We've met three of them already, Mr Andrews,' I said. 'His wife, Debra; Jane Lawless; and Ruth Strickland.'

'Oh, do call me Gerald, please. You don't mind if I call you Harry, do you? I feel that we have quite a lot in common, even though we've never met.' He twitched the corner of his mouth, as though aware of the interpretation I would place on his comment.

'Not at all,' I said, 'but to get to the point of my seeing you, have you any idea who might've wanted to kill Foley? It sounds like a routine question, and I suppose it is, but very often we find that there has been some disagreement that has culminated in violence.'

'A few husbands, I guess.' Andrews repeated what Debra Foley had said and smiled again. 'Sorry. That was a joke and in rather poor taste. I know the theatrical game is a cut-throat business, but I doubt that an actor would have resorted to murder,' he added, echoing what Gail had told me on many occasions. 'I think Jane Lawless was married, but that wouldn't have worried Lancelot and probably wouldn't have bothered her either. He tended to play the field, and I think Debra probably threw him out after he'd erred once too often. That was with a girl called Sally Warner, but I don't know what happened to her. Abandoned like all his other paramours, I suppose.' As our conversation progressed I noticed that he frequently primped the handkerchief in his top pocket and fussed with his tie. Whether it was nervousness or a continuing concern for his appearance was open to conjecture.

'But I presume that you can't really point the finger at anyone in particular, Gerald.' I wasn't going to admit knowing that Sally Warner was about to inherit Foley's substantial estate.

'No, I'm afraid not, Harry. He was a thoroughly dislikable man, and he'd made a few enemies on his way up. But if that were a motive for murder, half the leading actors in the country would've been slaughtered by now.'

'Well, thank you for your time, Gerald,' I said as Dave and I stood up. But as I reached for the door handle Andrews spoke again.

'I wonder if I could have a word with you in private, Harry,' said Andrews hesitantly, and glanced at Dave.

'I'll wait in the car, sir,' said Dave. He always called me 'sir' in the presence of civilians, as well as when I made some fatuous remark.

I sat down again and waited, fairly certain that Andrews didn't want to talk further about Lancelot Foley's murder.

'How's Gail, Harry?' There was a directness in the way Andrews posed the question, as though he wanted to get the matter over and done with as soon as possible. 'I've seen her from time to time, but the last time was just before Christmas.'

'She's very well, Gerald.' It was news to me that Andrews met up with Gail occasionally, and I wondered where this conversation was going. But I didn't have long to wait.

'You obviously know that she and I were divorced some years ago, but it was inevitable.'

'She told me something about you being in bed with a nude dancer when she got home from the theatre one afternoon,' I said, just to let him know that I knew.

'What?' Andrews' stunned expression could not have been other than genuine. 'Is that what she told you, Harry?' But then he gave a nervous little laugh.

'Isn't it true, then?'

'Not exactly.' Andrews primped his pocket handkerchief and touched his tie again. It was definitely nervousness this time. 'Gail was the one who was in bed when I got home from the theatre unexpectedly. With a man.' Once again, he ran his hand through his hair.

'I didn't realize that there were too many male nude dancers around.' It was a lame comment, but I was so taken aback by what Andrews had told me that I couldn't think of anything else to say.

'He wasn't a dancer, Harry, although he was nude at the time. He was the assistant stage manager at the Granville Theatre, which is where she was appearing at the time, and Gail eventually admitted that the affair had been going on for a while. I probably wouldn't have minded so much if it had been another actor.' Andrews paused momentarily and chuckled, attempting to make light of a delicate situation. 'There again, perhaps I would.'

'I see. This comes as something of a surprise.' I wasn't sure that I believed what Gail's ex had told me. But on the other hand, Gail had always been a passionate and inventive lover, and I knew from my years with her that she wasn't the sort of girl who would be prepared to go for too long without sex. And that worried me because it made me wonder what she did when I was tied up in a case and didn't see her for a week or two. And what did she get up to when she went to Nottingham, supposedly to see her parents? Damn this man Andrews. He'd succeeded in planting a seed of doubt in my mind; but perhaps that was his intention.

'I can understand you doubting my account of what happened, Harry, but if you ask Gail I'm sure she'll admit it. Eventually.'

'She told me that you'd stopped her from getting any decent acting parts. Is that true?'

Andrews smiled his tolerant little smile again, and once more primped his pocket handkerchief. 'Why should I do such a thing? But after Gail and I were divorced, I married a casting agent. She knows about Gail, and I suppose she might've had something to do with it. Women can be very vindictive when the mood takes them. And that, of course, brings us back to Lancelot Foley. I'm not a detective, but if I were, I'd have a good look at the women in his life.'

'Thanks for the advice,' I said, somewhat tersely.

'Sorry if I've spoiled things for you, Harry.' Andrews stood up and offered his hand.

'Thanks for telling me anyway.' After a moment's hesitation I shook hands with him.

'And perhaps you'd tell Gail that I'll do what I can to get her a part. If she really wants to go back to the theatre, that is.'

I walked out to the car, turning over in my mind the story that Andrews had told me and wondering if it were true or whether it was an attempt on his part to engineer a break-up with Gail. Or maybe it was designed just to destabilize my relationship with her. But if any of that were true, it begged the question why.

I thought back to Gail's appearance in *Scatterbrain* at the Granville Theatre when I had met her. And I wondered if the ASM there had been the only man with whom Gail had been having an affair. She was, after all, a damned attractive woman.

'Everything all right, guv?' asked Dave as I slid into the passenger seat.

'Fine,' I said.

Dave knew about Gail's divorce, and Gail and Madeleine, Dave's ballet dancer wife, often talked on the phone. Diplomatically, he said nothing further, but he must've guessed that Andrews' request for a private chat must have had something to do with Gail.

'Where to, guv?' asked Dave as he started the engine.

'Back to the factory, Dave.' CID officers always call their office 'the factory'.

Linda Mitchell, the senior forensic practitioner, was waiting for me in the incident room when Dave and I got back to Belgravia police station.

'Have you by any chance got some good news, Linda?' I asked hopefully.

'I think it's possible that I have, Mr Brock.'

'That'll be the first today.' I could certainly do with something positive. I have to admit that I was somewhat disturbed by what Gerald Andrews had told me, and was having some difficulty in believing it.

'We found a fingerprint on Foley's walking stick.'

'Whose is it?' Was this, I wondered, the piece of the jigsaw that would solve our murder for us?

'We don't know,' said Linda. 'It's not on record. All I can tell you with certainty is that it's not Lancelot Foley's print.'

'Well, that's something, I suppose. All we have to do now is find the owner of the print.'

'Mind you, Mr Brock, it could be anybody's. But the chances are that it was the murderer's, if he picked up the walking stick and threw it into the excavation where Foley's body was found.'

'I'm surprised that the killer wasn't wearing gloves in this weather.'

'If he's the sort of hard case who goes round snapping people's necks, he probably wouldn't wear 'em anyway,' said Dave. 'Just in case he meets another macho man.'

'If we ever find this killer, Linda,' I said, 'would that print stand up in court?'

'Without a doubt. The fingerprint examiners got a clear sixteen points. It was probably the snow and ice that preserved it so well.'

'Where's the commander, Colin?' I wondered if I should bring him up to date.

Wilberforce glanced at the clock. 'Gone home, sir.'

'Of course.' I knew that the commander always left on the stroke of six o'clock. He wouldn't want to get into trouble with Mrs Commander, if she was as much of a harridan as the photograph on the commander's desk seemed to indicate. 'In that case, I think I'll do the same. Tomorrow morning we must really get our teeth into this enquiry.'

'I've got toothache, guv,' said Dave.

One of the few advantages of having moved from Empress State Building at Earls Court to Belgravia police station was that we had private parking spaces.

I started my car and set off for Surbiton, knowing that my journey of about twelve miles would take forever, particularly as it had begun to snow again. Crawling my way through the evening rush hour, I inched over Albert Bridge, wound my way slowly through the gridlocked Wandsworth one-way system, and negotiated the snarled-up Robin Hood roundabout until eventually I reached the A3, after which I had a fairly clear run. I finally arrived at my flat at gone half past seven.

After my conversation with Gerald Andrews, I'd decided against calling at Gail's house in Kingston; I needed a day or two to think over everything that he had told me. Furthermore, it had planted a nagging thought in my mind: was Gail's affair with the assistant stage manager still going on? I even wondered if she was still seeing Gerald Andrews on the sly. On the other hand, Andrews could have been lying to me in order to preserve his own reputation.

With that jumble of thoughts racing through my mind, I had momentarily forgotten that I'd given Gail a key to my flat so that she could come and go as she pleased. I had a key to her house, too. It was a mark of how far our relationship, and our mutual trust, had progressed. But I had a nasty feeling that that was all about to come to an end.

The first thing that caught my eye when I opened my front door was a brown leather coat and a pair of knee boots. And I thought I could detect a whiff of Chanel Coco Mademoiselle, Gail's favourite perfume. She was here, and to put it beyond doubt, I heard her voice.

'I'm in the kitchen, darling. I rang the office, and they said you'd left for home, so I thought I'd come round and get you dinner. There's a whisky next to your chair in the sitting room. I'll be with you shortly.'

I put the whisky on hold and walked through to the kitchen. Gail, who is five foot ten inches tall and has long blonde hair and a superb figure, was standing at my cooker. She was wearing a red polo-necked sweater, a very short skirt and black tights that showed off her long legs to perfection. But she also had a devious mind, which was perhaps even more devious than I had imagined.

'Hello, darling.' Gail hugged me and gave me a lingering kiss. With a sigh, I yielded and ran a hand up her leg beneath her skirt.

'Later,' she said, smacking my hand away.

Being the pushover I am, the idea of having a row became less palatable. Nevertheless, I was determined to get her side of the story.

'Are you dealing with Lancelot Foley's murder, darling? I saw a bit about it on TV last night.'

'Yes, I am. Did you know him?'

Gail and I had had supper, several glasses of Malbec, and now we were in bed. It was only half past nine, but as I've already said, I'm a pushover for a pretty girl. And Gail is a temptress.

'I never met him, thank goodness,' said Gail, 'but he had a reputation in the theatre.'

'A reputation for what?' I asked, turning on my side to face her. From what I'd learned so far, I thought I knew. And I was right.

'For being a womanizer. I was told that any of the girls unlucky enough to be appearing in a play with him called him "the theatre handyman". These stories get about, you know. The advice was never to find yourself in a dressing room alone with him.'

'I met Gerald Andrews today,' I said, finally deciding to broach a subject that had been nagging away at me for most of the evening.

'Did you, darling? How is he?'

That was certainly not the reaction I'd expected. 'He seemed well enough. As a matter of fact, he said he saw you just before Christmas.'

'Yes, I ran into him in Oxford Street when I was buying your Christmas present. Didn't I mention it?'

'No, I don't think you did.' I eased myself up on to one elbow. 'He told me a rather strange story.'

'Well, you had to find out sooner or later, I suppose.' Gail put her hands behind her head and gazed at the ceiling. 'No doubt he told you that it was *he* who came home and found *me* in bed with a fellah.'

'Yes, he did actually.'

'It was quite true,' admitted Gail with disarming frankness. 'He caught me at it.'

'But why did you make up a story that made you look like the innocent party?' This conversation was not going at all in the way I'd anticipated.

'Harry, darling,' she said, drawing her hands down and turning to face me, 'I fancied you the moment you walked into my life that day at the Granville, and you don't honestly believe I was going to tell you that my marriage broke up because of *my* adultery, do you? Better for us both to have started with a clean slate, don't you think? Anyway, have you told me about all the women you'd slept with between your divorce and when you met me?' She paused, and in the absence of an answer, went on. 'No, I didn't think so. And before you deploy your interrogation skills any further, I might as well tell you that it was the assistant stage manager at the Granville Theatre. But I expect Gerald told you that too. It was a brief fling, and it was all over before I met you.'

'Oh, what the hell!' I said, greatly relieved that Gail had been honest about her affair. And she was right about me too: I hadn't mentioned the girls I'd slept with between my divorce and meeting her. And there had been a few, apart from the few *before* my divorce. My first wife was Helga Büchner, a German physiotherapist, who had straightened out my shoulder after a dust-up with a crowd of youths when I was a uniformed PC. We were married within weeks, but she insisted on working after the birth of our son Robert and would leave him with an obliging neighbour. One day, however, the boy fell in the neighbour's pond and drowned; he was only four. There had already been adultery on both sides, and finally we divorced so that Helga could marry a doctor with whom she'd been having an affair for some time. All I got out of the marriage was the ability to speak fluent German, but it had been a high price to pay.

I was in Belgravia by nine o'clock the next morning and settled in my office with a pile of paperwork and a cup of coffee. Now that I'd cleared the air with Gail I felt much more like getting on with my murder enquiry. And today was the day that Dave and I would go to Farnham to interview Sally Warner, the woman who was about to inherit Lancelot Foley's millions. And if she happened not to be at home, I'd get Dave to ask a few questions locally. He's very good at making enquiries wrapped up as 'market research'.

'Got a minute, sir?' DS Lizanne Carpenter appeared in the doorway.

'What is it, Liz?'

'Yesterday, sir, Nicola and I picked up some information that might turn out to be useful,' she said, and went on to tell me what she had learned from the Dixey twins who lived opposite Debra Foley in Chorley Street.

'And they reckon she goes out most afternoons, do they?'

'Except Sundays, sir.'

'There are matinees on Wednesdays and Saturdays, so that could account for her going out on those particular days.'

'That would tally, sir. The Dixey twins said that a taxi always comes for her at about one o'clock on Wednesdays and Saturdays. But on those days, she was always dressed smartly, rather than dowdily.' Liz paused before making a suggestion. 'What about an observation on the Foley woman, sir, to see what she does with her other afternoons? D'you think we'd learn anything?'

'From what I remember of Chorley Street when I called at Debra Foley's house, Liz, I think it would be a bit too tricky for an obo. Not much cover. You'd show out in minutes, especially if there are other residents who look out of their windows as often as your Dixey twins seem to.'

'We could ask the Dixey twins if we could keep obo from their sitting room, sir.'

'I doubt that that would help, Liz. Debra might go to the end of the street and take a taxi. Apart from anything else, I get the impression from what you say that these two old ladies are gossips. The last thing we want is for one of them to go beetling across the road to tell Debra Foley all about the Old Bill taking an interest in her. No, I think we'll have to mount a proper obo. If I can get it arranged in time, are you up for it today?'

'Yes, sir. Nicola's in the incident room now.'

'Good. What about Charlie Flynn? Is he about?'

'Yes, sir. I'll tell him you want to see him.'

Although Detective Sergeant Charles Flynn was a former Fraud Squad officer, he could turn his hand to most aspects of criminal investigation. And that's not something you can say of all coppers, despite the hierarchy believing that every member of the Metropolitan Police is an omnicompetent officer.

'You wanted me, guv?'

'I want you to set up an obo, Charlie, this afternoon.'

'Right, guv. Where and when, exactly?'

'In Chorley Street. I'm very interested in Debra Foley's strange goings on. According to Liz Carpenter, Debra dresses up like a bag lady when she goes out on weekday afternoons, apart from Wednesdays, Saturdays and Sundays. Get hold of one of the Job's nondescript vehicles, and get the rundown from Liz and Nicola Chance, who'll be accompanying you. They'll give you the SP.'

SEVEN

It is some forty or so miles from Belgravia to Farnham. Traffic on the London side of Guildford on the A3 had been reduced to a crawl, and progress was further delayed by an accident on the A31 between there and Farnham. But even having the benefit of what Dave called his 'positive driving', it took over two hours for us to get there.

Overcroft Lane proved to be on the outskirts of Farnham in an area that the residents undoubtedly preferred to call a 'village'. The Surrey Constabulary had replied to our request for information about Sally Warner by confirming her address, and that there was nothing in local police records to her detriment.

The bungalow where she lived was a well-kept detached dwelling. The long front garden was immaculate, the paintwork was in pristine condition and the curtains, behind each of the double-glazed casement windows, were identical. A Ford Focus – this year's model – was on the drive. That and the condition of the bungalow prompted a number of possibilities: Sally Warner was married to a reasonably wealthy man; or had a private income; or possibly had been given an allowance by the late Lancelot Foley.

The woman who came to the door appeared to be in her mid-thirties and was quite tall. Her straight blonde hair touched her shoulders and, although simple, had probably cost her a fortune to have it styled that way. Like Debra Foley and Jane Lawless she was possessed of a perfectly proportioned full figure, and her appearance confirmed, yet again, that Lancelot Foley had a fondness for big women. It caused me to wonder what attractions for Foley, apart from the obvious, that the comparatively skinny and rather plain Ruth Strickland possessed.

The woman surveyed us critically: a tall well-dressed man – even if I say so myself – and a hunky six-foot black man. 'If you're reporters, I've got nothing to say. You're wasting your time, so please go away,' she said sharply, and started to close the door.

'We're police officers, madam,' I said, and showed her my warrant card.

'Oh, I'm so sorry.' The hostile countenance was immediately replaced by a welcoming smile.

'It's Miss Warner, is it?' I asked, having introduced myself and Dave.

'I actually call myself Mrs Warner, although I'm not married, but I'd be quite happy for you to call me Sally. Come on in,' she added, and showed us into the sitting room. A young blonde girl, probably about eight years old, in jeans and a red T-shirt, was sitting cross-legged on the floor in front of the television, an earnest expression on her face.

'Run along to your room, Cindy, and watch the television there just while I talk to these gentlemen. Then we'll have some lunch, poppet.'

Without a word Cindy stood up, picked up a worn teddy bear, and spent a moment or two examining the pair of us closely with the innocent curiosity that only a child of that age possesses.

Dave squatted down and faced the girl. 'He's a nice bear, Cindy. What's his name?'

'It's not a "him" it's a "her". You should know that,' said Cindy crossly. 'And her name's Jemima.'

'Don't be rude, Cindy,' cautioned Sally.

'Whoops! Sorry,' said Dave as Cindy marched off.

'She's got a bit of a cold so I've kept her off school,' explained Sally Warner. 'D'you have any children, Sergeant?'

'Unfortunately, no,' said Dave. He and Madeleine had been trying for a baby for some time, but without success. Madeleine had some wild idea that her physical exertions as a ballet dancer may have had something to do with her inability to conceive, but her gynaecologist had dismissed that as fantasy, suggesting that her physique was more likely to be beneficial to childbearing than not.

'Now, what can I do for you?' asked Sally Warner. 'I suppose it's something to do with Lancelot's murder.'

'How well did you know him, Sally?' I asked.

She smiled, as if at some suddenly recalled memory of events of years ago. 'Lancelot and I had a rather torrid affair about nine years ago, and Cindy is the result,' said Sally frankly, displaying no embarrassment at her disclosure. 'Not that she knows that Lancelot is her father, nor will she until she's old enough to take it in.' She paused and smiled again. 'You've probably heard that he's left me all his money. Everyone else seems to have found out. According to his solicitor it's over fifteen million pounds. I didn't know Lancelot had that much money, and I certainly didn't know he was going to leave it all to me. I'm still trying to get my head round it.'

'I didn't know that,' I lied, not wishing to reveal that Foley's lawyer had already given us this information. 'Presumably, that's why you thought we were from the press and had come to talk to you about your new-found wealth.'

'I've been plagued with reporters, begging letters and more telephone calls than you can shake a stick at ever since the news of Lancelot's murder was in the press. God knows how they got to hear of my inheritance. I suppose they'll find out that he paid me quite a substantial allowance, too.'

'It's quite amazing,' I said, but I was certain that despite the recent Old Bailey trials, the press was still happily hacking away at the mobile phones of people whose activities or indiscretions they regarded as newsworthy.

'Had you seen Mr Foley recently?' asked Dave.

Sally Warner studied Dave for a second or two. 'He'd visit me from time to time, but mainly to see Cindy. I told her that he was an uncle.' She paused and gave a mischievous chuckle. 'I had an uncle like that when I was small.' She paused again, reflectively this time. 'Sorry. Now, where was I? Oh yes. Lancelot would stay the night when he could, but we had to be discreet about it because of Cindy. It was usually on the nights that she had a sleepover with one of her school friends.'

'I believe he has a house in Farnham somewhere,' I said, well knowing that to be the case.

'Yes, he has, and it's only a couple of miles away, but Lancelot and I didn't dare meet there in case his wife turned

up. We'd always hoped to get married, but that bitch Debra
wouldn't give him a divorce. She had a dog in the manger
attitude; she didn't love Lancelot, but neither would she let
him go. I suppose it had to do with his money, but she'll have
had a shock if she's found out that he left it all to me. Lancelot
and I did discuss his moving in at one time, but what with his
theatrical obligations it would've been unworkable, particularly
now that Cindy's started to ask questions. And you know what
gossip columnists are like. With Lancelot as well known as
he was, they'd have had a field day splashing it all over their
tawdry rags.'

'When did he last visit you?' Dave asked again.

'About three weeks ago, I suppose, just before his new play
opened.' Sally's reserve finally crumbled, and she emitted a
convulsive sob, reached for a box of tissues and dabbed at her
eyes. 'I'm sorry,' she said, 'but it's all come as an awful shock,
and I really don't know how I'm going to break it to Cindy.
He was always so good to her, bringing her presents and
generally spoiling her. As a matter of fact, I had to tell him
off about it. It doesn't do to spoil a kid the way he did.'

'Our job is to find out who killed Mr Foley, Sally,' I said.
'Do you have any idea who might've wanted him dead?'

'I've racked my brains since it happened to try to find a
reason, but I've no idea at all.'

'Did he seem in any way different when last you saw him?'
asked Dave. 'As though he was worried about something? Or
did he discuss any problems with you?'

'No, not at all. He was always very sweet to Cindy and me,
but from what he said it seemed that Debra gave him a hard
time. By all accounts she's a bit of a tartar. God knows why
he married her, but I suppose it had something to do with the
theatre. She's on the stage too, you know.'

'Yes,' I said, 'I did know that. As a matter of interest were
you in the profession?'

'Yes, but not for long. I got sick of the backbiting, the deceit
and the envy. And the extramarital affairs that seemed to be
the norm in the theatrical world.' She paused. 'Not that I've
any room to talk. Anyway, I got out and did some modelling.'
Sally shot a brief smile at Dave. 'And before you say anything,

Mr Poole, there's quite a demand for big girls like me on the catwalk.'

'I'm pleased to hear it,' said Dave, whose wife Madeleine was a petite principal dancer with the Royal Ballet.

'I take it you never met Debra Foley, Sally,' I said.

'No, and from what I've heard of her, I'm not sorry. According to Lancelot she's had more than a few affairs and didn't hesitate to tell him so. In fact, she flaunted them. She didn't seem to care how much she hurt him.'

'Thank you, Sally,' I said, having decided that she had little to offer that would assist us.

'D'you know when the funeral will be, Mr Brock? I'd like to go if I can get someone to look after Cindy,' she said as she showed us to the front door.

'I'll let you know, but it may be some time before the coroner releases the body.'

I left the house wondering how Lancelot Foley had managed to charm so many women, but at the same time alienate so many men. On reflection, it was probably the one that brought about the other.

'It seems that our Mr Foley played the field, Dave,' I said as we drove out of Farnham. 'Sleeping with Sally Warner and then with Jane Lawless and, it would seem, making vague promises of marriage to each of them.'

'And if Ruth Strickland's to be believed, he conned her in the same way,' said Dave, and after a moment's thought, added: 'Some people have all the luck.'

'You should have become an actor, Dave,' I said.

'Yeah,' said Dave. 'Instead of which I finished up joining the cast of a pantomime.'

At ten minutes to one that same afternoon, just as Brock and Poole were leaving Sally Warner's house at Farnham, a van drove into Chorley Street in Belgravia and parked a few yards down the road from where Debra Foley lived. The van was dirty, and the name on the side was that of a non-existent plumber, but the vehicle was actually owned by the Receiver for the Metropolitan Police District. For the benefit of any nosy passer-by, and to allay suspicion, the telephone number

on the side of the van was connected to the murder investigation team's offices at Belgravia police station where only the
incident room sergeant would answer any calls. He was adept
at assuring potential customers that it was indeed a plumber's
van, but that the said plumber was unable to deal with any
plumbing problems at present as he was fully booked for the
foreseeable future. I once enquired why there was a phone
number on the van at all if it was going to cause that much
trouble. The reply was that it would be even more suspicious
if a plumber *didn't* have a number on his van. I suppose there's
some logic to that, but I can't see it.

The driver was Charlie Flynn, attired in stained overalls and
a baseball cap, and once he had parked the van he joined DS
Carpenter and DC Chance, who were seated in the back out
of sight. All three officers were now in a position to keep
observation through the spy holes in the van's bodywork.

Any police officer who has undertaken a static observation
will tell you that it is one of the most boring tasks there is.
Being seated for hours on end in the back of a cold van in
winter, or a swelteringly hot one in summer, is a mind-numbing
job inclined to sap any enthusiasm for detective work that still
existed among the watching officers. And just to make it worse,
very often such observations came to naught.

Liz Carpenter and Nicola Chance, however, enjoyed a reputation for having the luck of the devil, and so it proved on
this occasion.

The observation van had not been in position for more than
twenty minutes when Debra Foley emerged from her house.
The manner in which she was dressed accorded exactly with
the description given by the Dixey twins. Her hair was covered
by a head scarf, and she wore a shapeless mackintosh. She
carried a shoulder bag that had obviously seen better days,
and her identity was concealed by dark glasses.

As she walked quickly along the pavement, Flynn moved
back to the driver's seat, started the engine and moved off
slowly, following the target at a discreet distance.

'Here we go, girls,' he yelled as Debra Foley turned the
corner and hailed a taxi.

On one occasion, Flynn had to jump a red traffic light to

avoid losing their quarry, but after a mile or so the taxi stopped outside a block of flats called Keycross Court in Keycross Road. The van stopped some way away, and the three officers watched as Debra Foley paid off the cab and entered the building. A few minutes later a light was switched on in a first-floor window, followed by the Foley woman, clearly visible to the watching officers, lowering the Venetian blinds.

'What d'you reckon we should do now, Liz?' asked Flynn.

'I think we should wait for a while, Charlie. According to the guv'nor, Jane Lawless told him that our Debra was not above "entertaining" gentlemen. By which I suppose she meant that Debra was an amateur tom.'

'By her appearance I'd say she was at pains to disguise herself, Skip,' said Nicola to Liz Carpenter. 'But I suppose that being an actress she's fed up with being recognized in the street.'

Charlie Flynn scoffed. 'It's not as if she's an internationally known Hollywood star, is it, Nicky? She's not even on television. She'd be more likely to be recognized if she was a weather girl.'

The officers stayed for half an hour and were about to call off the observation when they saw a man walking down Keycross Road towards the apartment block. He was attired in a short weatherproof coat and wore glasses and a cloth cap. Several times he looked over his shoulder, and his whole demeanour was best described as furtive. When he reached the main door of the building Debra Foley had entered, he stopped, pressed a button on the intercom system and spoke a few words. Then he took one last look over his shoulder and hurried inside.

'I'm sure I've seen that bugger on the *Question Time* programme on television,' said Flynn. 'Yes, got it. He's an MP, and his name is James Corley.'

'Are you sure?' asked Liz.

'Positive,' said Flynn.

'Good heavens!' exclaimed Nicola. 'What an evil world we live in. Who would have thought that an MP would consort with a prostitute?' She glanced at Liz Carpenter. 'What do we do now, Skip?'

'Go back to the factory and tell the guv'nor,' said Liz. 'I've got a feeling that this is all getting a bit too heavy for a mere sergeant.'

Charlie Flynn, Liz Carpenter and Nicola Chance appeared in my office just after Dave and I had returned from Farnham and were discussing our recent interview with Sally Warner.

Charlie Flynn gave me an account of what he and the two women had learned from their observation.

'But there's no proof that this MP, James Corley, entered the same apartment as Debra Foley, is there, Charlie?' I said.

'No, guv,' said Flynn, 'but he looked as guilty as hell and kept glancing over his shoulder. And he wouldn't be visiting a constituent because his constituency is up north somewhere.'

'And right now they don't have an MP in Debra Foley's constituency, sir,' said Carpenter. 'There's a by-election pending.'

'Maybe he was canvassing on behalf of the candidate,' suggested Dave. 'Did you wait for him to come out?'

'No, Dave, but he looked very nervous,' said Flynn, making the point again.

'If he's a politician, he's entitled to look nervous these days,' said Dave.

'Well, it certainly looks as though Debra's up to something,' I said thoughtfully. 'Dave, find out what you can about that block of flats. I want to know who rents that apartment, whether there's a telephone line into it, and anything else that might come in useful.'

'I don't think she'd use a landline phone if she's really on the game, guv,' said Dave. 'You can bet that her punters use an untraceable mobile to call her, and she's bound to use an untraceable mobile as well. There could be reputations at stake, and they'd want to avoid being hacked by the press. They probably don't use names either when they make the arrangements. People like that have got no consideration for us poor coppers.'

'You're probably right, Dave, but find out what you can.'

'D'you want us to carry on with the obo, guv?' asked Flynn.

'Not for the moment, Charlie. We don't want to alert Mrs Foley to the fact that we have an interest in her.'

'I don't think there's much danger of that, guv'nor.' Flynn sounded mildly defensive, as though his observational skills had been called into question.

'I'm not suggesting you've been spotted, Charlie, or are likely to be. I'm thinking more that the Dixey twins might've alerted Debra to our interest. What d'you think, Liz?'

'Quite possibly, sir. I reckon Thelma and Norma Dixey enjoy a good gossip, and I wouldn't be surprised if they'd made a point of telling Mrs Foley about our visit. And if not Mrs Foley, then some of the others in the street, who might pass it on.'

'I think you could be right, Liz. We'll wait until Dave turns up something for us to go on.'

Dave had not wasted any time. At nine o'clock on Friday morning he came into my office with details of the apartment that Flynn and the two women officers had seen Debra Foley entering the previous day.

'Keycross Court, the block of flats in Keycross Road, is owned by a large property company, guv,' Dave began. 'They were a little reluctant to give me the information to start with, but I eventually persuaded them.'

'I'm sure you did, Dave.' I had been witness to Dave's powers of persuasion on more than one occasion.

'You're going to like this, guv'nor. Believe it or not, the apartment on the first floor where Liz spotted Debra Foley is leased by a woman named Vanessa Drummond.'

'Which is Debra Foley's stage name,' I said.

'Yes, funny that, but it gets better, guv. I wandered round to Keycross Road to have a look at the set-up. Access is controlled by an entryphone system, and the name Corinne Black is on the bell push for Vanessa Drummond's flat.'

'What's that all about, I wonder,' I said, musing aloud.

'She's on the game, sir.'

'Yes, I had reached that same conclusion, Dave.' I spoke a little tersely because I knew why he had called me 'sir' again. 'Jane Lawless suggested that Debra Foley might be turning tricks for wealthy gentlemen as a sideline, although I did wonder if it was pure malice.'

'If it's true it's probably more profitable than acting,' said Dave. 'I dare say she charges more for a night's performance in the sack than she's paid for a week's performance in that play she's in.' And remembering what time she had arrived there yesterday added, 'Or for a matinee on her back.'

'Even so, she's taking a hell of a risk of being recognized by one of her tricks.'

'It's a double-edged sword, guv,' said Dave. 'None of them could boast about having bedded her without showing out that they pay for sex. According to Charlie Flynn, one of them appears to have been James Corley MP, and I don't somehow think he'd want his name splashed all over the tabloids.'

'No,' I said thoughtfully, 'but he might be prepared to talk to us.'

Dave pursed his lips. 'That could be a bit dicey.'

'Maybe,' I said. 'Have a look in *Who's Who*. See if he's married, and if he is he might be persuaded to have a frank and open discussion with us. Particularly if we mention that it's a murder enquiry.'

'Well, I'll say this for you, guv'nor, you certainly go in with both feet.'

'Look at it like this, Dave. Debra Foley is the widow of a murder victim, and she's openly admitted that she and Lancelot as good as hated the sight of each other. And that's borne out by some of the other people we've interviewed. On that basis, and with what she's said so far, we're quite justified in pursuing all leads, however tenuous.'

'Well, I hope you're right. By the way, I checked with BT,' Dave continued, 'and although there's a telephone line into her apartment, it's not connected. So I was probably right that she arranges all her appointments through an untraceable mobile.'

'Yes, but how does she reach her clients? She's not the sort to leave her business card in telephone boxes.'

'What telephone boxes are these, sir?'

Dave made a good point. Since the proliferation of mobile telephones, the number of telephone boxes in the capital and elsewhere had been reduced markedly. Apart from anything else, it was now an offence for prostitutes to advertise by leaving their cards in phone booths.

'Potential tricks must get to know of her by word of mouth, then,' I said.

'We could ask her,' suggested Dave.

'That's not a bad idea, Dave. We could drop in on her one afternoon.'

'Really?' The inflection Dave put on that one word indicated that he did not much care for the idea. 'I'll have a look in *Who's Who*, guv. We've got a copy in the incident room. See what it says about this Corley bloke.'

Dave returned a few moments later clutching a copy of the large volume.

'James Corley is aged thirty-eight,' he said, summarizing the relevant entry, 'and is married with two children. He's been the Member of Parliament for Lampton East – that's up north somewhere – for the past five and a half years.'

'Is there an address for him?'

'Yes, guv.' Dave looked up and grinned. 'House of Commons, London SW1A 0AA. But the company that owns the flats confirmed that Corley doesn't have an apartment there, so he can't claim that that's where he lives.'

'It was too much to expect that he'd put his home address in *Who's Who*. So I suppose we'll have to see him at the Commons. Some people can be very unhelpful.'

'Perhaps he's just shy. But to be serious, guv'nor, I hope you know what you're doing.' Dave looked unhappy. 'All right, so he visited that block of flats, but there are twenty-four apartments there, and Corley could have visited any one of the other twenty-three. We haven't got a shred of evidence to prove that he visited Debra Foley alias Corinne Black. And in the unlikely event that he does admit to seeing her, he might claim that he was a friend or just a "talker". Anyway, he won't have committed any offences, so he doesn't have to tell us a damned thing.'

It was well known in the murky world of police work that the clients of prostitutes sometimes wanted only to talk to a naked girl and nothing else. And were prepared to pay for the privilege. Don't ask me why, but it happens.

'It's all right, Dave. We'll put it to Debra Foley first. But I'm not thinking of charging Corley with anything. Unless, of course, it was him who murdered Lancelot Foley.'

'When are you thinking of seeing Debra Foley again, then?' asked Dave.

'This afternoon, if she's going to be there. I'll talk to Charlie Flynn.' Followed by Dave, I went out to the incident room. 'Charlie, take an unmarked Job car and park outside the flats in Keycross Road. If she turns up, give me a bell, and Dave and I will have a chat with her.'

An hour and a half later, Flynn rang. 'No go, I'm afraid, guv. She hasn't shown.'

'OK, Charlie, knock it on the head. We'll have to try next week.'

EIGHT

On Monday I had to attend the coroner's court for a preliminary hearing.

Dave and I made our way to Horseferry Road and were there by nine o'clock.

'In the matter of the death of Lancelot Foley.' The coroner peered around the almost empty courtroom. 'Is the officer in the case here?'

'Detective Chief Inspector Harry Brock, sir, Murder Investigation Team attached to New Scotland Yard,' I said, having moved swiftly into the witness box.

'I've not convened a jury this morning, Mr Brock, as I presume we are a long way from a full hearing. Perhaps you will be so good as to give me an interim report.'

I outlined, as succinctly as possible, what had been learned so far. I made no suggestion as to suspects and no indication as to when the enquiry was likely to be completed. It is unwise to provide a coroner with anything other than the unvarnished truth.

'Finally, sir,' I continued, 'as all scientific examination has been completed to the satisfaction of police, I ask for the release of the deceased's body to the family.'

'So ordered.' The coroner consulted his register and made an entry. 'I shall adjourn this hearing until Monday the eleventh of March, Mr Brock. If by that time, you are unable still to provide further details, advise my officer and I'll arrange another date.'

We were out of the court and on our way back to Belgravia police station by twenty minutes past nine.

Once there, I telephoned Debra Foley and informed her that she was now free to arrange the funeral and asked her to advise me of the date, time and place. An hour later, she rang back to say that Lancelot Foley's cremation would take place next

Wednesday the thirteenth of February at ten thirty at Golders
Green Crematorium.

'The ashes of quite a few famous actors are spread there,'
she said. 'He'll be in good company.'

'You arranged that very quickly, Mrs Foley,' I said.

'The sooner the better is my view on things like this, and
I was lucky that the crematorium had a slot at that time.' Debra
made it sound as though she'd been fortunate enough to find
a parking space. 'And to coin an apt phrase, the undertakers
were waiting in the wings.'

'Will the service be held at Golders Green or somewhere
else?'

'There won't be a service. Lancelot was an atheist.'

And with that Debra Foley slammed down the phone, leaving
me with the impression that she couldn't wait to dispose of
her late husband in mind as well as body. And presumably
move on to her next conquest.

On Monday afternoon I sent Detective Sergeant Flynn to keep
observation once again outside the apartment block in Keycross
Road. But this time he did not have long to wait.

At twenty minutes to two, he rang in to say that Debra
Foley had just stepped out of a taxi and entered the building.
And a few minutes later, he had seen her closing the Venetian
blinds in the window of the flat that we now knew she had
leased in the name of Vanessa Drummond.

'Stay put, Charlie,' I said, 'and let me know if you see
anyone else entering the building.'

At five past two, Flynn rang in again. 'I've just seen a
Mercedes stop outside the apartment block, guv'nor. A well-
dressed man of about forty alighted and went into the flats.
He had to use the entryphone to get in, although I couldn't
see which bell he pushed. But the fact that he had to be let
in seems to indicate that he's not a resident, or else he's lost
his key.'

'Hang on there for a while, Charlie. I'd like to know when
this guy leaves. In the meantime, I'll have Dave check on the
registration of the Merc.'

I had another call from Flynn at four o'clock to say that

the unknown caller had left minutes ago. I told him to return to the office.

'It's likely that your man is called Charles Tate, Charlie,' I said, when Flynn showed up in my office. 'The Merc registration is in that name, along with an address in Kensington. Dave's also done an electoral roll check on Tate's address. He lives there with someone named Elizabeth Tate, presumably his wife or daughter.'

'Or mother or sister,' said Dave.

'Have we any idea what he does for a living, Dave?'

'Not yet, sir,' said a somewhat exasperated Dave. 'I've only just found out who he is, but if he can take a Monday afternoon off, he must be in a good line of business.'

'Unless his line of business was the reason he was calling at Keycross Road,' I said.

'Possibly,' said Dave doubtfully. 'Maybe he's her pimp,' he added, always willing to see the worst in people.

'It doesn't matter if he is. He's only a means to an end in solving a murder. If he is a pimp we'll hand that aspect of the case over to the local nick to deal with.'

'But what are we going to do about him?' asked Dave.

'Pay him a visit,' I said. 'This evening.'

'On what grounds?' Dave was clearly unhappy about the direction in which I was taking this enquiry.

'Offences against the Ways and Means Act,' I said.

There were residents' parking bays outside Charles Tate's house, and his top-of-the-range Mercedes was in one of them; a sure sign that he was at home. Perhaps.

'Yes, please? What is it you are wanting?' The door was answered by a rather plain, square-jawed young woman who appeared to be little more than twenty years old. Those few words were sufficient to tell me that she was foreign and most likely employed as a household drudge under the guise of being an au pair.

'We'd like to speak to Mr Tate,' I said. 'Mr Charles Tate.'

'Yes. Come in, please.'

'What's this about, Hannah?' As we entered the house, a woman joined us. Certainly not the type to have appealed to the late Lancelot Foley, she was a slight, neat woman, probably in her mid-thirties, with an air of fragility about her, and was attired in white trousers and a black jumper. She had a delightfully husky voice.

'These gentlemens come to see Mr Tate, missus.'

'The word is "gentlemen", not "gentlemens", Hannah. "Gentlemen" is the plural, so you don't have to add the letter "s". And I'm called madam not missus. How many times do I have to tell you?' Mrs Tate corrected the girl in the sort of tones that a school teacher might have used: tolerant but stern. 'May I ask what this is about?' she asked as she turned to face us.

'We're police officers, madam,' I said as Dave and I produced our warrant cards, 'and we'd like to have a word with Mr Tate. Your husband, I take it?'

'Yes, he is.' The woman looked suddenly concerned. 'Is there something wrong? Oh heavens, it's not my son, is it? Has there been an accident? He's away on a school trip to the Swiss Alps, and he's only fifteen, you see.' It was apparent that the Tates were the sort of family that only ever expected to see the police at their door when they were bringing bad news. *And that,* I thought, *might just be the case, if Charles Tate has been doing what I think he has.*

'No, it's nothing like that, madam. In fact, it's merely a routine enquiry.' I always enjoyed making that reply. It was completely meaningless, but, curiously, rarely questioned.

'Please come in.' Mrs Tate escorted us into a sitting room where her husband was watching television. 'Charles, these gentlemen are from the police. They'd like to speak to you.'

Charles Tate almost leapt from his chair, clearly agitated at our arrival, but I think he sensed why we were there. 'What's wrong?' he asked. 'Has something happened to Leon, Elizabeth?' I agreed with Charlie Flynn's estimate that he was probably no older than forty, and his attire indicated that he wasn't exactly on the breadline: designer jeans, a paisley shirt, a cashmere sweater, and a pair of Gucci loafers. And I'll bet he paid a damned sight more for a haircut than I did. The furnishings in the room were expensive, too. That and the house, and the Mercedes, were all marks of a successful businessman.

'No, Mr Tate,' I said. 'As I explained to your wife we are making routine enquiries.'

'What about? How d'you think I can help?'

'It concerns an apartment block in Keycross Road called Keycross Court.'

'Keycross Court?' Tate gave a masterful display of perplexity. 'I don't think I know it. Where is it?'

'It's in the Belgravia area, Mr Tate,' said Dave helpfully.

'Ah, yes, of course.' Tate cast a glance in his wife's direction. 'Rather than interrupt my wife's viewing, shall we go into the study?' And without waiting for an answer, he led the way quickly into a room at the back of the house.

The study was decorated with tasteful wallpaper, and the woodwork was pristine white. It was thickly carpeted and had several leather armchairs. The obligatory computer stood in the centre of a leather-topped desk.

'Do take a seat, gentlemen,' said Tate smoothly as he sat down in the captain's chair behind the desk. Perhaps he felt safer being separated from us by a desk. 'Why should you think I know anything about this apartment block you were talking about?' He continued to maintain an air of lofty disdain, as though we had made an honest mistake, but I detected an underlying nervousness.

'We're investigating a murder at one of the flats in Keycross Court, Mr Tate.'

'A *murder*! What, at that block of flats?' For the first time since we'd arrived, Tate's mask of confidence slipped momentarily. 'Whereabouts?'

'Corinne Black . . .' began Dave slowly, skilfully sidestepping the question about the locale.

'Oh no!' said Tate, cutting across what Dave was saying. 'I don't know anything about Corinne being murdered. I only saw her this afternoon. Surely you can't think that I had anything to do with that.' Tate was clearly appalled and was probably visualizing himself in the dock at the Old Bailey already.

Nice one, Dave, I thought. *You've got him by the short and curlies.*

'You know Corinne Black, then,' I said, capitalizing on the admission that Dave had forced out of Tate.

'Yes, I do,' said Tate, lowering his voice. 'Does my wife have to know anything about this?'

'Not unless you tell her,' said Dave, 'or someone else does.'

'When was Corinne murdered?' Tate was clearly having difficulty coming to terms with what he believed we were talking about.

'Oh, it's not Miss Black who's been murdered,' I said, 'but we believe that it may have been one of her clients who was responsible for the murder.'

'Who has been murdered, then?'

'Lancelot Foley.'

'The actor? But according to the newspapers that happened in Chelsea last week.'

'You're quite right, Mr Tate,' I said, 'but we believe there is a connection with someone who has visited Keycross Court.'

'But how did you know I'd been there?' Tate was now completely confused, as we'd intended he should be.

'We've been keeping observation on that block of flats ever since Lancelot Foley's murder,' said Dave convincingly, 'and your car was seen there this afternoon. And you were seen entering the premises.'

'Oh, God! Does this mean I'm in trouble? I have a reputation to maintain, and if anything got into the press about this . . .' Tate left the sentence unfinished, but he didn't have to say anything else. His concern was quite apparent.

'I take it you know nothing of this murder, Mr Tate,' I said.

'No, absolutely nothing.'

'What exactly were you doing at Keycross Court?'

Tate ran a hand through his hair, and then tugged at the bottom of his pullover. Little beads of sweat broke out on his forehead. 'I was visiting Corinne,' he said eventually.

'For what reason? Is she a friend?'

'For sex,' said Tate, his voice barely above a whisper.

'Oh, she's a prostitute, is she?' I asked, feigning innocence.

'I wouldn't have put it quite that bluntly,' said Tate, recovering slightly. 'She provides female companionship.'

That was a definition of the sex trade I'd not heard before, and I hoped that Dave would not burst out laughing.

'How did you hear that she was a prostitute?' I asked, determined not to resort to euphemism.

'Oh, hell! You make it sound so sordid. A friend of mine told me about her.'

'What's his name?' demanded Dave, pocketbook at the ready.

'I'm not prepared to give you that,' said Tate, a measure of his initial confidence returning.

It was the answer I'd expected, but it was of no consequence anyway. 'As a matter of interest, how many times have you visited her?'

'About four or five, I suppose,' said Tate reluctantly. 'In the afternoons.'

'Afternoons? I take it you're retired, then.'

'Good heavens, no. I have an import and export business.' Tate took a card from a small box on his desk and handed it to me.

'And how much did you pay Corinne for her services?'

'Five hundred pounds each time,' said Tate quietly, 'and worth every penny.'

'In cash?' I asked.

'No,' said Tate. 'Credit card.'

'Oh dear!' I said quietly. Once again I was astounded that men who were so sharp and successful in other areas of their life could be so stupid as to leave a paper trail like that. And if James Corley MP *was* another of Corinne's clients, he probably paid her in the same way.

'Will she be prosecuted?'

I assumed that Tate's question was prompted by the fear that his name might come out in any court proceedings.

'No,' I said. 'As Miss Black entertains men and they give her what she would undoubtedly say were gifts, it doesn't amount to an offence. And provided she works alone, the premises can't be classified as a brothel. Thank you for your time, Mr Tate.'

'I'll show you out.' Tate seemed relieved that that appeared to be the end of the matter.

As we arrived at the front door, Elizabeth Tate emerged from the sitting room. 'Is everything all right, Charles?' she asked, her face registering concern.

'Perfectly, Mrs Tate,' I said, answering for the woman's husband. 'In fact, Mr Tate wasn't able to assist us at all. But we're obliged to follow up every lead. Your husband explained that he has business interests in Keycross Road.'

'That's all right, then,' said Elizabeth, and returned to the sitting room.

'Thank you, Inspector,' said Tate. 'I'm most grateful for your tact and discretion.'

'I'm a *chief* inspector,' I said.

Once we were in the car and on our way back to Belgravia police station, Dave asked, 'What exactly did we achieve by that little charade, guv? It seemed like a monumental waste of time.'

'What we achieved, Dave, is to establish as fact that Debra Foley is a prostitute. And that opens up a whole new line of enquiry. That she's on the game, albeit in a selective sort of way, means there may be a connection between her hiring out her body and the murder of Lancelot Foley.'

'Good heavens!' exclaimed Dave. 'Who'd have thought it, sir? Still, I think you've just lost her one of her customers. I doubt that Tate will be going anywhere near her again.'

On Tuesday morning, I gathered my team in the incident room to brief them on the current state of the enquiry.

'So far,' I began, 'we've established that Debra Foley, using the name Corinne Black, is engaged in prostitution at an apartment in a block of flats called Keycross Court in Keycross Road. And we have to thank DS Carpenter and DC Chance for obtaining the information that led us to the flat where Debra meets her clients.'

'Are we going to do Debra Foley for that, guv'nor, or the owner of the apartment block?' asked DS Tom Challis. 'Or even both of them?'

'No, Tom. It's of no concern to Homicide and Major Crime Command, and I doubt that the local nick would be all that interested either. There are hundreds of call girls working in London, and if they're solo operators no offence is committed by the owner of the block of flats unless there are two or more women working there, in which case the premises would be defined as a brothel. Apart from anything else, prostitution itself is not an offence, only soliciting for it. But you lot know all that, don't you?'

'They talk of little else in the canteen, guv'nor,' said an anonymous voice, a comment that raised a laugh.

'Our only interest,' I continued, 'is whether Debra Foley's prostitution has any bearing on the murder of Lancelot Foley. As I said to Sergeant Poole, where there's prostitution there's usually crime.'

'What about James Corley, the MP?' asked Dave. 'Is he still in the frame?'

'No longer a person of interest, Dave,' I said. 'We don't know for sure that he's one of Corinne Black's tricks – he could've been visiting any of the flats – and it doesn't matter if he was having it off with her. We've found out what we wanted, and it's better to leave sleeping dogs tucked up in their kennels, especially as Corley has a voice in the House of Commons. We can do without a complaint from that source.' Despite the commander's love of paperwork, I could visualize him having a heart attack if a docket marked Parliamentary Question landed on his desk.

'So what's next, guv'nor?' asked Kate Ebdon.

'Next is a full background check on Debra Foley, her relatives and her friends. I'll leave that to you, Charlie,' I told Flynn. 'Once we see what that turns up, we'll know which way to go next. At the same time, I want a thorough background check on Lancelot Foley. The same for him: relatives, associates and any other dirt we can dig up. And that's a job for you, Tom,' I said to Challis, 'but work with Charlie because the two are bound to overlap. Use as many of your colleagues as you need to, because time is of the essence. The trail is already getting cold.' I knew from experience that the more time that passed after a murder, the more difficult it was to identify the killer. The ideal was to crack it in the first twenty-four hours. 'And, finally, you may wish to know that Lancelot Foley will be burnt to a cinder at Golders Green Crematorium tomorrow at half-past ten.'

'D'you want me to come with you, guv?' asked Dave.

'Yes, but only to drive and observe. I've no doubt that the

press will be there in force, and we don't want to look too
obvious by going in mob-handed. Debra Foley tells me that
there won't be a religious service, but I suppose someone
might be leaned on to say a few words in the form of a eulogy.'
I glanced across the room at DI Ebdon. 'You and I will be
there, Kate, to see if there's anyone among the congregation
who interests us.'

'I'd better get the mothballs out of my Old Bailey suit,
then,' said Kate.

'One other thing, guv,' said Dave. 'I ran a check on Charles
Tate's business with Companies House. All legit and above
board, apparently, and making a healthy profit into the bargain.'

'No wonder he can afford to pay Corinne Black five hundred
quid for a screw. Right, we can cross him off the list.'

NINE

When Kate Ebdon and I arrived at Golders Green Crematorium on Wednesday morning it had begun to snow hard again, and with it came a chill wind.

'I'm very pleased you ordered me to stay in the car, guv,' said Dave, somewhat smugly.

Kate leaned across and whispered a few obscene suggestions in his ear.

'Certainly, ma'am,' said Dave, and laughed. 'Now, or later?'

Kate could always be relied upon to dress as the occasion demanded. Her appearances at the Old Bailey would see her attired in a smart two-piece suit, with discreet gold earrings and hair carefully coiffed. This morning she was wearing the same ensemble, together with her fur Cossack hat, a knee-length double-breasted camel overcoat with a large collar, high boots and a black umbrella that she opened as we left the car. It was at this point that I realized I had omitted to bring that essential piece of equipment with me. But, as Gail frequently and sarcastically pointed out, I'm a man. I sighed and turned up the collar of my overcoat.

There were a number of cars in the crematorium parking area. Among them I spotted a Rolls Royce, a Maserati, and at least two Porsches. Kate discreetly made a note of the index marks. There were more cars on the other side of Hoop Lane, immediately opposite the entrance, and I knew that Dave would be taking the details and would probably have a list of their registered keepers by the time we returned to the car.

The glitterati of the acting profession and its hangers-on had come to pay their respects. As was to be expected, there were the usual number of paparazzi, and a couple of television journalists with attendant cameramen.

There was already a sizeable crowd of mourners making their way towards the crematorium chapel. I recognized one well-known footballer, a chat show host and a couple of Z-list soap opera stars, although I doubt that their presence would have pleased Lancelot Foley. I'm sure he would have been happier to see some members of the Royal Shakespeare Company there, but they'd probably decided to give this event a miss.

But then, with all the unctuousness of a slug, I saw Fat Danny slithering towards me wearing his usual outfit: dirty mac and the battered, greasy trilby without which he was never to be seen.

Fat Danny has the dubious reputation of being the chief crime correspondent of possibly the worst tabloid in Britain, although I think he actually revels in such opprobrium. He has no scruples and certainly no dress sense, and I suspect that he only rarely takes a shower.

'Hello, Mr Brock, Miss Ebdon.'

'Don't bother to raise your hat, Danny,' said Kate sarcastically.

Danny laughed nervously.

'What are you doing here, Danny?' It was an unnecessary question; I knew why he was here. It wasn't to pay his respects – he had no respect for anyone – but because he'd guessed that *I* would be here.

'Have you come to make an arrest, Mr Brock?' Danny asked in his usual wheedling tone.

'Down Under, Danny, we cook journos like you on the barbie and then throw the remains to the roos,' said Kate.

'Oh, you do have a way with words, Miss Ebdon.' Danny laughed nervously again; he'd never quite got the measure of Kate, but he was not alone in that. 'But seriously, Mr Brock, have you got anything for me? I mean, you must have something. You're bound to be pulling out all the stops for a big case like this one.'

'Danny,' I said, 'this case is no different from any of the others. It doesn't matter who the victim is; we devote all our abilities to finding the killer.'

'Although we might not try too hard if you were the victim, Danny,' said Kate. 'Anyway, it would take forever to wade through the list of your known enemies.'

'Yes, but—'

'I suppose you were responsible for that appalling headline in that rag you have the temerity to call a newspaper,' I said.

The headline in question had proclaimed: LANCELOT FOLEY MURDERED IN LONDON STREET. Beneath it in a smaller typeface was the tasteless comment: *Famous Actor Exits Stage Left – For Good!*

'Yeah, that was mine. You've got to have something that'll get the punters to buy the bloody rag.' Fat Danny was unapologetic and unrepentant.

'I thought it was your style, Danny, but I notice you didn't have the guts to put your name to it. Now, I have a barbecue to attend, so make yourself scarce before I nick you for obstructing police. And for writing bad copy. Oh, and another thing: I should go out the back way, if I were you.'

'Why's that, Mr Brock?'

'Because Sergeant Poole is at the front, and he's in a very bad mood today.'

We stood aside, along with the last of the stragglers, as the hearse bearing Lancelot Foley's mortal remains nosed its way towards the chapel. The coffin was covered in flowers, in the centre of which was the BAFTA award he had won a few years previously. I assumed that someone would have the sense to retrieve it before the coffin disappeared into the furnace.

Kate and I waited until most of the mourners had traipsed into the chapel, and then followed at a discreet distance.

We stood at the very back of the congregation. I spotted Debra Foley and Jane Lawless seated as far away from each other as was possible, but there was no sign of Sally Warner, who, I supposed, had wisely decided not to risk a confrontation with either Lancelot Foley's widow or his final paramour. Also present were most of the cast of *The Importance of Being Earnest*. Sebastian Weaver was there, too, but sitting alone several rows back.

I noticed that no one was wearing obvious funeral attire; presumably, the shunning of mourning black was a theatrical thing. In the circumstances, it seemed that Kate and I were the only ones I thought to be fittingly dressed for a funeral.

As we waited for the coffin to disappear into the furnace, I reflected on my father's funeral. Fred Brock had spent his whole working life as a motorman on the London Underground driving trainloads of indifferent commuters on varying sectors of the Northern Line between Morden and Edgware or High Barnet. Four weeks after his retirement he'd died of pulmonary emphysema, leaving my mother Sheila with nothing but a stack of bills and me with a bundle of porn magazines. He'd never been much of a churchgoer, but my mother had insisted on a decent Christian burial for the old boy. And so it had been: a church in Tooting, a congregation in black, a clergyman to speak the obsequies and a reception at a local pub. One of the bosses from the Underground had been there, along with several of Fred's former colleagues, and a representative of the National Union of Railwaymen.

What a contrast with today's proceedings. Many of those present seemed to be regarding the whole affair as a jolly and were, no doubt, looking forward to the wake, where they could drink themselves senseless at someone else's expense.

Suddenly, I realized that it was all over. There had been no eulogy, no words extolling the late Lancelot Foley's artistic talent or attributes. The coffin and its contents had been converted into ashes, and that was that.

Kate and I hastened back to the car whence we could keep watch on the departing congregation. Most got into cars and drove away, but there were one or two souls who set out on the five-minute walk to Golders Green Underground station.

Almost last to emerge was Debra Foley, holding the BAFTA award. She was accompanied by a man of around her age, maybe a little older. He was on the short side, maybe five foot nine, and stockily built, and there was the indefinable air of a soldier about him. He and Debra appeared to be having a heated argument as they crossed the road, and then the man ushered Debra into a BMW, after which he got into the driver's seat. I assumed that he had been too late to find a space in the crematorium's car park, and I knew that he and Debra had not arrived together; she had been one of the first at the crematorium, and I'd seen her alighting from a taxi.

'Shall I follow it, guv?' asked Dave as the BMW moved away.

'Yes, until I get details of the registration,' I said, and

telephoned the incident room. Within seconds Colin Wilberforce had consulted the Police National Computer and was able to tell me that the registered keeper was Robert Miles with an address in Harrow.

'Another of Debra's fancy men, guv?' suggested Dave as I passed on this information.

'Or another of her clients,' said Kate. 'They seemed to be having a bit of a blue, though.'

'Miss Ebdon wishes you to know that they're having an argument, Dave.' I was becoming quite proficient at translating Australian. 'OK, you can break it off now. They'll only be going to the wake, wherever that's being held. We'll look into Mr Miles when we get back to the factory.'

Kate Ebdon had left her hat and coat in the office she shared with DI Len Driscoll, and exchanged her knee boots for high-heeled shoes before appearing in the incident room, but she was still in the elegant figure-hugging black suit and black tights that she had worn at Lancelot Foley's cremation. She hadn't released her shock of flame hair from its neat ponytail; neither had she removed her earrings.

The team were accustomed to seeing their lady inspector in jeans and a white shirt with her hair loose. They'd never before seen her attired in such a glamorous outfit. There was a stunned silence followed by a discreet round of applause.

'Wow!' exclaimed Charlie Flynn. 'You look terrific, ma'am.'

'You should wear that outfit more often, ma'am,' said Tom Challis, his mouth open in admiration. 'I reckon that's what you Australians would call "fair dinkum"!'

Kate put her hands on her hips and pushed one leg forward in a classical pose. 'Why don't you bludgers stop yabbering and get on with what you're supposed to be doing?' she said, but I suspected that secretly she was pleased at the compliments, the more so as they came from fellow officers who usually tended to be sparing with remarks of admiration or even sympathy.

It brought to mind an incident years ago when I was a detective sergeant on the Flying Squad. One of the team had been shot during an abortive bank raid. When he returned to duty after three months' sick leave, the DI looked up and asked him if he'd enjoyed his holiday. And that was all, but that's the way coppers are.

'I've been doing some background checks on Robert Miles, sir,' said Colin Wilberforce, bringing us back to the matter in hand. 'Charlie Flynn and I put our heads together and did a few searches. Robert Miles is Debra Foley's brother. He's two years older than she is, and he's ex-army.'

'Do we know which branch of the army he was in?' I was thinking about the manner in which Foley had been murdered, and I wondered whether Miles had been a member of what is euphemistically dubbed 'special forces'.

'Not yet, sir.'

'What does he do now?'

It was Flynn who replied. 'We don't know that either, guv, but I'm making further enquiries.'

'Good. Let me know as soon as you get anything.'

But we didn't have to wait for that information.

At three o'clock that afternoon, a man rang the incident room asking to speak to the officer in charge of the Lancelot Foley murder case, as he had important information. I told Wilberforce to put the call through to my office.

'This is Detective Chief Inspector Brock. I understand you wish to speak to me.'

'I'm pretty sure I know who killed Foley,' said the man.

'Are you able to give me a name?'

'I'm not prepared to discuss this over the phone, Mr Brock. Walls have ears. Or, put more accurately, interested parties hack mobile phones. I'm out and about at the moment, but could you call at my place at precisely eight o'clock this evening? Incidentally, don't mention my name over the phone. I noticed that your car followed mine as we left Golders Green this morning, and then broke away. Presumably, you've done a check on the police national computer, so I'm sure you know my address.' And with that, the line went dead.

Colin Wilberforce put his head round the door. 'I did a check on that call, sir. It was an untraceable mobile.'

'I thought it would be, Colin. But thanks anyway.'

For a moment or two I sat thinking about the call. I was in

no doubt that it was Robert Miles to whom I had been speaking, even though he had been very covert in our short conversation, particularly about revealing his identity. The more I thought about it, the more I wondered about his military background. It was fairly plain that he had been trained to a higher standard than most soldiers and had learned about the art of survival in all its forms. And possibly how to break a man's neck.

But then another thought occurred to me. Could Miles actually be the murderer, and was he luring me into a trap? I didn't think he'd have had any qualms about murdering his brother-in-law if the price was right. The apparent ruthlessness with which Foley had been killed led me to believe that his killer would stop at nothing to avoid capture, and I was sufficient of a realist to believe that he'd kill a police officer without a second thought. After all, a murderer can only serve *one* life sentence, no matter how many of them he receives.

I decided to take no chances and sent for Dave Poole, Charlie Flynn and Tom Challis. I related the gist of my conversation with Miles and told them of my concern that it might be a set-up.

'Dave, you'll come with me,' I said, 'and Charlie and Tom will follow in a separate car. And I want you tooled up.'

Now came the difficult part: I had to get the commander's authority for the issue of firearms. Reluctantly, I made my way to his office.

'Ah, Mr Brock.' The commander set aside the file he was reading with, I imagined, the same degree of reluctance that I had approached him to seek his permission to draw weapons. 'Is there some progress?'

I told the commander about the phone call from Miles without elaborating; otherwise he'd offer me advice about matters of which he knew very little. Right now, I was in no mood for one of his ill-informed little homilies on crime detection.

'In the circumstances I think it would be wise if we were to carry firearms, sir.'

Predictably, the commander pursed his lips. 'D'you think that's absolutely necessary, Mr Brock?' He gave me the sort of look that implied it wasn't too late for me to change my mind.

'I do, sir,' I said firmly. I was not prepared to be messed about, and if necessary I'd go over his head and speak to the deputy assistant commissioner. The DAC was a real detective and knew the dangers that could face working detectives. 'I could go to the DAC if you'd feel happier about it, sir,' I added, putting my thoughts into words.

'No, no, that's all right, Mr Brock. You may draw firearms.' My veiled threat had its effect; the commander was frightened of the DAC. He opened the file he'd been working on, indicating that as far as he was concerned the interview was over.

'In writing, sir, if you please.' I handed him the requisite form.

'Is that really necessary?'

'Yes, sir. One must think ahead. If in the meantime you had a heart attack and died, it would be difficult to prove that firearms were authorized. It's particularly important in case we shoot someone.'

'Oh, um, yes, very well.' The commander appeared shocked that I thought he might succumb to a fatal coronary, and that we might actually *use* firearms. God knows what he'd do if someone actually died at the hands of police. He took the form and scribbled his signature on it.

I returned to the incident room and told the three sergeants to go ahead and draw weapons, and I drew one myself.

It was fifteen miles from Belgravia to Robert Miles's address in Harrow, but we'd be travelling during the end of the evening rush hour, and there was no telling how long the journey would take. I decided that to be on the safe side we'd leave Central London at seven o'clock.

TEN

It was a quiet road in Harrow, an area of London described by its residents as a leafy suburb, more out of self delusion than reality. The BMW that we had seen at the crematorium was parked on the drive of a very ordinary detached house. The property could have belonged to a middle-class, middle-income, middle-management, upwardly mobile man with a medium sized family. A man who was struggling to pay the mortgage, the golf-club subscription and the school fees of his children at an overpriced second-rate private school. All in all, the occupants could have been a family desperately trying to keep up with the neighbours and impressing them by hosting lavish dinner parties they could ill afford.

But I was certain that Robert Miles did not fit into that category.

That his car was on the drive seemed to indicate that Miles was at home, even though it was only a quarter to eight. He had been specific about the time: eight o'clock.

I'd radioed Flynn and Challis and told them to park a few yards down the road, but to alight and cover Dave and me as we approached the house. When we reached the front door, I noticed a CCTV camera covertly positioned in the porch. Dave, pistol held discreetly against his leg, stood to one side of the door.

I rang the bell, and then I moved to the other side and drew my firearm. It was not unknown for a suspect – and right now Miles was one – to open fire through a door. There was no answer. I tried again, but there was still no answer. I signalled to Flynn and Challis to move up and told them to cover the door. All the windows were closed and, I suspected, locked and alarmed.

'We'll try round the back, Dave.' We moved round to the side of the house and were confronted by a pair of six-foot high wooden gates that were wide enough to admit a vehicle. I tried one of them, but it wouldn't budge. 'It's locked.'

'Yes, sir,' said Dave, and without hesitation placed his hands on top of one of the gates and vaulted over. I think he must've been taking lessons from his ballet dancer wife.

'Any luck, Dave?' I asked, but there was no reply.

A few minutes later, I heard some object being dragged towards the gate, and I imagined that Dave was moving something to stand on. Then his head appeared over the top. 'D'you want the good news or the bad news, guv?'

'Start with the good news, Dave.'

'There isn't any, but the bad news is that there's a body lying on the floor in the room at the back. I'm pretty sure it's Miles, and it looks as though he's snuffed it. Either that or he's smashed out of his brains from all the booze at Lancelot's wake.'

'Oh, bloody marvellous,' I exclaimed. 'Any sign of blood?'

'No, guv.'

'Is there any chance of getting into the house at the back?'

'No way. Everything's locked up. We'd even have a job smashing a window: they're triple-glazed.'

'I'll get Charlie and Tom to give me a hand and see if we can break in through the front door. You hang on there, Dave.'

'I was planning on doing that . . . sir.'

I returned to the front of the house to find that Flynn and Challis were in conversation with two uniformed constables. A police car was parked across the entrance to the drive.

'These two officers got a call from a concerned neighbour opposite, guv, who saw a suspicious looking black man—' Flynn stopped and dissolved into laughter. 'Sorry, guv,' he said, once he'd recovered. 'She saw a sussy looking black guy hopping over the back gate and seemed to think he was breaking in. I explained who we were and where we're from.'

'We're *about* to break in, Charlie.' I turned to the two PCs. 'Have you, by any chance, got a forty-pound key in your car?' I asked, using police slang for a battering-ram.

'Never go anywhere without one these days, sir,' said one of the PCs, and fetched the rammer from the boot of the police car. 'Front door, sir?' He didn't ask if I had a warrant, but as

I was the senior officer I suppose he didn't really care. I'd be the one carrying the can if it all went pear-shaped.

'Yes, please.'

The PC swung the battering-ram against the door, but it took several blows before it finally gave way, with a splintering of the woodwork surrounding the lock.

Telling the uniformed officers to stand well back, Flynn, Challis and I drew our pistols and entered the house.

Once we were satisfied that the ground floor was clear, I sent the two sergeants to search the upstairs while I made for the back door. It was safeguarded by two huge deadbolts of the sort more often seen in American apartments and that secured the entire width of the door.

'This place is like a fortress, Dave,' I said, when he joined me. 'And the front door's got deadbolts on it similar to the back door.'

'How did you get in, then?'

'Only the latch was on. The deadbolts hadn't been engaged.'

We went through to the room at the back of the house where Dave had sighted the body. Several armchairs and a settee, all in black leather, were placed at intervals around the room, on a thick pile carpet. A small bookcase contained a number of popular paperbacks, none of which indicated any particular interest that Miles may have had. There were no signs of a fight having taken place, and nothing appeared to have been disturbed. Each of the windows, which were triple-glazed, as Dave had said, was secured with high-quality window locks. As I'd surmised, they were protected by an alarm system. Miles was obviously a man who took no chances.

'Why the hell didn't the alarm go off when we broke in?' I said, thinking aloud.

'It wouldn't, would it?' said Dave. 'Miles obviously turns it off when he's at home, sir.'

A quick examination of Robert Miles's body confirmed that he was indeed dead, and to my unpractised eye it appeared that his neck had been broken; it was certainly positioned at an unnatural angle. And that was how Lancelot Foley had been topped too, but I'd have to wait for Dr Mortlock to confirm it.

'Looks very much as though he was got at before he could tell us what he knew, Dave.'

'I reckon the guy who killed Foley must've found out that Miles was going to grass on him.'

'And that means that his phone was hacked, despite all his precautions. Miles said he was out and about until eight, but that was probably an excuse to cover a meeting here with whoever topped him. He was very specific about the time.'

'We'll have to see if any fingerprints are found that might help us,' said Dave. 'But I'll bet my pension none will be.' He made a call to the incident room requesting a full murder-investigation turnout. 'The supporting cast is on its way, guv.'

Flynn and Challis joined us. 'All clear, guv,' said Flynn. 'Nothing appears to have been disturbed anywhere, so I don't reckon it was a burglary. On the other hand, if the murderer was looking for something in particular, he was certainly a tidy bastard. There was no sign of a search; not that that means there wasn't one.'

'I don't see how anyone *could* have got in,' I said. 'The place is as tight as a drum.'

'That leaves only one alternative,' said Dave. 'Whoever topped Miles must've been known to him and was let in. When he left he just closed the front door after him. That would explain why only the night latch was on, the deadbolts hadn't been engaged and the alarm was dormant.'

'I think you're right, Dave. I get the impression that Miles was so security conscious that he wouldn't have left those bolts undone.'

'What exactly is going on here?' A youthful inspector appeared in the doorway. His attitude was one of pompous officialdom.

'And you are?' I asked.

'The late-turn duty officer, and who are you?'

'Detective Chief Inspector Brock, Murder Investigation Team.'

'Ah, I see, sir.' The inspector wrote it down in his pocket-book and then waggled his pen at Dave. 'And who are you?'

'Colour Sergeant Poole, ditto . . . sir.' Dave frequently described himself thus when he sensed that he was dealing with a graduate-entry accelerated promotion officer who set great store by diversity and political correctness.

'I see,' said the inspector with a frown. He was probably wondering how to deal with a black sergeant who made racist remarks about himself. But he obviously decided not to try and instead turned to me. 'Can you tell me what's going on, sir?'

I explained that we were dealing with a murder, but that was all. The rest had nothing to do with him. 'Perhaps you'd be so good as to arrange for your officers to guard the property, Inspector. And I'd be obliged if you'd wait outside. You're contaminating a crime scene.' It was a fact of life that rubber-necking police officers were more likely to corrupt a scene than anyone else.

'Yes, sir, sorry, sir.' Somewhat red faced, the inspector withdrew, doubtless to collect more names.

'While we're waiting for the team, Dave, we'll have a word with the woman opposite who put up the suspects call.'

Dave got the details from the PCs who'd responded to the call, and we crossed the road.

The woman who answered the door appeared to be in her late twenties and wore jeans and a crop-top. A small child clutched the woman's right leg and gazed up at Dave and me with wide-eyed innocence. Another child, a little older, stood behind his mother and peeked round her.

'Mrs Hughes?'

'Yes, I'm Emma Hughes.'

'We're police officers,' I said. 'I'm Detective Chief Inspector Brock, and this is Detective Sergeant Poole. We'd like to talk to you about the house opposite.'

'Have you got any identification?' Mrs Hughes was clearly the cautious type. I wished there were more about like her; it would make our job that much easier. Trusting tenants all too often gave bogus police officers, utility workers and sundry other would-be thieves unfettered access to their properties. And would subsequently complain that the police weren't doing enough to protect them.

Dave and I produced our warrant cards, and I was pleased to see that the woman examined them closely.

'Please come in.' Mrs Hughes smiled as she opened the

door wide and showed us into a sitting room that was over-poweringly hot. The central heating must've been on full blast. The Hughes family was obviously not worried about paying its energy bills. 'You'll have to excuse the mess, but I was in the middle of housework. I work part-time at a nursery school, and I never seem to have time to catch up.' She spent a few moments rushing around gathering up children's toys, maga-zines and some odd pieces of clothing. 'Do sit down,' she said breathlessly, and flicked a stray lock of hair out of her eyes. Glancing at her children, she said, 'Now, sit down over there and keep quiet while I talk to these gentlemen.'

'Do you know the man who lives opposite you, Mrs Hughes? A Mr Miles.'

'Not to speak to. We only moved in about three months ago, and we've not really had time to get to know anyone. As I said, I work part-time, and my partner works long hours in Wembley.'

'I understand that you called the police earlier.'

'Yes, I did. I saw some men at the house looking through the windows, and then I saw one of them jump over the side gate. I thought they were up to no good, so I dialled nine nine nine.' Emma blushed and put a hand to her mouth. 'I feel such a fool now that I've found out it was you.'

'There's no need to be embarrassed, Mrs Hughes,' said Dave. 'I can assure you that the police are always grateful for calls of that sort. We don't mind genuine mistakes, and we'd rather have that than miss something important.'

'Have you ever seen anyone calling at the house opposite, Mrs Hughes?' I asked.

'I'm not one for spying on my neighbours,' said Emma, a little defensively, 'but I have noticed men calling there from time to time. They seemed like businessmen, always smartly dressed.' Emma Hughes paused in thought. 'But, come to think of it, I've never seen a woman there. I suppose the man must live alone.' She paused again. 'Oh my God! Is he one of those paedophiles? You hear such terrible stories about these men who abuse young children. Is that why you're here?'

'I don't think that he was a paedophile, Mrs Hughes,' I said. 'In fact, he has been murdered. That's why we are here.' That wasn't quite the truth, but Mrs Hughes didn't need to know that we'd come across Robert Miles's dead body almost by accident. The thought that Miles might've been a paedophile was a wild but intriguing one; it hadn't occurred to me, but the idea opened up the possibility that his death might have had nothing to do with the murder of Lancelot Foley. Unless Foley was *also* a paedophile . . .

I dismissed those idle thoughts from my mind; the situation was complicated enough as it was.

'Murdered! Oh, good heavens. When did this happen?'

'That's what we're trying to find out,' said Dave. 'Did you see anyone calling at the house today, particularly within, say, the last few hours? Did you perhaps see a car parked outside the house?'

'No, I'm afraid not. As I said, I've been busy around the house.'

'Have you *ever* seen a car parked outside the house? Apart from Mr Miles's BMW, which would probably have been on the drive.'

'I'm sorry, no. I don't seem to have been much help, do I?'

'But you have, Mrs Hughes,' I said. 'However, we may need to speak to you again, and it's possible that you may later recall having seen something. In the meantime, we'll let you get on with your housework.' I gave her one of my cards. 'If you do think of anything, perhaps you'd give me a ring.'

The team had arrived by the time Dave and I returned to Miles's house. Kate Ebdon had turned up with DS Lizanne Carpenter, DCs John Appleby, Nicola Chance and Sheila Armitage. I sent them off to make house-to-house enquiries, but if the usual success rate obtained, we would learn nothing. When the police start asking questions, they suddenly find that everyone minds their own business. The truth of the matter is that they don't want to get involved.

Linda Mitchell and her evidence recovery team were already there and had got busy. Photographs were taken, video recordings were made of the interior, and every likely surface was examined for fingerprints.

Five minutes later, a complaining Dr Henry Mortlock drew

up outside the house. 'You do pick the most inconvenient times to find dead bodies, Harry,' he said.

'I'll try and do better next time.'

'Where is it?'

'Follow me, Henry.'

Mortlock spent a few moments walking round the corpse and taking temperatures before examining the body. He made a few notes and stood up. 'I would say – with the usual reservation, Harry – that Miles's death was similar, in every particular, to the way in which Lancelot Foley was murdered. But,' he added cautiously, 'I'll confirm that once I've carried out the post-mortem.'

It was almost midnight by the time that the technicians of murder had completed their tasks. There was no point in keeping my team there, and I decided that a thorough search of the house and its contents would begin tomorrow when they were fresh.

I rang the incident room and told Gavin Creasey, the night-duty sergeant, to get hold of DI Len Driscoll and tell him to start searching Miles's house tomorrow morning at eight o'clock. I then instructed Tom Challis and Charlie Flynn to meet him here.

'You and I, Kate, will break the news to Debra Foley first thing tomorrow.' I walked out to the car and looked around until I spotted the late-turn duty officer. 'We're leaving now, Inspector,' I said. 'I'd be grateful if you'd arrange to have the premises guarded back and front until my officers return in the morning.'

'All night, sir?' The inspector's face expressed alarm at this request; he'd now been on duty two hours longer than he should have been. 'But it'll mean taking men off patrols, sir, and we're short-handed as it is.'

'As Sir William Gilbert so graphically put it, Inspector, a policeman's lot is not a happy one,' I said, 'but that's your problem. Good night.'

ELEVEN

K ate and I arrived at Chorley Street a little after nine on Thursday morning.

I pressed the intercom. 'We'd better get it over with, Kate,' I said, while we waited for an answer. I was not relishing telling Debra Foley of her brother's death.

'Yes?' There had been a lengthy delay before Debra Foley answered.

'It's the police, Mrs Foley. May we come in?'

There was a buzzing noise as the lock was released. I pushed open the door, and Kate and I mounted the stairs.

Debra was standing in the doorway of her sitting room. 'What d'you want now?' she demanded truculently. Although she was attired in a peignoir, she had made time to put on some make-up, but her hair was untidy. I assumed that she'd just risen from her bed.

'I'm afraid we have some bad news for you, Mrs Foley,' I said.

'Oh, really?' Debra responded sarcastically, as though doubting that we could be the harbingers of something even worse than the death of her husband. Not that she had seemed all that distraught by his demise when we had broken that news to her. She would probably be more upset to learn that all her husband's money had been left to Sally Warner, if she hadn't heard already. She turned from the door, leaving us to follow her.

'It's about your brother, Mrs Foley,' I began.

'Oh? What's Bobby been up to?' Debra arranged herself carefully in the centre of the settee so that her peignoir parted sufficiently to reveal her legs, and ran both hands through her unruly hair.

'I'm sorry to have to tell you that he's dead,' said Kate. She was never one to pussyfoot around when it came to breaking bad news.

'No, no! It can't be true.' Debra dissolved into tears, great sobs wracking her whole body. 'No, I don't believe it.' The thespian poise and studied behaviour that had been a feature of our previous interview with her vanished in an instant, and she quickly covered her legs. This time she was not acting. 'What happened?'

'He was murdered, Mrs Foley.'

'But this can't be. I only saw him yesterday at Lancelot's funeral. You were there.' Debra pointed an accusing finger at me.

I was always mildly surprised that people would say they'd seen someone yesterday, as if that would somehow disprove that they were dead today. I suppose it's shock that causes them to make irrational remarks.

'It happened sometime between you last seeing him and yesterday evening. We went to his house at Harrow at eight o'clock and found him there. He was already dead.'

'Why should you have gone to see him?' Debra gazed up at me, with a tear-stained face and traces of her mascara running down her cheeks.

'He telephoned me and asked me to call on him at eight o'clock.'

'But why? Why should he have wanted to see you?'

I weighed carefully whether I should tell her the real reason, but decided that to do so might well elicit some useful information.

'He said he knew who had murdered your husband, Mrs Foley, but he declined to tell me over the phone.'

'But how could he possibly have known that?' Debra Foley's face assumed an exaggerated quizzical expression, but the thought did cross my mind that she had poked about in the dressing-up box of her mind, pulled out something marked 'quizzical expression' and put it on.

'That is something we hope to find out,' I said.

'Are you sure you know nothing about your husband's murder, Mrs Foley?' Kate asked.

'How the hell should I know anything about it?' Debra's face became a mask of fury at the very suggestion. 'Don't talk such bloody nonsense.'

I decided that there was nothing more to be derived from this rather fractious interview. 'I'll let you know when the coroner has released your brother's body, Mrs Foley,' I said, and we left.

'I think she knows more than she's telling, guv'nor,' said Kate, once we were in the car and on our way to Harrow to join the search team.

'We've been through the house with a fine-tooth comb, guv'nor, and found nothing of evidential value. So far, that is,' said Len Driscoll by way of a greeting when Kate and I arrived at Miles's house. 'It's obvious from our initial survey that this guy was a very tidy man and a very careful one. His clothing's all been put away with military efficiency, and there are no papers or correspondence to be found anywhere.'

'I rather expected that somehow, Len,' I said. 'Was there anything on his answering machine?'

'There wasn't one, guv. In fact, there's not even a landline. We found his mobile, but he's one shrewd operator; the record of calls made and received has been deleted.'

'I suppose there's always the possibility that Linda's crew might come up with some fingerprints, but in view of what you said about Miles I'm not holding out much hope.' It was a depressing thought, but it looked as though we wouldn't find anything in Miles's house that would point us towards his killer.

But then Charlie Flynn found a safe in the loft.

'It's only a small safe,' he called down, 'but it's got a combination lock, guv'nor, and I doubt we'll be able to get into it without help. It looks pretty substantial.'

There is an old wives' tale prevalent among crime writers and the producers of police shows on television that this problem is easily resolved. A detective with a stethoscope, it's suggested, can twirl the dial and hear the tumblers clicking over. I can tell you that it doesn't work; I've tried.

'Get on to the lab, Dave,' I said, 'and tell them I want the services of a locksmith ASAP. They should have a list of reliable ones.'

It was twelve o'clock before the expert arrived, and we told him where the safe was situated. After asking whether the loft was boarded, how much headroom there was, whether there was adequate lighting and finally muttering something about health and safety, he deigned to climb the ladder. After testing it thoroughly.

'Go up with him, Charlie,' I said, 'so that you can testify at the trial as to what was found in the safe.'

'If there ever is a trial,' commented Dave gloomily.

I don't know how the locksmith did it, but ten minutes later he descended from the loft. 'All yours, guv'nor,' he said and made for the door.

'Hold on, squire,' said Dave. 'I need a statement from you before you leave.'

After further muttered complaints, the locksmith made his statement and left, bitching about how long he'd have to wait for the police to pay his bill.

Charlie Flynn came down from the loft. 'This is all there was in the safe, guv,' he said, holding out a laptop computer.

'Want me to have a go at it, guv?' asked Dave.

'No,' I said. 'We'll let the boffins work their magic on it. If we mess about with it we might wipe it clean.' A comment which, I suspected, only served to demonstrate how little I knew about computers.

The pitiful expression on Dave's face confirmed it. 'Very good, sir,' he said. 'By the way, I checked the surveillance cameras, including the one in the porch at the front door.'

'And you're going to tell me that you found a clear shot of the killer approaching the house whereby we can identify him?'

'We would've done,' said Dave, 'except that the clever bastard took all the tapes with him.'

We spent another couple of hours at the house before I decided that there was nothing else to be found. Nevertheless, I arranged for the local police to maintain a guard on the premises for a further twenty-four hours just in case something on Miles's computer caused us to look over the property again. I also lumbered them with getting the front door mended and the property secured. As to the disposal of the house and its contents, that would be a matter for Debra Foley, or whoever Miles had nominated as executor of his will. If he'd made a will.

Taking Miles's laptop with us, we returned to our offices at Belgravia, and I sent a message to Linda Mitchell with a request that she send a computer whizz-kid over to us to try to decipher the laptop's data.

I also received the depressing but unsurprising news that the house-to-house enquiries in the vicinity of Miles's house had gleaned nothing whatsoever. But that was not surprising; there is a widespread 'we keep ourselves to ourselves' culture whenever the police seek witnesses to a crime.

It was mid-afternoon before a young man reported to the incident room and announced that he'd come to look at the computer. He appeared to be about nineteen, was skeletally thin, and was a martyr to acne. To my surprise he wasn't wearing an anorak, but he did sport an earring.

'I'm Lee Jarvis, Mr Brock, resident nerd with the Metropolitan Police,' he said, with refreshingly self-deprecating humour. 'You got a laptop you want opening?'

I sat him down at a spare desk, and Dave handed him the computer.

For several minutes he studied it without touching it. Then he turned it over and over and continued to study it, at one point taking out a jeweller's glass to peruse the serial number. Finally, he placed it back on the desk, opened it and allowed his hands to hover over the keys with all the finesse of a concert pianist about to embark on Rachmaninov's Second Piano Concerto. Then he began to play. 'It's encrypted,' he announced eventually.

'Does that mean you can't get into it?' I asked, disappointed that our only lead was about to defeat our expert.

'Nah!' Lee grinned at me. 'No problem,' he said. For the next ten minutes or so he played about with various keys and then referred to a small notebook. I presumed it contained his personal troubleshooting solutions on how to deal with a vexatious computer. He returned to the keyboard and eventually gave a shout of triumph. 'We're in,' he exclaimed. After a few minutes scrolling back and forth, he made a further announcement.

'There's a load of stuff on here, Mr Brock.' He rubbed his hands together, his face working with enthusiasm for his job.

Robert Miles's computer did indeed contain a wealth of information, but whether this data would assist us was another matter.

'What have you got, Lee?'

'I've turned up this guy's log. It's the best place to start, I've always found. This one's particularly good because he's recorded in detail everything he's done and everything he's going to do.'

'I'm especially interested in the last month.' I leaned over Lee's shoulder and stared at the screen of Miles's computer.

'On the second of January this year he was contacted by someone called Bill Anderson.' Lee looked up at me. 'There's a note against that entry that says "re Corinne".'

'Are you sure?' The entry didn't make sense to me. Why should someone called Anderson speak to Miles about a woman who was, in fact, Miles's sister? Was Anderson Corinne's pimp? Or, even more macabre, was Miles?

'Look for yourself.' Lee pointed at the relevant item. 'And there's another entry on the tenth of Jan: "Visited Corinne at Keycross Court. Mission aborted."'

'What the hell's that all about, I wonder? Is there an address book anywhere on there, Lee?'

Lee scrolled through the data. 'Sure is. There's his contacts list,' he said, pointing at the screen.

'See if there are any details for this Bill Anderson.'

'Yep, it's all here. It lists a Colonel William Anderson, and his address is shown as Wisteria Cottage, Reeching Lane, Romford, Essex. I suppose that's the same bloke.'

'Any other details about Anderson? Telephone number, for instance?'

'No, Mr Brock, that's it.'

'It looks like this Anderson has some serious questions to answer, Dave.'

'And so does Corinne Black, alias Debra Foley, otherwise known as Vanessa Drummond,' said Dave. 'So where do we start, guv?'

'I've come across Anderson's name previously, guv,' said

Tom Challis, who had been standing around in the incident room while Lee was interrogating the laptop. 'And so has Charlie Flynn.'

'D'you mean he's got form?' I stood up and eased my aching back. I'd been bending over Miles's computer for too long.

'Not under that name, as far as I can tell,' said Challis. 'But you asked Charlie and I to do background checks on the Foleys, and oddly enough the name Anderson was in Lancelot Foley's address book. The one you got from Jane Lawless. It lists Anderson's same Romford address.'

'Were there any other interesting names in that book?'

'I don't know about interesting, guv, but there were three other men's names that we're still looking into. According to entries in the diary section of Foley's Filofax, he played poker with Anderson and these other guys about once a month.'

'What the hell is the connection, then?' I asked. 'Debra Foley's brother has Corinne's and Anderson's names and addresses on his computer, but Anderson was a poker-playing partner of Lancelot's.'

'Perhaps they met before Debra split up with Lancelot,' suggested Kate. 'Maybe they had dinner or something like that.'

'It's possible, I suppose,' I said dubiously, 'but Debra didn't strike me as the sort of woman to throw dinner parties.'

'No, but Anderson might've been at a first-night party after the Foleys' play opened,' said Kate. 'I think it's the sort of thing these theatricals do.'

'Oh, they do,' I said. 'Believe me.' Gail was still on several lists, even though she'd been 'resting' for some time now, and I'd been dragged along to several of these junkets. But it wasn't my scene; I'm not a great admirer of the average luvvy.

'Not the sort of thing they do at the ballet, though,' said Dave, with a superior sniff.

'You're a snob, Dave,' said Flynn.

'None of this actually explains why Robert Miles had a meet with Anderson "re Corinne", according to Miles's computer,' I said. 'Or why, a week later, Miles recorded on his laptop diary: "Visited Corinne at Keycross Road. Mission aborted." None of it makes a lot of sense.'

114 Graham Ison

'We could ask Anderson, guv,' suggested Dave.

'I think not. At least, not until we've done more background digging on him. He might be the man responsible for the murders of Foley and Miles.'

'There's more here, Mr Brock,' said Lee. 'Going back to Monday the ninth of July last year, there's an entry about Zimbabwe.'

'What's it say, Lee?'

'"Spoke to Anderson re *Operation Zimbabwe Overthrow*. Mission aborted. Financier pulled out."'

'So Anderson's a bloody mercenary, and so was Miles,' I said. 'It doesn't take much imagination to work out what was planned for Zimbabwe. We'll definitely have to go carefully when we look into Anderson's affairs. We might even have to involve the Foreign Office. And that would be a pain in the neck.'

'D'you need me any more, Mr Brock?' asked Lee.

'I don't think so, Lee, and many thanks for your invaluable assistance. Can my officers go through the laptop now? I mean, is it all decoded, or whatever you call it?'

'Yes, it's all in plain,' said Lee, and wandered off.

'So what do we do about Anderson?' asked Dave. 'Observation?'

I shook my head. 'I don't think so.'

'Spin his drum, then?'

'If his place is anything like Miles's house, Dave, and he's got surveillance cameras, he'd see us coming and hide any damning evidence in such a way that we'd never find it. And then he'd sit in his safe room until we went away. I'll put money on this cottage of his being isolated, and as a mercenary he'll know all about self-preservation. We'd never be able to break in. As for an observation, I reckon he'd spot a tail within minutes. He's probably done counter-surveillance training at some time.'

'We've got to do something, guv.'

'Yes, and that means sitting and waiting. The first thing we must do is find out as much as we can about him. He's bound to be ex-military. I'll leave it to you, Charlie, but it might be a good idea to start with the military police.' Flynn was an absolute wizard when it came to trawling through paper, and if there was anything to be found he would find it. 'Dig up what you can, but in no way must Anderson be alerted to our interest. In the meantime, Dave, you and I will speak to the manager at the theatre and see if there was a first-night party and who was there.'

'Might not Andrews be a better bet, guv?' asked Kate.

'Maybe, but we'll try Sebastian Weaver first.' For personal reasons I was reluctant to approach Gerald Andrews again.

Dave and I arrived at the Clarence Theatre at about three o'clock that afternoon and made our way to the manager's office.

'Oh, God! Not more bad news.' Sebastian Weaver stared at me with an expression of despair on his face.

'Not this time, Mr Weaver,' I said. 'When was the first night of this play?'

'The seventh of January,' said Weaver without hesitation. 'And it's bloody well closing at the end of this week. Bookings have gone through the floor. I thought that Lancelot's murder would've brought in the ghouls, but it wasn't to be.'

'Was there a first-night party?' Dave asked.

'Yes, there was, but not here. It was at the Waldorf in the Aldwych. No expense spared. As a matter of fact, I think that Lancelot Foley paid for most of it. But there won't be a last-night party, that's a racing certainty.'

'Have you got a list of who was there?'

'I've got a list of those who were invited. In addition to the cast, of course,' said Weaver. 'But I dare say there were a few gatecrashers. All sorts of hangers-on turn up at these junkets. They twitch at each other.'

'I think you mean tweet,' said Dave mildly.

'Were you there?' I asked, deciding not to ask Dave about tweeting; I'd rather the social networking scene remained a mystery.

'Of course I was,' said Weaver, as though it would have been an affront for the theatre manager not to be invited. 'It went on until two in the morning.'

'Perhaps we could have a copy of the list, then,' said Dave.

Weaver opened a drawer in his desk and ferreted around, eventually producing a tatty piece of paper. 'There you are,' he said. 'You can keep it as a memento of yet another theatrical flop. Mind you, there have been so many flops recently, it probably won't be worth the paper it's written on if you try to auction it.'

Dave handed me the list. 'He was there, sir,' he said and pointed at Anderson's name. 'Invited by Lancelot Foley.'

I glanced down the list. Debra Foley's name was there, obviously, but Robert Miles had also been a guest. 'I reckon that makes our friend the common denominator, Dave.'

'I graduated in English, sir,' said Dave. 'Not maths.'

Back at Belgravia, I sat in my office and contemplated just how we were to get tabs on such a shadowy figure as Bill Anderson. I tend to get impatient in situations like these, but I knew that I'd have to wait and see what information Charlie Flynn turned up.

But then another thought occurred to me. Suppose the murders of Foley and Miles had nothing whatever to do with Anderson. Were we dealing with a serial killer who went around breaking people's necks just for the sheer hell of it? I walked out to the incident room.

'Colin.'

'Sir?' Wilberforce swung round from the computer and faced me.

'I was wondering if there have been any other murders with the same MO as the two we're dealing with.'

But the efficient Wilberforce dashed that idea without the need to refer to his computer. 'No, sir. I checked.'

Oh well, it was worth a try.

Dave looked up from his desk. 'I know you said we mustn't go anywhere near Anderson, guv, and I agree, but why don't we speak to Debra Foley? Miles's log showed that he visited Corinne Black on the ninth of January. And we know that's the name Debra uses for her sex business.'

'I still can't work that out, Dave. Why should Miles make an entry about visiting his sister and then mark it "mission aborted"?'

'Perhaps he didn't know it was his sister until he got there, guv'nor.'

'Yes, you could be right.' I'd often said in the past that Dave thought of the things I didn't think of, and it looked as though he'd just done it again. I glanced at my watch; it was too late to catch Mrs Foley today. 'We'll pay her a visit at Keycross Road tomorrow afternoon. That should surprise her.'

Dave laughed. 'Especially if she's flat on her back with a guy on top of her,' he said.

'I get the impression that she'd be a bit more inventive than the missionary position.'

'I don't know about that, guv,' said Dave. 'If what Miss Ebdon said about Corinne's weight is right, she'd suffocate the poor guy if she was on top.'

TWELVE

Detective Sergeant Challis came to see me just after lunch, the next day.

'I've followed up on the names in Lancelot Foley's address book that you got from Jane Lawless, guv. The only one I was able to reach was a guy called Hubert Darke.'

'What did he have to say, Tom?' I asked.

'He's one of Foley's regular poker partners, and he told me that the other three were William Anderson, Gavin Townsend and Dudley Phillips. I got Darke to give me a description of Anderson, but it would be good for at least a hundred other guys.'

'We know that Anderson's in the wind somewhere,' I said. 'But have you tracked down the other two?'

'Not to speak to, guv. At the moment I'm relying on what Darke told me. And he told me that Townsend is in Australia at the moment.'

'What's he doing there?'

'According to Darke, Townsend is a professional yachtsman and is around forty years of age. Darke reckons that he's due back this week. Apparently, he told Darke that he was taking part in some Antipodean yacht race. I wouldn't have thought that February was the right time of year for it, even Down Under, so it might be a moody excuse.'

'Not necessarily. The Sydney to Hobart yacht race begins on Boxing Day each year. Anyway, that's irrelevant. What does Darke do for a living?'

'He's something in the City, guv. He wasn't very forthcoming, but I suppose he's a broker, a financial adviser or a banker, or something that gets big bonuses every year. If his drum at Hinchley Wood is anything to go by, he's not short of cash.'

'What about Phillips, Tom?'

'Dudley Phillips is a fashion designer and has a studio or

workshop, or whatever it's called, in the Commercial Road and lives over the shop, so to speak. Got a bit of previous: one for burglary and two for petty theft, guv. But the last one was fifteen years ago, so they're spent, anyway.'

'Thanks, Tom. You can leave it with me. I'll see them and see if they shed any light on Foley's murder.'

Dave and I arrived in Chorley Street at half-past two and parked a little way down the road from Debra Foley's house. At twenty minutes to three she emerged, dressed in the dowdy outfit that Liz Carpenter had told me she usually wore when going to the flat where she would 'entertain' gentleman. She walked round the corner and hailed a cab.

Dave started the car and followed at a safe distance. It didn't matter too much if we lost her in traffic; we had a good idea where she was going.

As we had hoped, the cab set her down at Keycross Court. Once she had gone inside, we gave her time to close the Venetian blinds and, we thought, to change into attire more suited to her alternative profession.

Twenty minutes later, I pressed the bottom button on the intercom system.

'Caretaker.' The voice crackled through the speaker.

'Police.'

There was no reply, but the door lock was released. We entered the apartment block and took the lift to the first floor. I rang the bell of Corinne's flat, and Dave and I stood to one side of the door, thus avoiding being seen through the spy hole.

Seconds later the door was opened by Debra Foley. To say that she was minimally attired was perhaps erring on the side of exaggeration. She was wearing a thong, a suspender belt, black nylons, stiletto heels, a short diaphanous negligee, and nothing else.

'Christ Almighty!' she exclaimed. 'What the hell are you doing here?' She closed her negligee tightly around herself and held it closed. Not that it did much good in terms of covering her near nakedness. Her ample breasts were still plainly visible. 'How did you get in?'

'*Mrs Foley!*' I said, feigning surprise. 'What on earth are *you* doing here? We've actually come to see Miss Black, Miss Corinne Black. Is she here?'

'I'm Corinne Black.' Debra Foley made the admission with a sort of 'you've caught me out' resignation in her voice. 'Corinne Black's another of my stage names.' I doubt it sounded convincing even to her.

'I never knew that,' said Dave, stifling a laugh. 'May we come in, or would you prefer that we conducted our conversation out here in the hallway?'

Without a word Debra turned and walked into the sitting room, leaving us to follow. Dave closed the front door.

The sitting room was large but sparsely furnished and, unsurprisingly, lacked the lived-in look of permanent residency. The carpet was cream, as were the curtains, a contrast to the two armchairs and the settee that were both upholstered in black leather. Two small tables with lamps on them completed the furnishings, but there were no ornaments anywhere.

Having recovered her poise after greeting us in a state of undress, Debra Foley invited us to sit down and then left the room, returning a minute or so later attired in a full-length kaftan. She seated herself in the centre of the settee and crossed her legs. Although the kaftan had long slits on either side, she made no attempt to display her legs as she had done on the other occasions I had interviewed her.

'I hope this won't take long,' she said, as if warning us that she was not available for a lengthy interview. The way she'd been dressed when she opened the front door indicated quite clearly that she was expecting a client.

'Have you moved here from Chorley Street, then, Mrs Foley?' asked Dave, with a masterful display of feigned innocence.

'Yes, as a matter of fact I have,' said Debra airily. 'The other place was too big once I'd thrown Lancelot out, and it seemed silly to keep such a big house. Apart from anything else, the play's closing at the end of the week, so I probably won't be here for much longer, anyway.'

'I suppose you'll be going back to your house in Farnham, then,' said Dave.

'It's not mine any more,' snapped Debra. 'That bastard husband of mine has left all his money – it was over fifteen million pounds – to that wretched woman Sally Warner. I suppose it includes the house because the deeds were in Lancelot's name, but some of the furniture is mine. Naturally, I shall contest the will, but it'll take time and money. I've plenty of the former now, but not much of the latter. The only redeeming aspect of it all is that Jane Lawless won't see a penny of it either.'

I was rapidly tiring of this woman's insistence on playing centre stage, and I decided to put a stop to it.

'Mrs Foley,' I said, deliberately injecting a tone of weariness into my voice, 'please don't take me for a fool. You're using this apartment for the purposes of prostitution.'

For a moment, Debra stared at me, a carefully contrived expression of astonishment on her face, before giving vent to a response that demanded all her acting skills for its explosive delivery. 'That is an outrageous suggestion!' she exclaimed vehemently, as though addressing the gallery with an impassioned deathbed monologue. 'How dare you come here and accuse me of such a thing! I shall certainly lodge a formal complaint. Just because you're a policeman doesn't mean you can walk in here and make slanderous allegations like that. Whatever makes you think that I would demean myself in that way? I'm an actress!'

There's no doubt about that, I thought.

'We are investigating the murders of your husband and your brother, Mrs Foley,' said Dave, 'and it was necessary to keep observation on your Chorley Street house. And it was you who led us to this apartment. We then made further enquiries. That's how we know.'

'I can't imagine why you thought you'd find Lancelot's murderer here,' said Debra. 'I told you why I've opted to live here, and I've visited from time to time to make sure that everything would be ready when I did move in. What on earth makes you think I'm a prostitute? It really is the most bizarre idea.' Her mental script demanded that she laugh gaily at this point, and she did.

'The way in which you were dressed when we arrived, for

a start,' Dave said. 'It looked as though you were expecting a client, but instead we turned up.'

'You caught me in the middle of getting dressed.'

'You can stop pretending, Mrs Foley,' I said, not wanting to give the woman a chance to create more spurious excuses. 'We've observed several men coming here, and we're in no doubt that they're coming here for the purpose of having sexual intercourse with you.' There was really no point in pursuing this discussion, but I wanted to unnerve the woman before moving on to the real purpose of our visit.

'Why shouldn't I have gentlemen friends? Lancelot and I were separated, so you can't blame a girl for looking elsewhere to satisfy her needs. And you can't prove that it was me these men were coming to see. If I were you I'd have a few words with the woman who lives on the top floor. If you really want to talk to a prostitute, I suggest you start with her.'

'And I dare say the men paid you by credit card,' I said. 'These things can be checked, of course.'

Debra glowered at me, but remained silent.

'And we're probably going to talk to James Corley, too.' Dave took a chance on the MP being another of Debra's clients, based upon what DS Charlie Flynn had reported.

'Oh, I get the picture.' Debra leaned back in the settee and conjured up a disdainful expression. 'And now, I suppose, you're going to tell me what I have to do to make all this go away,' she said sarcastically, all pretence having now vanished. 'What's it to be – one at a time or three in a bed? Tied to the bed? Once a week? Twice a week? Actually, I rather fancy you, Sergeant.'

Dave laughed, which was not what Debra had expected. 'We're not the slightest bit interested in having sex with you, Mrs Foley.'

'Oh, and why the hell not?' Her reaction was one of anger, probably because no one had ever turned down such an offer before.

'That's not why we're here,' I said. 'You aren't committing any offence by hiring out your body.'

'Then what the hell *are* you here for?' Debra had been caught wrong-footed and was probably feeling rather silly,

having made the offer she had and thus revealing herself in
her true light.

'Why did your brother Robert visit you here on Thursday
the tenth of January this year?'

'My brother came here? I don't think so . . . No, that's not—'
Debra said haltingly, and then stopped. My question, coming
so suddenly and at variance with anything we'd discussed so
far, clearly flustered her. But, being the actress she was, she
quickly recovered from having fluffed her lines and improvised.
'No, you're wrong. It couldn't have been here because I was
still at Chorley Street. But I do remember now. He did call
there to ask how the play was going. Yes, that would have been
it. The play opened on the seventh of January, you see. Yes, I
remember now,' she said again, 'it was Chorley Street.'

'He came here to *this* apartment, Mrs Foley.' I was becoming
heartily sick of this woman's prevarication. 'What other reason
could he have had for making an entry on his computer to say
that he had called on Corinne at Keycross Court? And you've
already admitted that Corinne is another of your so-called
stage names.'

'I've really no idea what you're talking about, Chief
Inspector.' Debra spoke carelessly, but her expression revealed
her concern at learning that her brother had recorded the visit
on his laptop. She was probably wondering what else he'd
made a note of. 'In any case, I don't see that it matters whether
Bobby came here or to Chorley Street.' She made a point of
glancing nervously at her wristwatch, as she had done at
intervals throughout the interview. 'I'm sorry, but I'm expecting
a friend at any minute.' In other words, she wasn't prepared
to talk about it any more.

'Very well, Mrs Foley,' I said. 'But we will be coming to
see you again. There are other matters we need to discuss.'

As we walked across the forecourt to our car, a man came
towards us. Whatever reason he had for doing so, he suddenly
turned, placed one foot on a low wall and pretended to tie a
shoelace. Once we were past him, he hurried towards the
entrance to the flats.

'Did you see who that was, Dave?' I asked, when we were
in the car.

'Yes, it was James Corley the MP, and he's probably just remembered that he's wearing slip-ons. Very difficult to tie shoelaces that aren't there.'

'He must know that he'd be recognized sooner or later, Dave. He's always on TV, shooting his mouth off about something or other. Some guys are suckers for punishment.'

'D'you reckon Corinne's into that sort of thing as well, then, guv?'

I decided we would wait in the car for a few minutes before leaving, for no better reason than a desire to satisfy my idle curiosity. Sure enough, I was rewarded almost immediately. James Corley spent a few minutes talking on the intercom. Several times he turned to look around. When he'd finished his conversation, he turned and ran down the path. He contrived to look absolutely furious, disappointed and worried all at the same time.

'Oh dear!' said Dave. 'He looks as though someone's stolen his lollipop.'

'I imagine that he's just had a tongue lashing from Debra before she sent him on his way, Dave. As we mentioned his name to her, she'll have blamed him for telling us that she was on the game.'

'Nor hell a fury like a woman whose trick has just shopped her to the wicked police. I wonder what she'll do now, guv. You told her that she's not committing an offence, but I wonder if she'll decide to give up anyway.'

'I'm not sure she can afford to, Dave. We knew about Lancelot leaving everything to Sally Warner, so it's quite possible that Debra really hasn't got a penny of her own. And now that the play's closing she won't have an income. No, I reckon she'll go on the game full time.'

Debra Foley looked out of the window and watched as DCI Brock and DS Poole walked down the path towards their car. But as she did so, her afternoon client, James Corley, came into her field of vision. She was thankful that he was late, otherwise he would have arrived when the police were with her. She watched the police officers get into their car, but was concerned that they did not drive away immediately.

Suddenly, she realized what they were doing. Despite what they'd said about her not committing an offence, she was certain they were waiting for sufficient evidence to charge her with prostitution or even with something more serious.

The intercom buzzed. 'Yes, who is it?'

'It's me, Corinne, James Corley.'

'I'm sorry, James, but you can't come in.'

'Why not? I have got the right date and time, haven't I? Or have you got someone with you?'

'The police have just been here, and they're outside now in their car watching everyone who calls on me. Someone's told them that I entertain gentlemen.' Debra paused before levelling an allegation that she believed to be true. 'Was it you, James?'

'Christ, no! Of course it wasn't me. Why the hell would I show out by telling them I'd been screwing you?' Corley was suddenly beset with panic. 'Is there a back way out of here, Corinne? I mean, can you let me in, so that I can pretend I'm going to see someone else?' An awful panorama of disaster unfolded in his mind's eye: arrest followed by appearances in court and the ruination of his career. But despite being a legislator, James Corley was not too well versed in the law and did not immediately realize that his only danger would be the tabloid press.

'No, James, you'll just have to go back down the path.' Despite his denial, Debra was still convinced that it was Corley who had informed the police about her activities. But had she thought it through, she would have realized that it didn't make sense; Corley would have been committing political suicide by telling the police that he had regular sex with a prostitute.

There were, however, more important and more pressing things on her mind. After she had finished her conversation with a shocked Corley, she took a small black book from her handbag and thumbed through it until she found the mobile phone number she wanted.

'Hello?'

'Bill, it's Debra.'

'Well, well,' said William Anderson, 'are you free for the afternoon? I feel like dropping in on you to have a bit of fun.'

'It's the police, Bill, they've been here. They know that my brother came here, and I'm sure they know it was to murder me. But we know that he didn't know it was me, and that's why—'

'For God's sake slow down, Debra,' said Anderson sharply. 'You're not making a lot of sense.' He became suddenly serious. And very worried.

'They said something about having got the information about his visit from his computer. Apparently, they found it when they searched his house after he was murdered,' Debra continued, blurting out the words breathlessly, forgetting all she had learned at drama school about pacing her delivery and not gabbling her lines.

'Did they mention Lancelot at all?' asked Anderson.

'No, they didn't, but it wouldn't surprise me if they suspected something. They waited outside for a while after they'd been here. Bill, I'm frightened. I'm sure they suspect us both. They pretended to talk about my little sideline, but I'm certain there was more to it than that. I'm sure they know what's happened. I just know that they're going to arrest me soon!'

'Dammit!' exclaimed Anderson. 'I didn't know your brother had a computer. If I told him once I must've told him a dozen times not to keep anything that the police might find if any of our operations went belly up. It seems that your stupid bloody brother has handed it all to them on a plate.' He had searched Miles's house after he'd murdered him, but found nothing that was likely to connect him with the murder. Unfortunately for him, such was his hurry, he'd had no time to look in the loft.

'It wouldn't have happened if Bobby hadn't been murdered,' said Debra pettishly.

'Well, I didn't kill him.' Anderson saw no reason to confess to Debra Foley that he'd killed her brother. She had caused him enough trouble already, and he wondered just how much this garrulous woman had told the police. It seemed to him that she opened her mouth as often as she opened her legs. 'There's only one thing for it, Debra. We'll go away for a while until the dust settles.'

'But where? Where will we go?'

There was a moment or two of silence. 'Paris for a start,' said Anderson. 'I know just the place.' There was another pause. 'Meet me at St Pancras railway station as soon as you can. And I mean as quickly as you possibly can. There's no time to waste. You must leave immediately.'

'Whereabouts at St Pancras, Bill? Under the clock?'

'Oh, for God's sake, woman, this isn't a bloody film; this is for real. Meet me in the Champagne Bar. I'll get tickets for the Eurostar service to Paris. If we go before the police really start looking for us, we should be in the clear.'

'But will it be safe, Bill?'

'Of course it will. I've got contacts all over the world. We'll just keep moving, and I assure you, Debra, that I know how to keep one step ahead of the law. We'll spend a night or two in Paris, and then we'll go on down to the Riviera. How d'you fancy champagne on the beach? I'll even buy you a new bikini. Now, be a good girl; pack just one overnight bag and meet me at the station.'

'But if we're staying longer, Bill, I'll need more than an overnight bag,' complained Debra. 'I'll need a change of clothes and all sorts of other things. And then there's—'

'One bag, no more,' said Anderson, cutting in sharply. 'I'll buy you anything else you need, Debra, but don't waste any more time or we won't get a train. And we might even get arrested. Oh, and make sure you're wearing your wedding ring.'

Although Anderson had tried to make it sound as though he was inviting Debra Foley for a romantic holiday, he had other plans in mind. She had become a liability, and he had no intention of allowing her to endanger him any farther.

After she had finished her phone call to Anderson, Debra embarked on the difficult problem of packing. It was easy enough when she went on a theatrical tour and there was no limit to what she could take, but Anderson's stricture of one overnight bag made the choice of what to pack much more difficult. It was with some misgivings she eventually managed to assemble the essentials, secure in the knowledge that Bill had promised to buy her anything she wanted.

Quickly changing into a navy-blue trouser suit and remembering just in time to take her passport with her, she put on the black leather overcoat that an admirer had bought her a year or so ago. She telephoned the caretaker and asked him if he'd be a sweetie and call her a taxi and perhaps he'd take her bag down for her as well.

Debra Foley arrived at St Pancras International Station at half-past four. Pushing her way through the crowds, she entered the Champagne Bar, renowned for being the longest in Europe, and looked around.

Anderson came rushing towards her. 'Thank God you made it. I've got tickets for the four fifty-two train for Paris, but we'll have to get a move on.'

'Where are we going to stay?' asked Debra as they hurried towards the train.

'All arranged,' said Anderson, 'and I've even booked dinner in the restaurant.'

'You've grown a beard,' said Debra as they boarded the train.

'Seemed sensible,' said Anderson.

THIRTEEN

It was half-past eight when Anderson and Debra Foley arrived at the Santa Barbara Hotel in the rue de Castiglione. After the porter had placed their two overnight bags on the luggage rack and accepted a generous tip with profuse thanks, they went straight to the restaurant.

As the couple had eaten on the train, they limited their meal to a plate of *moules marinières* and French fries, accompanied by a bottle of Muscadet.

During the leisurely meal the two of them laughed and even joked with each other. In Debra's case, it was a feeling of relief that the imminent danger had been averted and that she could afford to relax. In Anderson's case, however, it was to give the impression to everyone else in the hotel that they were just another carefree married couple enjoying a romantic break in Paris.

It was ten o'clock when they went up to their room.

'I'm tired after that journey, Bill,' said Debra, stifling a yawn.

'Maybe,' said Anderson, 'but don't forget you have to pay off your debt in kind.'

Debra performed an erotic striptease before allowing Anderson to throw her on to the bed and take her.

Forty minutes later, an exhausted Debra finally fell asleep face down. But she was destined never to wake up.

Anderson leaned over her, seized her head and twisted sharply. 'No one puts William Anderson in danger,' he said quietly.

Quickly dressing, he picked up his overnight bag and walked out to the corridor. Having previously reconnoitred the layout of the hotel he did not pause, but calmly descended to the ground floor by the service stairs and out of the emergency exit into the rue de Castiglione. He walked a few yards, turned a corner, hailed a taxi and asked to be taken to the gare du Nord.

When the cab driver dropped him at the station, he waited a few minutes before hailing another cab. This second cab took him to a different Paris hotel, where he booked a room for the night and produced a genuine American passport in the name of Geoffrey Crawford, born Brunswick, Ohio, forty-one years ago. The first thing he did was to shave off his beard, by which time it was midnight, and to all intents and purposes William Anderson had ceased to exist. The following day, he moved hotels again.

'Anderson is ex-army, guv'nor,' said DS Flynn, the moment I walked into the incident room, 'and he's got an interesting history.'

'Come into my office, Charlie,' I said, and signalled to Kate and Dave to come in as well.

'Anderson is forty-one years old, and was a captain in an infantry regiment, but was cashiered seven years ago,' said Flynn, once we were all settled.

'What for?'

'Striking a non-commissioned officer is what it says in the records, but they were only the bald facts. I had quite a long chat with the military police sergeant-major who investigated the case, and it seems that Anderson's wife was carrying on an affair with a colour sergeant in Anderson's battalion when it was based at Aldershot. Instead of doing the sensible thing when he found out, Anderson went round to where this NCO lived and knocked hell out of him in front of the bloke's wife and kids. There was a court martial, during which a military police lieutenant testified to having received a formal complaint from Mrs Anderson that her husband had assaulted her on several occasions over the preceding year. Anyway, the upshot was that Anderson was found guilty of grievous bodily harm with intent, and conduct unbecoming an officer and a gentleman, and was cashiered.'

'I don't suppose the army knows what he's been doing since he got the boot?'

'The only thing this sergeant-major had heard from the army rumour mill was that Anderson had been involved in some dodgy mercenary work, but he didn't know where or when.

But word is that he'd been recruiting ex-soldiers for some job as recently as nine months ago.'

'If that entry on Miles's computer is anything to go by,' said Dave, 'it looks as though Anderson and Miles were thinking about doing a job in Zimbabwe. It was called Operation Overthrow, and that can mean only one thing as far as that country's concerned.'

'Yes, maybe, but we don't want to get involved in politics, Dave,' I said. 'Let's just concentrate on finding out who killed Foley and Miles.'

'We know that Anderson was at the first-night party,' said Dave. 'Let's suppose it was no more than a case of Debra meeting him there and the pair of 'em going to bed together. We don't know that there's any more to it than that.'

'Much too simple,' said Kate Ebdon. 'It doesn't explain why Robert Miles should have made an entry on his laptop about seeing Corinne and then adding "mission aborted". I think that Debra ought to be interviewed again, possibly even under caution.'

Kate was right, of course, and she was just the woman to do it.

'Good idea, Kate,' I said. 'Bring her in and find out what she knows.'

'I think a better idea would be if Nicola Chance and I called on her tomorrow. If we like what she tells us, we'll arrest her.'

Leisure time is always at a premium when I'm involved in a murder enquiry, but there was little more that could be done that evening. I decided to take Gail out for a meal while I had the chance, and I phoned her and asked where she'd like to go. To my surprise, she'd said that she'd rather eat at home and would prepare a meal. But she'd sounded unusually nervous, and I thought that she had something to tell me. Something that would not please me.

I drove out of the Belgravia area and made towards Surbiton. The snow had given way to rain, and it was a miserable drive home. Consequently, it was almost eight o'clock by the time I reached my flat, having used up my entire stock of swear words on the journey. There is something about rain that has an adverse effect on motorists: they seem to lose any common-sense they may have possessed in the first place.

There was one of Gladys Gurney's charming little notes on the worktop in my kitchen. Gladys is my personal domestic saviour. She has been looking after my flat for years now, although I hardly ever see her. But her presence is felt through the notes and the immaculate state of my apartment.

Dear Mr Brock
    I give your fridge a bit of a clear out. All the stuff what was in there was well out of date. I hope you don't mind, but I was rather you was hungry than poisoned.
    Yours faithfully
    Gladys Gurney (Mrs)
    P.S. I put Miss Sutton's bra in the wardrobe on the left hand side.

I changed into a clean shirt, grabbed a bottle of wine and dashed out of the door. I cut through Surbiton railway station and was lucky to find a cab on the rank.

'Sorry I'm late, darling,' I said, having let myself in with the key I now possessed to Gail's Georgian town house. That description is actually a euphemism for a three-storey terraced property that was built sometime in the seventies. 'Traffic was terrible.'

'I'm about to serve, if you'd like to pour the wine.'

We sat down to another of Gail's superb meals, but there was something missing. And I don't mean anything culinary. She was amazingly quiet this evening, which was quite out of character. Usually, it's difficult to stop her talking, especially when we haven't seen each other for a day or two, but she'd hardly said a word since I arrived.

Eventually, I put down my knife and fork. 'What is it, darling? There's clearly something on your mind.'

'I've been offered a contract in Hollywood,' said Gail. Just like that. No frills, no wrapping it up.

'What?' That had come right out of the blue, like an unfore-seen punch to the solar plexus. 'For how long?'

'Six months, darling. Possibly longer if it's a success.'

'But . . . I mean, how did that happen?'

'It was actually your fault. After you'd talked to Gerald Andrews the other day, I got a call from him. He said you'd told him that I thought my ex had a grudge against me and that was why I hadn't got any decent parts. So he pulled out all the stops and spoke to his wife. She's a casting agent – but you know that – and up came this opportunity to appear in a TV soap that requires a quintessential Englishwoman for the part. It's not a very big part, but it's a start; a rung on the Hollywood ladder, if you like.'

I was absolutely stunned by this news, but I suppose I shouldn't have been surprised. Our relationship was heavily laden in my favour. I dropped in whenever duty allowed and good old Gail was there, ready and waiting to provide a meal or to jump into bed with me. Now it looked as though it was all coming to an end. I knew damned well that if she trotted off to Los Angeles she'd likely be wooed by some rich American who owned a ranch and three or four houses, each with an indoor swimming pool for when the outdoor one couldn't be used. Doubtless there'd be a garage full of cars, and a stable full of horses with opportunities to go riding every day. And it was all my fault.

'Are you going to take it?' I asked.

'I think I'd be foolish not to,' said Gail.

'I agree,' I said, 'although I'd rather you didn't.'

'It's all right for you, Harry,' said Gail. 'You've got an interesting job, but one that takes you away from me for days – weeks, even – while I sit here twiddling my thumbs. You know I've been dying to get back into the theatre, and a job in television is just as good. In fact, it probably pays better, especially in the States.'

'What will you do about this place?'

'Let it out, I suppose.'

'When is this all due to start? The TV programme, I mean.'

'They want me to fly out on Monday.'

'But that's only three days away.'

'You don't want me to go, do you, Harry?'

'No, I don't, but I think you should. You're quite right about your career. If you don't take this opportunity, you might never get another.'

'I knew you'd understand, Harry. After all, I'm not getting any younger.'

We finished our meal in silence, and at half-past ten, I stood up. 'I'd better be going. I've still got a murder to solve.'

'Won't you stay the night?'

'No, I don't think so. I've an early start in the morning.'

'Yes, I suppose so. See you in six months' time, then, Harry.' Gail gave me a lingering kiss.

'Yes, six months.'

But, to be brutally honest, we both knew that the relationship was over. Gail had got bored with her aimless life and had probably become bored with me too. I took the key to her house from my key ring and placed it on the table. Curiously, she did not return the key to my flat that I had given her, and I clung to a vestige of hope that I might see her again. But deep down I knew that I was fooling myself.

Having learned from Sebastian Weaver that the afternoon's matinee had been cancelled through lack of bookings, Ebdon and Chance opted for calling at Keycross Court on Saturday afternoon. They waited in their car a few yards down the road, but by four o'clock the woman had not made an appearance.

'Damn!' said Kate. 'Just our luck that on the one day we were waiting for her to turn up, she doesn't show.'

'I suppose she could've come earlier than usual, ma'am,' said Nicola.

'Possibly. Let's go and bang on the door. I don't intend to spend all this arvo hanging around waiting for her.' Kate rang the bell several times, but eventually had to admit that Debra Foley wasn't there, or if she was she was probably 'working' already. 'There's a resident janitor here,' she said. 'We'll have a word with him. See if he knows anything.'

The janitor, a bald-headed man of about fifty with bushy eyebrows and a jolly, rubicund expression, gazed enquiringly at the two young women at the door of his flat on the ground floor.

'We're looking for Corinne Black,' said Kate, once she had identified herself and Nicola Chance as police officers.

'I think she's gone away for a bit, love,' said the janitor, thumbs in the armholes of his unbuttoned waistcoat. 'She asked me to help her down with her bag and put it in the taxi for her.'

'When was this?'

'Yesterday afternoon, about half-past three, I suppose.'

'Did you hear where she was going?' Nicola asked.

'No, sorry. She must've told the driver once she was in the cab. She give me a couple of quid for helping, though.'

'Shall we try Chorley Street, ma'am?' asked Nicola, once she and Kate were back in their car.

'Might as well, Nicky, although I doubt she'll be there,' said Kate. 'It looks as though she's done a runner. Pity, really, because I was hoping we'd catch her wearing the outfit she was wearing when the guv'nor called here yesterday. She wouldn't like coming face to face with another woman when she was dressed like that. That would have thrown her off balance.'

'Not if she's bisexual,' said Nicola.

'Well, she'd be out of luck with me,' said Kate firmly, 'because I'm not.' She put the car into gear and pulled away from the kerb.

But the two detectives fared no better in Chorley Street. There was no answer to repeated knockings, as the police are wont to write in negative reports.

'She could've gone to the theatre already, I suppose,' suggested Nicola.

'It's possible, even though the matinee's been cancelled,' said Kate, 'but I've got a nasty feeling about this.'

They pulled up in front of the Clarence Theatre. As they got out of the car, Kate was approached by a young policeman, who looked as though he'd just escaped from the forcing factory known as Hendon training school.

'You can't park your nice car there, love,' he said.

Kate moved closer to the PC, invading his personal space. 'D'you usually address members of the public as "love"?' she asked in menacing tones. She was becoming increasingly frustrated by her lack of success in finding Debra Foley, and the unfortunate policeman happened to be in her line of fire. And it was he who got the broadside.

The PC made the mistake of smiling. 'I didn't think a pretty girl like you would mind,' he said as he appraised Kate's attractive figure.

'Well, I do bloody mind, cobber.' Kate put a hand in the pocket of her jeans and took out her warrant card. 'Detective Inspector Ebdon, Murder Investigation Team.'

'Oh, I'm sorry, ma'am.' The PC's smile vanished immediately, and his face coloured with embarrassment.

'But since you've taken such an interest in this car, sport, I've got a job for you,' said Kate. 'While I'm in this theatre, I want you to watch over it very carefully because it belongs to the Commissioner. If it's missing, either through theft or because some enthusiastic traffic warden has removed it to the police car pound, or it is damaged in any way, I shall come and find you.' She stared pointedly at the policeman's identifying numerals. 'And I'd better not find a ticket on it when I get back.'

'Yes, ma'am,' said the policeman nervously, and breathed a sigh of relief as the abrasive Australian DI moved away.

Kate led the way upstairs to the manager's office and pushed open the door without knocking.

'Oh no!' exclaimed Sebastian Weaver as he recognized Kate Ebdon. 'Not more bad news.'

'Not to my knowledge,' said Kate, 'but I'm interested in having a word with Debra Foley. I know this arvo's performance has been cancelled, but is she here?'

'She's upped sticks and gone, Inspector.' Weaver slumped in his chair, rather like a teddy bear that's just had all the stuffing knocked out of it. He spent a moment or two mopping his brow with a huge red handkerchief, which he then used to clean his spectacles.

'Gone where?'

'Your guess is as good as mine.' Weaver picked up a sheet of paper and handed it to Kate. 'The selfish cow sent me an email. There, read it.'

Kate scanned the short message and noted that it was dated

yesterday and timed at 15:07 hours. It merely said that Vanessa Drummond would be unavailable for the remaining days of the production as she had urgent family business to attend to abroad.

'That wasn't long after the guv'nor and Sergeant Poole visited her at Keycross Court,' said Kate, turning to Nicola Chance. 'And if she has gone abroad she'll have gone already. Probably sometime last night.'

'We've cancelled the remaining performances anyway,' said Weaver. 'It won't cost much in returns because not many punters had booked to see it. Even when we were papering the house it was still half empty.'

Kate gazed at the peeling wallpaper in the manager's shabby office. 'Pity they didn't paper in here while they were at it.'

Weaver gazed at Kate in apparent despair, wondering whether this was some sort of Australian wind-up or that she really didn't know. 'Papering the house means giving away free tickets, Inspector,' he said with a sigh.

'Really? Good job the drongo who brought me to see it didn't know that.' Secretly, Kate was quite pleased that the insufferable bore who'd treated her to expensive seats at the theatre had also shelled out a substantial amount for dinner afterwards. And got nothing in return.

FOURTEEN

'I obviously frightened her off,' I said, when Kate Ebdon had given me the news that Debra Foley had disappeared.

'D'you want me to check the airports, guv?' Kate asked.

'It's an outside chance, but you might get lucky,' I said. 'It would help if we knew which airport or which airline. It'd be like looking for a needle in a haystack.'

'I wonder if she'll come back for Robert Miles's funeral, guv,' said Dave.

'We don't know when or where that'll be,' I said. 'The coroner shouldn't have released the body yet.'

'I'll try the undertakers in the Harrow area,' said Dave. 'It's just possible that Debra Foley had put matters in hand before she did a runner.'

It was a setback. I'd had no alternative but to interview Debra Foley again. With twenty/twenty hindsight, however, I realized that it had been a mistake to have mentioned the entry on Miles's computer and to have posed the question about her brother's claim to have visited her in her persona of Corinne Black. Unfortunately, in so doing, I had obviously disturbed the woman so much that she'd felt impelled to disappear. But what was she running *from*?

All of which was pure speculation. She might have had a perfectly justifiable reason for taking off so suddenly and would return after the weekend. But I had my doubts. I suspected that the 'urgent family business abroad' was untrue.

'Dave, before you do anything else, check with Eurostar. Whenever we're told that someone's gone abroad we automatically think of airlines, but Eurostar carries a lot of passengers to Europe. Might be worth a go.'

Dave spent ten minutes on the phone before he came back with the answer.

'That was a good guess of yours, guv'nor. She left yesterday

afternoon on the sixteen fifty-two hours Eurostar service for
Paris. I had a thought and checked another name while I was
about it. You'll be interested to know that a certain William
Anderson travelled to Paris on the same train. Neither of them
had booked in advance.'

'Well, well,' I said.

'I wouldn't get too excited, guv,' said Kate. 'It could be a
coincidence. There are probably thousands of William
Andersons in the English-speaking world.'

'And even in Australia,' said Dave.

'Watch it, *Sergeant*,' said Kate sternly, but unable to maintain
the pose, began to laugh.

'A trip to Paris, then, guv?' asked Dave hopefully.

'No. At least, not yet. In the meantime, I'll get Mr Driscoll
to get search warrants for Chorley Street and her apartment
at Keycross Court, and then I'll make a phone call to Henri
Deshayes. That'll do for a start.'

Capitaine Henri Deshayes of the *Police Judiciaire* in Paris
was an old friend. We had worked together on several cases
in the past, and we had visited each other in London and Paris.
As a result, Henri's glamorous wife, Gabrielle, had become
firm friends with Gail. Both had a common interest, as
Gabrielle had been a dancer with the famous *Folies-Bergère*.
Unfortunately, they also had a shared interest in fashion and
would spend hours visiting the haute couture establishments
of Paris. And there are many of them. Rather than trail round
after them, Henri and I would usually make an excuse of
urgent police work and promptly repair to the nearest bar.

'If the Anderson we're interested in is the one who went to
Paris last night, guv,' said Dave, 'wouldn't it be a good idea
to get a warrant for his place at Romford?'

'Not until we know for certain that it's him. If we go there
and he's at home, we could blow the whole thing.'

It was now getting on for seven o'clock, too late to obtain
warrants. 'As I suspect him of being a mercenary, Dave, I'll
get a superintendent's written order to search under the
Explosive Substances Act,' I said. 'But it's not too late to
speak to Hubert Darke. He should be at home on a Saturday.'

'Where does he live?' asked Dave.

'Hinchley Wood.'

'Just my luck.'

Tom Challis had said that if Hubert Darke's house was anything
to go by, he wasn't short of cash. And that was the impression
I got, too. It was a detached property in a tree-lined avenue,
with a long drive and space for turning in front of the house.
There were two cars in this turning circle: a Lexus and a
Bentley. Whatever it was that Darke did in the City it certainly
paid well, and I reckoned his bonus would make my annual
salary look like loose change to him.

'Mr Darke, Mr Hubert Darke?'

'Yes, that's me.' Darke looked at Dave and me with a quizzical expression. 'How can I help you?'

'We're police officers, Mr Darke, and we're investigating
the murder of Lancelot Foley.' I told him our names, and we
showed him our warrant cards.

'Oh, a dreadful business. Do come in.' Darke showed us
into a large, airy sitting room. 'This is my partner Tina,' he
said, indicating an attractive brunette who was reclining in an
armchair watching an animal programme on television. Tom
Challis had checked birth and marriage records for Darke and
had told me that he was forty-one. The woman he'd introduced
as his partner was actually his wife, and we knew that she
was fourteen years younger than Darke.

'I understand that you were a friend of Mr Foley,' I began
as we settled into comfortable armchairs.

'That's correct.' Darke glanced at his wife. 'D'you mind,
darling? The TV.'

'Sorry,' said Tina and used the remote to turn off the
television.

'As a matter of fact we used to play poker together about
once a month,' Darke continued. 'Usually on a Thursday
evening, except when Lancelot was working, and then it would
just be the three of us. But I told all this to that other policeman
who came here a few days ago.'

'Yes, I know,' I said. 'Sergeant Challis is one of my officers.
How well did you know Mr Foley? Did you socialize, or was
it just poker?'

'Mainly poker, but he did give us the occasional theatre ticket whenever he was appearing in a new show. As a matter of fact, Tina and I saw *The Importance of Being Earnest* only a couple of days before he was murdered. Oh, and we were invited to the first-night party at the Waldorf. That was on the seventh of January.' Darke paused. 'Can you think of anyone who would have wanted him dead, Mr Brock?'

'I was about to ask you the same thing, Mr Darke.'

'No, I can't honestly think of anyone. Mind you, he wasn't the easiest of people to get on with.'

'You can say that again,' said Tina. 'He was thoroughly objectionable. The sort of man who undressed a woman with his eyes, if you know what I mean.'

'There was just one thing, though,' said Darke. 'He and Gavin Townsend had a row at the last game.'

'The last poker game?'

'Yes. Gavin finished up owing Lancelot three hundred pounds or thereabouts, but he refused to pay up because he said that Lancelot had been cheating. It was the first time that any of us had made that sort of accusation against Lancelot, although the three of us had suspected it for some time. He was very good with cards, was Lancelot. It wasn't as if he needed the money, but I think it was a matter of principle. If he'd waived the debt, he'd more or less have admitted to cheating.'

'Did this row get violent?' asked Dave.

'They didn't come to blows, but it left a very nasty taste in the mouth. As a matter of fact, Gavin told Lancelot that he'd never play cards with him again, and that if he wanted his three hundred quid he could sue him for it. That, of course, was a ridiculous thing to say because you know better than me that gaming debts aren't enforceable at law.'

'No, but slander is,' said Dave quietly.

'I was told that Mr Townsend is in Australia,' I said.

'He was, but I think he's back now. He's a professional yachtsman. Beats toiling up to the City every day and struggling to put bread on the table.'

Darke didn't look as though he had to struggle very hard. His casual clothing – chinos, sweater and loafers – looked as though it had cost a fortune. I took a guess he wasn't a patron of high-street chain stores.

'When was this game, when Townsend accused Foley of cheating?'

'About three weeks or so before the murder as I recall.'

Dave took out his diary. 'If it was a Thursday, then it would've been the seventeenth of January. Would you agree with that?'

'Sounds right,' said Darke.

'Why wasn't he at the theatre, I wonder,' said Dave.

'He told us that he'd taken the night off. Apparently, it's something they do from time to time, to give their understudy a chance. At least, that's what Foley said.'

'And when did Mr Townsend go to Australia?' asked Dave.

'About two days after Lancelot's murder, I think, but I'm not sure.'

'I understood it was earlier than that.'

'No, it was definitely about two days after the murder because Gavin rang me and we discussed what a terrible thing it was.'

'What about William Anderson?' Dave asked. 'Have you any idea where we can find him?'

'No, I'm afraid I can't help you there. He was more of a friend to Lancelot than to the rest of us. A bit of a dark horse, actually. Talked vaguely of having a military background, hinted at membership of the SAS and disappeared for weeks on end. Always played his cards close to his chest, and I'm not talking about poker, either.'

In my experience, soldiers who had been in the Special Air Service *never* mentioned it, whereas those who hadn't been members of that elite unit often claimed that they had been.

'Thank you, Mr Darke,' I said, 'but there's just one other thing. Where were you on the night of Monday the fourth of February?'

'Good God, I haven't a clue. Just a moment.' Darke left the room and returned minutes later holding a desk diary. 'Well, I didn't have any appointments that evening, so I must've been at home here with Tina.' He glanced at his wife. 'D'you remember, darling?'

Tina laughed. 'You know I can never keep track of you.'
She glanced at me. 'He leads a hectic life, you know, Mr
Brock. He could've been anywhere.'

And with that unsatisfactory alibi, we left, but warned Darke
that we may need to see him again.

'What d'you think, Dave?' I asked as we drove out of
Darke's road.

'I reckon we need to have a close look at Townsend,
guv.'

In view of what we'd learned from Hubert Darke about the
argument Foley and Townsend had had over cheating, I decided
that it was imperative that we should interview the professional
yachtsman as soon as possible.

I had previously sent DI Driscoll to Westminster Magistrates
Court in Marylebone Road to obtain search warrants for Debra
Foley's Chorley Street house and her Keycross Court flat.
Although police like to execute search warrants very early in
the morning thereby catching suspects in bed, there was no
point in exercising ourselves too much in this case. We knew
that the bird had flown and the search would have to wait.

Dave and I made our way to the address that Challis had
given me for Gavin Townsend.

Townsend lived in a mews flat off Praed Street, Paddington.
The door was answered by a willowy blonde in white trousers
and a Breton sweater.

'Hi!' she said.

'We'd like to speak to Mr Gavin Townsend.'

'Oh, yah, right.' The blonde hung on to the door and leaned
backwards. 'Gav!' she shouted, 'there are two nice gentlemen
here to see you.' Turning back, she said, 'Follow me,' and led
us up a narrow staircase to the first floor.

The man who was standing at the top of the staircase was
wearing jeans and a heavy white cable-stitch pullover.

'We're police officers, Mr Townsend. DCI Brock and DS
Poole, Murder Investigation Team.'

'Come on in and take a seat,' Townsend said, and shook
hands with each of us.

'We'd like to speak to you about Lancelot Foley. We're investigating his murder.'

'Yeah, sure. I see you've already met Catrina, my first mate.'

'And your only one, I hope,' said Catrina. 'D'you guys want a drink?' she asked, addressing me.

'No, thanks.'

We sat down, and Dave pulled out his pocketbook ready to make notes.

'I understand that you've recently been in Australia, Mr Townsend,' I began.

'No. I was supposed to go, but the event was cancelled at the last minute. Can't say I was sorry; it's a long haul from London to Sydney.'

'We've been talking to Mr Darke,' said Dave, 'and he was under the impression that you'd been to Australia.'

'As I said, the event was cancelled. I didn't bother to ring everyone up and tell them that, though.'

'You and Foley, Darke and Anderson played poker together, I believe.'

'Yes, and Dudley Phillips, but that's all it was. Anyway, the circle's broken up now that Lancelot's dead and Bill Anderson has buggered off somewhere.'

'Mr Darke told us a story about a row between you and Mr Foley,' I said.

'Too bloody right there was. Lancelot Foley was a cheat, and I caught him at it red-handed. It was only a matter of about three hundred pounds, but I'm damned if I was going to pay him. He, of course, was equally adamant that he hadn't cheated, but I'd spotted him dealing off the bottom of the pack. He was damned good at it, I must admit, but I stood my ground. Lancelot, on the other hand, wasn't prepared to lose face, and not to have demanded payment would've been tantamount to admitting that he'd cheated. Anyway, I told him that I would never play cards with him again.'

'Did you come to blows over it?' I asked. Townsend looked as though he'd be quite useful in a fight, but Darke had denied that the argument had become physical.

'I wouldn't have demeaned myself,' said Townsend. 'I must

admit I was tempted, but I'd no intention of finishing up in court for damaging his matinee idol good looks.'

'When did you last see Lancelot Foley?' asked Dave.

'On that occasion, and I've not set eyes on him since. To be perfectly honest I disliked him intensely, and to be frank I don't know why I played poker with him for so long. I didn't go to his funeral because I'm not a hypocrite.'

I glanced at Townsend's blonde companion. 'Did you ever meet Lancelot Foley, Miss . . .?'

'Wall, Catrina Wall, but call me Cat. And to answer your question, yes, I did meet the creep. But only once, and that was at a first-night party.'

'I take it you didn't like him,' said Dave, with a smile.

'I couldn't stand the bloody man,' responded Catrina vehemently. 'He was the sort of guy who moved up close to you, peered down your cleavage and propositioned you, all in the space of about thirty seconds. I suppose he thought that all women would swoon at his feet, just because he was a well-known actor.'

'You didn't respond to his proposition, then?' Dave asked impishly.

'Oh, I did, but not in the way he expected. I told him, very quietly, to go away and perform an impossible biological act. But I phrased it a little more graphically than that. I also mentioned that my right knee could do some damage if he persisted.'

'What was his reaction?'

'He went away to try it on with some bosomy bimbo who'd come with a footballer, and he didn't speak to me again.'

'It's extremely dangerous to tangle with Cat, Chief Inspector,' said Townsend. 'And I speak from experience.'

'Liar,' said Catrina.

'One last question, Mr Townsend,' I said. 'Where were you on the night of the fourth and morning of the fifth of this month?'

'Good God, Chief Inspector, I have absolutely no idea, other than to say that I was in London.'

We left Gavin Townsend and his dangerous girlfriend. He had no alibi, but at least he'd been honest about the row he'd had with Lancelot Foley. But despite his denial, it was possible that he had murdered Foley.

As we had spent half the morning talking to Townsend, it was close to three o'clock before we started to execute the search warrants that Len Driscoll had obtained for us. We went first to Chorley Street. I sent for a locksmith, which would mean a delay, but I didn't want to smash open the front door to Debra Foley's house for no better reason than it would involve securing the premises after we'd finished. And that would mean a lot of paperwork. Eventually, one turned up and admitted us.

We went from room to room, but found nothing of evidential value anywhere, not that I'd expected to. There were no messages on the answering machine and no correspondence that would assist us.

We went from there to Debra's one-bedroom flat at Keycross Court. On our visit there two days ago, we had only seen the sitting room. The bedroom was more interesting, but hardly surprising. The wardrobe contained a selection of colourful and erotic underwear, along with a couple of whips and a cane. The metal-framed bed was at least six foot wide by seven foot long, and judging by the restraints at the four corners it was obviously equipped for advanced fun and games. And there was a mirror on the ceiling above it. I don't suppose the owners of the property would be too happy about that.

But all we had learned from our search was that Debra Foley, in her alter ego as Corinne Black, was very much the professional call girl.

'It's a blowout, Dave.'

'Yes, sir.'

I did not hold out much hope that I would find Henri Deshayes at work on a Sunday afternoon, the French police being better organized than we are. But I tried.

I telephoned the *Police Judiciaire* in Paris and eventually made contact with an English speaking officer.

'This is Detective Chief Inspector Brock of Scotland Yard,' I began. 'I'm trying to contact *Capitaine* Henri Deshayes.'

'*M'sieur* Deshayes is now a commandant, *m'sieur*, and he is at this moment dealing with a murder at a hotel in the rue de Castiglione in the first arrondissement. I am expecting him to return shortly. I will ask him to telephone you, *oui*?'

'Thank you, *m'sieur*,' I said, and gave him the number.

It was gone six o'clock when Henri Deshayes rang me.

'*Bonjour*, 'Arry, how are you?'

'Busy, Henri, but I hear that you have a murder on your hands.'

'That's so. I was going to ring you anyway. My victim is an Englishwoman, and I think perhaps you can help me, *n'est pas*?'

'If I can. Incidentally, congratulations. I hear that you are now a commandant.'

'Thank you, 'Arry. No more than I deserved, of course.' Deshayes laughed. 'But, to be serious, the victim's name is Debra Foley.'

Ye Gods! That was all I needed. My enquiry into the murder of Lancelot Foley and Robert Miles had just got a hell of a lot more complicated.

'There is little else I can tell you,' continued Deshayes, 'apart from the fact that she had booked into this hotel with a man called William Anderson. But he has disappeared. Is it possible that you can find out more details to help me?'

'I know the woman, Henri, and there's a great deal I can tell you, but it's too complex a situation to explain over the phone. I'd better come over.' I hoped that I wouldn't meet opposition from the commander, who was as reluctant to spend the Commissioner's money as he was to part with his own.

'That's good. Why don't you bring Gail with you? Gabrielle will be delighted to see you both again.'

'I'm afraid that Gail's going to Los Angeles on Monday, to Hollywood, Henri. She's obtained a part in a television programme.'

'Will she be gone for long?'

'Six months, possibly longer.'

'Oh, *malchance*! I'm sorry to hear that. Never mind. When d'you think you can get here?'

'Tomorrow morning, I hope,' I said. 'I'll let you know when I'm arriving.'

I replaced the receiver and sat in thought for a moment or two. To telephone the commander at home would mean having to speak first to Mrs Commander who acted as a filter for her husband. And I didn't feel like explaining the complexities of the latest twist in my enquiry to her. I decided to be devious: I rang the deputy assistant commissioner at home.

'Sorry to disturb you on a Sunday evening, sir,' I said, 'but I can't seem to get hold of the commander.'

'That's all right, Harry,' said the DAC. 'What's the problem?'

I explained, as succinctly as possible, what had happened in Paris, but when I started to give him details of the Foley murder, he cut me short.

'I know all about the Foley job, Harry, and there's obviously a connection. I suppose you want permission to go to Paris.'

'Yes, sir.'

'Then go, Harry. Put in the report when you get back.'

It was always refreshing to speak to a real detective, and one who was conversant with the difficulties faced by working coppers who were frequently hamstrung by administrative niceties.

Having decided that I would leave Dave Poole in London to handle any enquiries at this end, I made another decision and telephoned Kate Ebdon.

'How d'you fancy a trip to Paris, Kate?'

'Bonzer!' exclaimed Kate. 'When?'

'Tomorrow morning. I'll ring you back with the details as soon as I've made the booking. There is one condition, though. No visiting dress shops.'

There was a pause before Kate said, 'Oh well, can't win 'em all, guv.'

I walked out to the incident room. 'Colin, I've got to go to Paris tomorrow morning, and I'm taking Miss Ebdon with me. Would you arrange the flight for me?'

'Of course, sir.'

Ten minutes later, Wilberforce put his head round my office
door. 'You're booked on BA flight three-oh-eight, sir. Leaves
Heathrow at ten forty-five hours and arrives at Charles de
Gaulle at one o'clock their time.'

'Thank you, Colin.' I rang Kate back and told her to meet
me at the airport.

FIFTEEN

The flight landed on schedule at one o'clock at Charles de Gaulle airport, and Henri Deshayes was waiting at the end of the walkway to meet us. Henri is about my height and age and possessed all the suavity of the typical middle-class Frenchman. His dress sense was impeccable, and today he was wearing a light-grey suit with a flower in the buttonhole. I had never once seen him looking like a *flic*, as the French are wont to call their policemen.

Kate had undergone a transformation from her customary outfit and had abandoned her shirt and jeans in favour of the smart black suit she had worn at Lancelot Foley's funeral. The same camel coat completed the picture of a well-dressed woman.

'This is Detective Inspector Kate Ebdon, Henri,' I said.

'It is a very great pleasure to meet you, Kate,' said Henri, bowing low to kiss her hand and as usual overdoing the Gallic charm. He glanced at me and added, 'You have the ability always to surround yourself with beautiful women, 'Arry. You must let me into the secret one day.'

'Wow!' said Kate, for once overwhelmed and, apart from that one word, rendered speechless.

Henri quickly ushered us through the controls by simply waving his badge at the immigration and customs officials, many of whom greeted him by name, and out to where a large police Citroën was waiting in an area where parking was strictly prohibited.

'First we have lunch, 'Arry, and then we can get down to business, *non*?' Henri gave the driver the address of a restaurant, and we were whisked through the Paris traffic with the aid of a siren and blue lights. 'I'm a highly paid policeman, 'Arry,' he said, chuckling as he turned to face us from his place next to the driver, 'and my time is much too valuable to be wasted sitting in traffic jams. And apart from anything else, I'm hungry.'

The restaurant, close to the Opera Garnier, was crowded, but the obsequious maître d'hôtel immediately found a secluded table for *'M'sieur le commandant.'*

Henri studied the menu and steered us through the minefield of various dishes which of course were all written in French, and advised us what to choose. He then turned his attention to the more important question of wine, a subject close to the hearts of all Frenchmen.

'And now, 'Arry, the murder.' When, an hour later, we had finished our meal, Henri swept the napkin from his collar with a flourish. 'On Saturday morning at ten o'clock a young chambermaid entered a room at the Santa Barbara Hotel in the rue de Castiglione to make the bed and clean the room. There was no "Do Not Disturb" sign on the door. The chambermaid found the naked body of Mrs Foley lying face down on the bed. You will note that I said on the bed, not in the bed; it would seem that the bed had not been slept in, although it had been disturbed. You understand this?' Henri raised an eyebrow, and I nodded. 'The pathologist was called and determined that the woman's neck had been broken and that she'd recently had sexual intercourse. The time of death was estimated to be between ten o'clock and midnight.'

'We know she was a prostitute as well as an actress, Henri. Any DNA?'

'Yes, but it is not recorded in our database. We suspect she had sex with the man William Anderson. He and Mrs Foley had arrived together and had booked a double room. The porter carried the luggage of both him and Debra Foley to that room, so we know they were sharing. The porter remembers them particularly because the man gave him a handsome tip. The man Anderson has since disappeared, but the porter and receptionist were able to give good descriptions and each manufactured a computer likeness, an E-fit.' He paused and put his head to one side. 'To say "manufactured" is a good word, 'Arry?'

'It'll do, Henri,' I said, unable to think of a suitable alternative.

Henri took a printout of the computer generated likeness from his pocket and handed it to me. A bearded man with horn-rimmed spectacles stared back at me.

'I'm afraid I can't help you, Henri. It doesn't remind me of anyone I know. I've certainly not come across anyone with a beard in connection with my enquiry.'

'A pity, but that is the trouble with pictures made from the computer. They are seldom any good,' said Henri, taking back the printout.

'Of course, it's possible that the suspect has shaved off his beard by now.'

'That is what I was thinking. I shall have other likenesses made without the beard and the glasses. However,' continued Henri, 'the *juge d'instruction* has authorized a murder investigation. As if it could be anything else,' he added with a chuckle. 'After all, it is not possible for a woman to break her own neck, *n'est pas?*' He paused again. 'Unless she jumps out of a window.'

'This William Anderson is almost certainly the same man in whom we have an interest, Henri,' I said, 'and it looks as though he's concerned in the murder of Lancelot Foley, an English actor and husband of your murder victim. There is also a connection with the murder of your victim's brother. We had already learned that Anderson and Debra Foley left London for Paris on the four fifty-two Eurostar service on Friday, and were together.' I went on to tell Henri as much as we knew about the murders of Lancelot Foley and Robert Miles.

'How was this Lancelot Foley murdered, 'Arry?'

'Strangely enough, he had his neck broken, and so had Robert Miles, Debra Foley's brother.'

'*Sacré bleu!*' exclaimed Henri. 'I think I need a cognac,' he said, and signalled for the waiter. 'Will you have a cognac, Kate, or would you care for something else?'

'That'll be ripper, thanks, Henri,' said Kate.

'Ripper?' For a moment Henri looked puzzled, but then he shrugged and ordered three cognacs.

'Have you any idea when Anderson left the hotel, Henri?' I asked, having decided that there was insufficient time to introduce Henri to the basics of Australian patois.

'No idea,' said Henri. 'There were certainly none of his belongings in the room when we arrived. I'm told that he and Mrs Foley had dinner together in the hotel restaurant the night before the woman's body was found, but none of the hotel staff know at what time he left the hotel. I think it's likely that he used the service stairs and went out through a door that leads directly to the street. He took his one item of luggage with him.' He laughed. 'And he didn't pay the bill.'

'We believe Anderson to be an ex-army officer who has since become a mercenary,' I said, 'so there's no telling where he might be now. In his profession, it's likely that Anderson is not his real name, anyway.' I gave Henri a few details of what we had found on Miles's computer without mentioning that there was much more on the laptop that we had yet to analyse. 'It was after I questioned Mrs Foley about that data that she vanished.' I explained about the mystery of Miles having visited Debra Foley at Keycross Court where she operated as a prostitute.

Deshayes nodded as he absorbed this information. 'I checked with our *police de l'air et des frontières* at your St Pancras station, and they told me that he travelled on a passport in the name of William Anderson. We have now circulated his name and description, and details of the passport to all airports, seaports and to the Eurostar terminal at gare du Nord.'

'That passport might be one of several he holds, Henri. Mercenaries are devious operators, and they're very good at covering their own tracks. In fact, I would hazard a guess that he's now travelling under a different name and has probably left France already. He may even have gone to Africa, which is where a lot of these mercenaries do their business.'

'It's possible,' agreed Henri. 'As I said, we put out a description immediately, but I think the bird he has flown. However,' he said, signalling the waiter for the bill, 'first you would like to visit the crime scene, perhaps?'

'Yes, please, Henri, and then we must find ourselves a hotel.'

'I have made a booking for you at a hotel in the first arrondissement near to *le trente-six*.'

'Near where?' asked Kate.

'The headquarters of the *Police Judiciaire* is at number thirty-six in the quai des Orfèvres, Kate, but it is always known as *le trente-six*: number thirty-six. Have you not read the famous Maigret stories?'

'Who the hell is he?' asked Kate, now thoroughly confused by Henri's rapid mixture of French and English.

'I'll explain later, Kate,' I said.

'I have booked separate rooms for you,' said Henri, with a mischievous smile. 'Was that correct, 'Arry?'

'Yes, it was, Henri,' I said firmly.

Debra Foley's body had been found in a first-floor room of the Santa Barbara Hotel in the rue de Castiglione. A police officer stood guard at the tape that cordoned off that part of the corridor and saluted at the approach of *Commandant* Henri Deshayes.

It was a typically modern hotel room: a double bed, built-in clothes closet, writing desk, two armchairs, en-suite bathroom and a television. Pictures of well-known Paris landmarks adorned the walls, and there was also a Wi-Fi connection for those guests to whom a computer was akin to a life-support machine.

'Nothing has been disturbed, 'Arry,' said Henri, 'apart from the removal of the body, of course. We searched everything that was here, but we haven't yet taken it away. Have a look round, if you wish.'

'Were there any fingerprints, Henri?'

Deshayes gave another of his expressive Gallic shrugs. 'Hundreds. I don't think the chambermaids here do much in the way of polishing. We are searching the database for those we found, but we're not in a hurry. I'm sure we know who killed the woman.'

'I think you're right, Henri,' I said.

Kate and I went through Debra Foley's small overnight bag, which was all that she appeared to have brought with her in the way of luggage. Her handbag yielded the usual contents that one expected to find in a woman's handbag, together with her passport. But there wasn't anything that might further Henri's investigation into her murder or our search for the killer of Lancelot Foley and Robert Miles.

'As I said when we were having lunch, I'm fairly certain that he went that way,' said Henri, once we were in the corridor again. 'That door,' he continued, pointing, 'leads to a flight of stairs. At the bottom is a door that leads straight on to the street.'

'Is that door not locked?' I asked.

'Alas, no. It is an emergency exit in case of fire, and it can only be opened from the inside. But it cannot be locked; that's the law.'

'And now he could be anywhere,' said Kate.

'I'll take you to your hotel now, 'Arry, and then this evening perhaps you and Kate will have dinner with Gabrielle and me. I will pick you up at seven o'clock.'

'Thank you, Henri. I'm looking forward to meeting her again. But you must let me pay for dinner.'

'No, 'Arry. You are guests in my country, and I pay. When next I come to London, you will pay.' And with that comment, Henri gave another of his throaty laughs. 'Anyway, Gabrielle is preparing the meal at our home.'

We had adjoining rooms at the hotel Henri had booked for us, and there was a communicating door between them. I suspected he had arranged that deliberately; in common with many Frenchmen, he was a grand romantic.

I'd taken a shower and had just got dressed when there was a knock at the communicating door.

'Come in, Kate.'

Kate Ebdon was attired in an elegant low-cut green dress that stopped just above her knees, black tights and high heels. Her usually unruly flame hair was neatly coiffed into a ponytail, and she wore tasteful gold earrings.

'Will I do, guv?' she asked.

'You certainly will, Kate, but stop calling me "guv". We're off duty now, and the name's Harry.'

'I meant, will I do up against Gabrielle? From what you told me about her on the flight over, I gather she's something of a fashion icon.'

'You've nothing to fear on that score, Kate,' I said, and glanced at my watch. 'Henri should be downstairs now.'

Kate returned to her room to pick up her clutch bag, and we took the lift to the ground floor.

Henri Deshayes was leaning on the reception counter and in earnest conversation with an attractively mature receptionist. After a last comment that caused the woman to laugh, he walked across to join us. For a moment or two he appraised Kate before slowly shaking his head. '*Magnifique!*' he exclaimed. 'Like I said, 'Arry, you have the art of surrounding yourself with beautiful women.'

'I bet you say that about all the girls, Henri,' said Kate, by now having got the measure of Henri's fulsome compliments.

'Only about beautiful ones like you, Kate.'

It was not far to Henri's apartment in one of the select parts of Paris. Gabrielle was waiting at the door with open arms.

'*Cher* 'Arry,' she said, giving me four air kisses. 'It is good to see you again, but I'm sorry that Gail is not with you. Henri told me that she is going to be a Hollywood star.'

'Maybe,' I said, not wishing to elaborate on what I thought might become a permanent and painful split. 'You are looking as glamorous as ever, Gabrielle.' She was too: a beautifully cut pearl-grey trouser suit over a matching high-necked sweater and a colourful thin silk scarf. 'I'd like you to meet my assistant, Kate Ebdon.'

'It is delightful to see you, Kate,' said Gabrielle, giving her a few air kisses. 'And so chic.' She stood back to admire Kate, and then turned to me. 'You have very beautiful policewomen at Scotland Yard, 'Arry. It must be a terrible temptation for you to be naughty, eh?'

'Harry doesn't need any temptation,' said Kate, and shot me an impish glance. I wasn't quite sure what to make of that.

Henri served champagne – the best, of course – and we sat and chatted for a good hour before Gabrielle announced that we should sit down to dinner.

We had always dined out on my previous visits to the French capital, and I had not therefore experienced Gabrielle's culinary skills. But the meal she prepared was sumptuous.

The starter was a delicious *soufflé au fromage* that simply melted in the mouth, with a Savoy wine to accompany it. The main course, a filet mignon, was out of this world, and Gabrielle was flattered when Kate asked what it was and how it was cooked. Gabrielle explained – in great detail – how she had prepared the noisettes of roast pork fillet and the Vichy carrots, and Henri insisted on telling her the origin of the vintage Buzet wine that he served with it.

'And now, Kate,' said Gabrielle, producing a selection of local cheeses, 'as 'Arry knows, in France we always serve the cheese before the dessert.'

'And with it,' said Henri, pouring yet another wine, 'the most delicious Coteau du Layon.'

Finally, Gabrielle served a delightful Paris-Brest. 'This is a very French dessert,' she said. 'It is choux pastry on the bottom and on the top with crème pâtissière in between.'

'Don't tell me that you have yet another wine to go with that, Henri,' said Kate.

'Of course,' said Henri, producing a bottle of Loupiac. 'This is quite definitely the only wine that is to be served with Paris-Brest.'

'Good on yer!' said Kate. 'I'll remember that just in case I'm ever tempted to have a go preparing it myself.'

'Oh, I didn't make the dessert,' said Gabrielle. 'I bought it from the local patisserie,' she added with disarming frankness. 'French woman can't be bothered making desserts. It is much easier to go round the corner and buy one.'

We returned to the sitting room, and Henri brought in coffee, cognac and a selection of chocolates.

Over the next hour or so, the drink flowed and the conversation sparkled. Gabrielle reminisced about her days as a dancer at the Folies Bergère, and Kate told Henri and Gabrielle about her childhood in Port Douglas, just north of Cairns in Queensland. She went on to describe the weather and how, when it was hot enough, she would go skinny-dipping in the Coral Sea.

'You mean you swam naked?' exclaimed Gabrielle, clapping her hands in glee. 'How wonderfully liberating.' And reading her husband's mind as only a wife of long-standing can do, she laughed and leaned across to slap the back of his hand. 'Stop looking at Kate like that, Henri.'

It was close to midnight when eventually we took our leave. I wanted to say that Gail and I would be delighted to entertain

Henri and Gabrielle when next they came to London, but I now had grave doubts about ever seeing Gail again. She had already left for Los Angeles by now.

One of Henri's police cars delivered us to our hotel, and it was as we were crossing the pavement that Kate staggered a little and cannoned into me. It was then that I realized she'd had too much to drink. The last thing I needed right now was a detective inspector from the renowned Scotland Yard collapsing in the foyer, and I was sure that Henri would have told the management who we were. I put an arm around her waist and held her tightly against me as, with some difficulty, I steered her through the revolving door and across the foyer towards the lift.

'You're very kind, Harry,' she mumbled as I supported her along the corridor to her room.

'Are you sure you're going to be all right, Kate?' I was really quite concerned at her having been overcome by the amount of wine that Henri had served. To say nothing of the cognac.

'I'll be apples,' slurred Kate, her Australian accent becoming even more noticeable. 'You know what, Harry?' She turned to face me. 'You're a beaut, mate. In fact, you're the best guv'nor I've ever worked for.' She was almost incoherent now, and she leaned against me, flung her arms round my neck and gave me a kiss. 'G'night, Harry, darling.' And with that she disappeared into her room, leaving me to wonder.

SIXTEEN

The next morning I decided to go down to breakfast without disturbing Kate; she probably needed the lie-in to recover from the excesses of the previous evening. To my surprise, however, she appeared in the dining room within minutes of my arrival, looking as perky as ever and showing no signs of a hangover.

'G'day, Harry,' she said, all bright and sparkly.

'Good morning,' I said. 'How are you feeling?'

'Bonzer, thanks.' Kate sat down opposite me and spread her napkin over her lap.

This was one of those civilized hotels that served champagne with breakfast, and a waiter appeared instantly and poured a glass for Kate and me.

Kate seized it in much the way that a drowning woman will reach out for a lifebelt. 'Ah, a heart-starter,' she said. 'Just what I needed.'

'No ill effects?' I queried, surprised that she showed no signs of her tipsy behaviour of the previous evening.

'No way. I went for a swim in the hotel pool.' Kate took a longish sip of champagne. 'I didn't see you there, Harry,' she said, eyeing me mischievously over her glass.

'I hope you were wearing a swimsuit,' I said drily, recalling her comments the night before about nude bathing in her home town.

'Too right. I brought my cossie with me. Too many wowsers down there for skinny-dipping.'

I raised an eyebrow.

'Prudes,' said Kate, and signalled the waiter for another glass of champagne.

We touched down at Heathrow at eleven o'clock on the Tuesday morning, and were driven straight to Belgravia police station by Dave, who had been waiting to meet us.

Kate disappeared into her office the moment we arrived and changed into her usual jeans and shirt, emerging once more her normal self. She was calling me 'guv' again, and made no mention of her amorous behaviour the previous evening. Neither did I.

'The commander said that he wanted to see you the moment you came in, sir,' said Colin Wilberforce, as I entered the incident room.

'I think I know what that's about, Colin,' I said. 'Have we had a memo from the DAC authorizing the trip Miss Ebdon and I made to Paris?'

'Yes, sir.' Wilberforce immediately put his hand on the document and passed it to me.

The commander went on the attack the moment I entered his office. 'What d'you mean by going to Paris without my authority, Mr Brock?' he demanded. He peered at me over his half-moon spectacles and gave the impression that he was spoiling for a fight.

Without comment I placed the DAC's memo in the centre of the commander's desk.

He seized it hungrily and scrutinized it carefully. For the moment I'd disarmed him, but he soon recovered. 'Why did you find it necessary to go over my head?' he enquired, staring at me accusingly.

'I couldn't get hold of you, sir, and in view of the urgency of the enquiry, I telephoned the DAC.'

'Well, I suppose that's understandable,' said the commander with obvious reluctance. 'As a matter of fact I took the lady wife to the opera on Sunday evening.'

'That would explain it, sir,' I replied blandly, relieved that he had unwittingly got me out of having to justify not having phoned him in the first place. 'What did you see? Which opera, I mean.'

'*Nabucco*. That's Nebuchadnezzar in English, of course. It was composed by Giuseppe Verdi in 1841,' said the commander airily, giving the impression of being the fount of all operatic knowledge.

'Programme notes are extremely helpful when it comes to knowing what the show is all about, aren't they, sir? You should talk to Doctor Mortlock; he's very knowledgeable about opera.'

'Mmm! Yes.' The commander wrinkled his nose. He didn't like being caught out, and he didn't like the opera being called a show. 'Anyway, what was so urgent that you and Miss Ebdon had to go rushing off to Paris?' he asked, changing the subject.

I explained about the death of Debra Foley in a Paris hotel room and that the police there were now actively looking for William Anderson, a mercenary. I mentioned in passing that the *Police Judiciaire* had requested that Interpol issue a red-corner circular for Anderson's arrest. I went on to add one or two facts about the progress of our enquiries in London, but I kept it as simple as possible in the hope that I would frustrate the commander if he was thinking of offering me any advice.

'But how can you possibly say that this man Anderson is a mercenary? There doesn't appear to be any evidence that would stand up in court.'

'I doubt that we'd need to prove it in court, sir, although there are foreign powers who may seek his extradition if he's taken part in any armed insurrection in their country. But as far as we are concerned it is merely a pointer that will eventually lead us to discovering the killer of these three victims.'

The commander was on it in a moment. 'But how d'you know that the same man killed all three, Mr Brock?'

'We don't even know it's a man, sir.' I thought I'd put that in, as the boss, unusually for him, had assumed the killer to be a man. Everything pointed to it; indeed, the murder of Debra Foley in Paris made it a certainty in my view. 'The modus operandi is similar in each case, sir,' I added, just for good measure.

'Yes, I see, quite so. Keep me informed, Mr Brock.'

From the commander's office I went into the incident room and brought the team up to speed on what Kate and I had learned in Paris. Colin Wilberforce updated the entry about William Anderson on the police national computer and at my direction marked it 'armed and dangerous'. I was pretty certain that he would be armed, and from what we'd learned about him so far I was happy to assume that he'd be dangerous.

Going back to my office, I made myself a cup of coffee

from my illegal coffee machine. The Yard's electricity police
don't like us using the Commissioner's power supply.

I sent for Kate and Dave, and then set about discussing
what we should do next. It was now two weeks since the
murder of Lancelot Foley and the only significant events since
then had been the murders of Debra Foley's brother, Robert
Miles, and of Debra herself. But we now had a front runner
in terms of a suspect. The method used in all three killings
had been similar, as I had told the commander, and the fact
that the elusive William Anderson was almost certainly a
mercenary pointed to him being the killer. But, in all this, the
one thing that was missing was motive. So far I'd been unable
to find any evidence that explained *why* the three victims had
been murdered.

'I don't see any reason why we shouldn't search Anderson's
house at Romford now, guv'nor,' said Dave. 'We might even
be lucky enough to find him there.'

'I'd be very surprised if he was there, Dave, but you're
right; I think we should search it. However, it's possible that
some of his henchmen might be there. I can't see a man like
Anderson leaving his property unguarded, whatever sort of
security system he's got in place.' I glanced at Kate. 'Is Len
Driscoll in this morning, Kate?'

'Yes, guv, he's in the office catching up on paperwork.'

There was something new about the way that Kate smiled
when she called me 'guv' now, almost as if we were conspira-
tors. If Gail didn't return from Hollywood, I wondered whether
Kate would . . .? No, I put that thought aside; if it came to
the notice of the commander he'd go ballistic. He had very
strong views about that sort of thing.

'Ask him to come in, Kate.'

Len Driscoll had the appearance of a successful businessman
rather than that of a detective inspector on the Murder
Investigation Team. Complex, often irritable and always
demanding, it was rumoured that he had been to one of the
better known public schools. He was tall and well dressed and
possessed the superior attitude of a man who was efficient at
his job, which he undoubtedly was, and scathing about the
inefficiency of anyone working for him or with him or even

above him. I always got the impression that his suave demeanour left even the commander feeling ill at ease.

There was a story circulating about him that when he was a DI on the Flying Squad he and his colleagues had arrested a robber, one of an armed team that the Squad had surprised when they were attempting to rob a betting shop. Although the robbery had been thwarted, one of the robbers had severely injured one of Len's detective constables with a sash weight he had used as a weapon, but had escaped with two others in the mêlée that followed.

Len did not believe that there was honour among thieves and, producing his pistol, he had given the one remaining robber the option of revealing the identity of his fellow villains or of dying right there. He mildly pointed out, in educated tones, that his death would be put down to having been shot in the course of the attempted robbery. The man revealed the names of the other robbers instantly, and they were all in custody in time for lunch.

'Len, I propose to search William Anderson's drum in Romford. But it's not going to be easy. What do we know about this place?'

'I ran a check with the local authority, and the council tax is paid by William Anderson, as are the utility bills. It's all above board, and payments are made by bank direct debit from an account held in Newcastle.'

'He obviously doesn't intend getting caught out on a technicality, then. I somehow doubt that Anderson will be there, but I don't think that the property will be empty, even so.'

'An armed response team then, guv, and perhaps a unit of the Territorial Support Group.' Driscoll started to make notes. 'How many of our own officers will we take with us?'

'As many as we can muster, Len. But only you, Dave, Kate and I will be tooled up.' I knew that Kate was a crack shot and would have been offended if I'd excluded her from the vanguard.

'And when d'you propose to go in?' asked Driscoll.

I glanced at my watch. 'I'll get a written order this afternoon, and I reckon we'll hit the place early tomorrow morning, say six o'clock. While I'm doing that, Len, perhaps you'd get

India Nine-Nine to do a sweep over the property so we know what we'll be up against.'

'Helicopter to do a surveillance sweep.' Driscoll spoke aloud as he wrote the instructions in his pocketbook. 'I'll go up with them, guv. A few photographs might come in useful.'

That evening, Driscoll came into the incident room with the photographs that had been taken by the helicopter's observer. I could see that Wisteria Cottage was at the far end of Reeching Lane, a turning off Romford Road.

'It might be called a cottage, guv,' said Driscoll, 'but it looks more like a bloody fortress with open ground all round it.' Producing another of the aerial photographs, he pointed out the property with a ballpoint pen. 'As you can see, there are CCTV cameras covering the front and the back, and there's a proliferation of aerials on the roof. There was no sign of habitation, but that doesn't mean it's empty.'

'From what little we know of Anderson, I'm bloody sure that he'd leave someone there to guard the place. I suppose there's no way it can be approached from the back, is there?'

'Not a cat in hell's chance,' said Driscoll.

'I can see that there's a lot of other property in Reeching Lane. Is that likely to be a problem?'

'I doubt it. The houses there are all of good quality, and they're spaced out, each with a fair bit of ground round them. Add to that the upmarket cars on the driveways, and I'd say they're not short of a bob or two in these parts.'

'What sort of gate to Wisteria Cottage is it that I can see, Len?' asked Kate, pointing to the photograph.

'A five-barred job, and it's probably alarmed. I couldn't see very clearly from the air.'

'Is it substantial?' I asked.

'I wouldn't think so. Looks like a standard gate.' Len grinned. 'Thinking of bulldozing it?'

'Why not? In for a penny in for a pound,' I said, 'but from what you say we won't be able to surprise anyone who happens to be there.'

'I don't see why we should mess about,' said Kate. 'Anderson's wanted for murder in France, and there's an Interpol red circular that says so. It's a pretty good bet that our own two toppings are down to him as well. If the joker's there, we don't want him to shoot through, do we?'

'So long as he doesn't shoot through me,' said Dave drily.

'I reckon the only way, then, is to ram the gate, rather than tiptoe up the garden path.'

'I suggest we assemble in Romford Road, guv'nor,' said Driscoll.

By six o'clock on the Wednesday morning everything was ready. I beckoned to the officers in charge of the ARU and the TSG and explained the plan that Len and I had worked out.

'There's a very strong cowcatcher on the front of each of my two vehicles, sir,' said the inspector in charge of the twenty-one officers comprising the TSG. 'I reckon they'll go through that five-barred gate like a knife through butter.'

'I hope you're right,' I said. 'OK, we'll move on my signal. I'll let you lead the way, followed by the ARU. And make it fast. My team will bring up the rear. But once we're in the grounds of this place, spread out the minute you alight. We've no idea what we're up against.'

I gave the two officers time to brief their respective units, and then gave the signal.

'Forward ho!' shouted Dave.

The leading TSG vehicle must have been doing at least fifty miles an hour by the time it hit the gate. There was a resounding crash as pieces of wood flew in all directions, and almost immediately a light went on in an upstairs room of Wisteria Cottage.

'I hope this *is* Anderson's drum,' observed Dave as we followed the small convoy into the area in front of the house. 'He might've moved.'

'A fine time to think of that, Dave,' said Kate, who was sharing the back seat with him. 'But Mr Driscoll said that he pays the council tax.'

As I had instructed, the vehicles in our little convoy fanned out immediately, and the officers, once deployed, spread out. We scrambled out of our car as fast as we could, and I was pleased to see that Tom Challis, Charlie Flynn and Nicola

Chance had exited their vehicle just as quickly and had moved
up so that they were close to the front of the house. Which
was extremely fortunate in view of what happened next.

Suddenly, an upper window was thrown open, and there
was a rattle of small-arms fire. I had time to see the windscreen
of the leading TSG vehicle hit and star over before we all
dived for cover at the front of the house, as the others had
done.

'I hope he doesn't think of dropping hand grenades out of
the window,' said Dave.

'Looks like he's got some sort of automatic rifle, sir,' said
the sergeant in charge of the ARU as he sidled up to me.
'We've got a stun grenade launcher with us. I reckon my lads
could get one through the window where he's standing.'

'Go for it,' I said, and turned to the TSG inspector who was
lying next to me. 'Might be a good idea to get some of your
chaps to go back to Reeching Lane, in case we've woken up
any of the locals and they start rubbernecking. There's going
to be enough report writing about this without having civilian
casualties to complicate things.'

'I should think we've woken up half Romford,' said the
inspector, and issued rapid instructions on his personal radio.

Looking sideways, I saw one of the ARU officers launching
a stun grenade. There was an immediate sound of an explosion
when the grenade passed through the open window where the
sniper had been standing. The TSG inspector and two of his
men rushed the front door with a rammer and made several
attempts to batter it down, but they were unsuccessful: the
door wouldn't shift.

Muttering an obscene oath, the inspector seized the rammer
from the PC and hurled it through one of the adjacent ground-
floor windows. Seconds later, ARU officers were inside the house.

It was silent for at least fifteen minutes, and I began to wonder
if there had been a problem, or, worse still, the stun grenade
had been ineffective. But then the ARU sergeant appeared at
the front door. He and another officer were holding a handcuffed
man who had the appearance of an ex-soldier. He was of medium
height, clearly fit and muscular, with a crew cut hairstyle, and
was dressed in battle fatigues and combat boots.

'This guy is the only one in the house, sir, and I've disarmed him,' said the sergeant. 'I've only had a brief look round, but I reckon there are sufficient weapons in there to equip a small army.'

'Good work, Skipper,' I said, and turned to the TSG inspector. 'Have this guy taken to Romford nick, searched and detained. I'll finish up here, and then I'll come and have a chat with him.'

'Right, sir.' The TSG inspector turned to one of his officers. 'Go and fetch the rammer from the sitting room, Jane, otherwise I'll finish up paying for the bloody thing.'

Jane laughed. 'We wouldn't want that, sir,' she said, 'because you'd have a whip round, and we'd all finish up paying for it.'

Taking the rest of the team with me, I entered the house and detailed Len Driscoll to conduct a systematic search with Charlie Flynn, Tom Challis, John Appleby and Nicola Chance, while I had a look round the rear of the property. 'But bear in mind that the place still has to be dusted for fingerprints.'

'Naturally,' drawled Driscoll, in such a way that implied that he knew his job and didn't have to be told.

The search party spent an hour working their way through the house, but the result was disappointing. As the ARU sergeant had said, there was a large steel cabinet on the first floor containing weapons, which was open, presumably as a result of our rifleman having taken a firearm from it in his rush to repel boarders. However, the stun grenade had disorientated him, and a quick blast from a taser pistol had made sure that he was no longer a threat to anyone.

It was indeed a small arsenal that the team had found. Uzi machine-guns, point-44 Remington magnum pistols, hand grenades and a stock of ammunition. The basement contained another cabinet, in which was found a number of rocket launchers. Altogether there was sufficient materiel to equip a small army which, presumably, was what Anderson had in mind. The quantity of weapons seemed to indicate that he was actually the head of a mercenary unit and, from what we had discovered, it was a substantial one.

Sadly, there was no computer to be found, and I could only imagine that if Anderson possessed one it was in the form of a laptop and he'd taken it with him. That was a wise move; by the look of the thug that the ARU sergeant had arrested, it would have been dangerous to leave a computer with him. As Dave suggested, he looked as though he might've eaten it.

After a couple of hours, I decided that there was no more to be learned from the house. Certainly, there was nothing to indicate William Anderson's present whereabouts, or even that he'd been there in the first place. We were clearly dealing with a consummate professional. However, I didn't think that the mercenary side of the enquiry was anything to do with me. I made a quick call to the Counter Terrorism Command, gave them the SP and told them that the house would be guarded until their officers arrived, after which it would be down to them. However, I did ask to be advised of any fingerprint or scientific evidence they found that might lead us to Anderson.

There was always a chance that the Counter Terrorist Command would say that this was not a terrorist threat and would bounce it back to us as a major crime. But the one thing our beloved commander *was* good at was administrative ping-pong.

I left Len Driscoll to mop up and return all the firearms that we'd drawn that morning.

It was eleven o'clock when Dave and I arrived at Romford police station, a long, low building in Main Road.

'The TSG brought in a prisoner earlier this morning, Skip. Has he told you his name?'

The custody sergeant smiled. 'Refused to say a word, sir. If he does eventually open up, you'll probably only get his number, rank and name.'

'Like that, is it? Have him brought up to the interview room, then. I'll see if my sergeant can charm a few words out of him.'

The custody sergeant glanced at Dave's six-foot well-built stature. 'Yes, he might just be able to do that, sir.' He turned to the gaoler. 'Get Number Three cell open and take its resident up to the interview room, lad. Tell him this nice chief inspector would like to speak to him.'

'And tell him he's got a gorilla with him,' said Dave.

'How are you spelling gorilla?' asked the sergeant.

SEVENTEEN

I decided that I would let Dave kick off with the questioning. He has a way of disorientating recalcitrant prisoners.

'Hello,' said Dave affably as he sat down opposite the sniper and smiled at him. 'I'm Detective Sergeant Poole, and this is Detective Chief Inspector Brock. We're both from the Murder Investigation Team. What's your name?'

'I've got nothing to say,' snapped the prisoner aggressively, speaking with a vaguely Irish accent.

'It doesn't really matter,' said Dave. 'It won't stop us from charging you with three murders. In fact, I've known quite a few murderers who didn't tell us who they were until after they'd started their thirty-year sentences.' Leaning forward, he rested his elbows on the table so that his arms were vertical, and he cupped his chin in his hands. 'D'you know, I went down to Dartmoor once to talk to a prisoner; he was Irish too. I remember it well because it was such a lovely sunny day with a cool breeze sweeping across the moor and little Dartmoor ponies frolicking about enjoying the balmy weather. Mind you, that was outside. It was a very different story on the inside . . . the inside of the prison, I mean. Dank, dirty, overcrowded and full of very nasty people. And the smell was unbelievable.' He continued to speak conversationally, almost as if he were discussing how he'd spent his holidays.

The prisoner sat up sharply and fidgeted with the front of his battle fatigues, and then sniffed and wiped his nose with the back of his hand. This sergeant had unnerved him. It wasn't supposed to be like this. He was expecting to be given a hard time, even to the extent of having a confession beaten out of him. 'I don't know nothing about no murders.'

'I'm not sure that's true.' Dave continued in the same chatty tones as before. 'I'm not talking about your mercenary activities, of course; what you get up to overseas doesn't really interest me. No, I'm talking about the two murders in London and the one in Paris.'

'I don't know what the hell you're talking about.' In his anguish, the prisoner's Irish accent had vanished, to be replaced by what subsequently proved to be his native Cockney, and he began to shake, his hands twitching nervously on the tabletop.

'Oh, don't worry about that, my dear fellow. Your lawyer will explain it all to you.' Dave glanced at me. 'D'you want me to charge him straight away, sir?' He looked at his watch. 'There's just time to put him up in front of the beak and get an eight-day lay down.' He faced the prisoner again. 'If all goes according to plan, you'll be in Brixton nick in time for tea. Won't that be nice? I do believe they have toasted teacakes on a Wednesday. So I've heard, anyway.'

'My name's Jim Finch, and I don't know nothing about no murders, like I said. And that's the God's honest truth.' Perspiration had broken out on Finch's forehead, and he looked decidedly worried. He tugged at his left ear-lobe.

'Oh, good. At last we can begin.' Dave turned on the recording machine and announced the date, time and place and who was present. 'Well, Jim—' He paused and leaned towards Finch. 'It's all right if I call you Jim, isn't it?'

'Yeah, I s'pose so.'

'Excellent. Well, now, Jim, perhaps you'd start by telling me where your guv'nor's gone.'

'I dunno. The colonel never tells me nothing.'

'This would be Colonel Anderson you're talking about, would it?'

'Dunno. He never told any of us what his name was. He was just known as the colonel.'

'Oh, there are more of you, are there?'

'Yeah, course there is. There's about eighteen altogether.'

'And do they all live at Wisteria Cottage?'

'Nah, course not. Just me. The colonel made me his sergeant-major, see. He put me in charge and told me to look after the place.'

'Many congratulations on your promotion, Jim.' Dave smiled at Finch again. 'But how does the colonel assemble his team whenever you're going off on a job?'

'He gives 'em a bell on his mobile.'

'Oh, of course he does. Silly me. When's the colonel coming back? Did he tell you that?'

'Dunno. Like I said, he never tells me nothing.'

'How long were you in the army, Jim?' asked Dave, suddenly switching his line of questioning.

'How did you know that?' Finch stared at Dave suspiciously. 'I never told you that.'

'Come on, Jim. It's written all over you. I can see you're a soldier through and through. You're fit, and you've got that bearing that tells me you know what discipline is all about. I can see that you're head and shoulders above mere civilians.'

'Yeah, well.' Finch grinned and preened himself. 'I done three years before me bit of trouble.'

'Oh, what bit of trouble was that?'

'Well, it was like when some gear went missing when we was in Afghanistan—' Finch stopped suddenly and screwed his face into a thoughtful mode. 'Or was it Iraq? Oh, I dunno. Never mind. Anyhow, they reckoned I'd nicked it, but it was 'cos I forgot to sign for it, see? But by then it was too late, and I got the elbow after I done six months down the glass-house.' Such was the effect of Dave's persuasive questioning that Finch evidently felt he owed him an explanation. 'That's the army prison down Colchester, see. It don't do getting banged up in there, I can tell you.'

'Interview concluded at eleven thirty-two,' said Dave, and turned off the recording machine. 'I think the intelligence quotient of our transient friend is such that he's unlikely to be forthcoming with anything of evidential value, sir,' he said, turning to me and deliberately using convoluted language in the certain knowledge that the obtuse Finch wouldn't understand a word of it.

'You're right, Dave. Go ahead and charge him with attempted murder.'

That announcement did, however, register with Finch. 'What attempted murder's that?' he asked, clearly shocked by this turn of events. He'd heard all about people getting fitted up by the Old Bill for something they hadn't done and imagined it was about to happen to him.

'Strange though it may seem, Jim,' said Dave, 'opening fire on police officers with an automatic weapon is a serious matter, and the court will find no difficulty in seeing it as attempted murder.'

'Oh, that,' said Finch. 'How long d'you reckon I'll get for that, then?'

'Well,' said Dave, 'let me put it this way: if I were you, I wouldn't book any holidays for at least the next ten years.'

We obtained Finch's date of birth and found out that he'd been born in Hoxton. Dave took his fingerprints and confirmed that Finch had been convicted of stealing weapons from an armoury while serving with the army in Afghanistan, for which he had received six months' military corrective training followed by a discharge with ignominy. Dave told me later that six months in a military prison was worse than five years in a civilian nick.

The resident Crown Prosecution Service lawyer at the police station agreed the charge of attempted murder, and Finch appeared before the magistrate at Romford court which was conveniently situated next door. He was remanded in custody to appear at Snaresbrook Crown Court eight days hence.

'Well, we didn't get much out of him, Dave,' I said as we drove back to Belgravia. 'But what little we did get might be of use to the Counter Terrorist Command.'

'I'll give 'em a bell when we get back, guv. I wonder whether Anderson will return to Romford eventually. I was wondering whether it was worth putting an obo on the place.'

'I don't think there'd be a good hiding place for an obo, Dave, and I'd like to think that Anderson will be nicked before he gets the chance.' I was absolutely convinced now that Anderson was the man wanted for all three murders. But he was going to be a difficult man to catch. From Dave's brief and largely unproductive questioning of Finch, it was apparent that Anderson was an extremely cautious man and played his cards close to his chest. That even his cohorts didn't know his true identity – whatever that was – probably rendered our entries on the police national computer virtually useless. It also meant that Henri Deshayes' Interpol circular was unlikely to bear fruit. We were looking for a man that the staff at the

Santa Barbara Hotel could describe, albeit sketchily, but who no one could identify.

I telephoned Henri at his office at the quai des Orfèvres and told him about our raid on the house in Romford, but disappointed him by telling him that we'd found nothing that would assist him in finding Anderson.

'There's something that you can do for me, 'Arry. The next of kin of Debra Foley must be told of her death, but we couldn't find anything in her belongings that indicated who that might be.'

'I've no idea either, Henri, but leave it to me and I'll get back to you.'

It was a problem, but only a minor one. Debra Foley's husband and her brother were both dead, and I knew of no other relatives.

I sent for Dave and explained the problem.

'The obvious person to talk to is Lancelot Foley's solicitor, guv. The one we spoke to about the great actor's will.'

It was three o'clock in the afternoon of what was proving to be a very long day when we arrived at the Chancery Lane offices of the solicitor.

I explained to Cynthia, the solicitor's receptionist, that we needed to see the senior partner urgently, and she ushered us into his office without demur.

'Ah, Chief Inspector, we meet again.' The solicitor rose from his desk and shook hands. I noticed that his desk was still devoid of paperwork. Turning to his secretary, he said, 'Cynthia, be so good as to telephone my next appointment and advise her that a sudden emergency has arisen. Arrange for her to make a fresh appointment.' Realigning his gaze on me, he asked, 'What can I do for you today, Chief Inspector?'

'Debra Foley, Lancelot Foley's widow, has been murdered, sir,' I said. 'The day before yesterday.'

'Oh dear.' The solicitor swept his handkerchief from his top pocket, held it to his mouth and coughed affectedly. 'I do act for her, but I'm afraid I don't hold her will if that's what you were after. In fact, she may not even have made one. It's very inconvenient when people die intestate. Creates a lot of difficulty for their legal representative, don't you know.'

'I'm not interested in her will,' I said. 'But we need to inform her next of kin of her death. D'you happen to know who that might be?'

'I see. That, of course, presents a problem. Do you have a death certificate for her?'

'I'm afraid not. You see, she was murdered in Paris.'

'Oh, how terribly inconvenient. But I need confirmation of her death before I can proceed further.'

I wondered what on earth he was talking about. I didn't think it was necessary for him to see a death certificate before telling us who Debra Foley's nearest and dearest were.

'There's no doubt that she's dead, sir,' said Dave, 'but if you need confirmation I can give you the telephone number of *Commandant* Henri Deshayes of the *Police Judiciaire* in Paris. He's dealing with her murder, and he's actually seen her dead body. In fact, he was there when she was certified dead,' he added, guessing that that would have been the case.

'Mmm!' The solicitor steepled his fingers and put them to his mouth, as though he were praying. Which he may have been. 'Perhaps, Chief Inspector, you'd be prepared to sign an affidavit that to the best of your knowledge Mrs Foley is actually dead. I am a commissioner for oaths, so it can be done straight away.' With a flourish, he produced a gold fountain pen from an inside pocket of his grey, discreetly pinstriped suit, as if to brook no argument on the matter.

'If that'll make you feel more comfortable, sir,' I said, still mystified as to why the lawyer thought it necessary to go through all this legal mumbo-jumbo just to tell me the identity of Debra Foley's relatives.

By way of reply, the solicitor took his spectacles from the little holder on his desk and extracted a form from a drawer in his desk. After he'd spent a few minutes writing, and had read it aloud to me, he produced a New Testament and I swore that the document I was about to sign was to my knowledge true in every particular.

'Good,' said the solicitor, putting the signed form back in his desk drawer. 'I have something for you, Chief Inspector.'

He rose from his desk and crossed the room to a large safe. Selecting a key from his key chain, he opened the safe and took out an envelope. 'This document, Mr Brock, was lodged with me by Mrs Foley, some considerable time ago. As you can see,' he continued, handing me the envelope, 'it is marked: "To be handed to the police in the event of my untimely death." I therefore do so, but I shall require that you sign a receipt for it.'

'Do you know what's in it?' I asked.

'Certainly not. By the way, I've no idea as to the identity of her next of kin.'

I waited until we were back at the office before opening the envelope and did so in the presence of Dave and Kate Ebdon. It's always a good idea to have a witness to the opening of strange envelopes of this nature. There are some barristers who seem to think that we make up things like that to bolster a flagging case.

The handwritten document, headed with Debra's Chorley Street address, but undated, made interesting reading. I scanned it quickly and then read it aloud to Kate and Dave.

> You will only be receiving this in the event of my murder.
>
> I am an actress, but I am also a call girl. I am not proud of it, but in my particular case the acting profession pays so poorly that I had to find a way of supplementing my income.
>
> My clients are sent to me by word of mouth, through a friend of mine whose name I prefer to keep secret. You will understand that it came as a terrible shock when one evening my husband, Lancelot Foley, arrived at the flat I used for meeting clients. Using a false name, he had booked me for the night and thought he was coming to have sex with Corinne Black, the name I used as a call girl. When he arrived and found it was me, there was a terrible row, and he threatened to divorce me and to let everyone know what I was doing.
>
> I told him that I was willing to divorce him, but that I wanted half his money to keep quiet or I would tell

everyone that he was living on my earnings as a call girl. He said he would tell everyone that I was a whore and that he would ruin me as an actress. I replied by saying I would leak a list of all the well-known names I'd slept with to the press, an MP and a judge among them, but I would sign the covering letter with his name, so it would appear that it was he who had given this information to the tabloid press. At that point he slapped my face and started to search the flat, looking for the list. But I knew he would never find it.

I heard nothing for a few days, or maybe a week, and then my brother Bobby Miles arrived at the Keycross Court flat, not knowing that the Corinne Black he was expecting to meet was actually his sister. He told me that the man he worked for had promised to pay him £25,000 to murder me and make it look like suicide. Bobby said that the contract on me – that's what he called it – had come from my husband, who had said that he wanted to stop me blackmailing him. Having found out that I was his sister, of course, Bobby didn't do anything about it. He told me the man he worked for was called Colonel William Anderson.

I asked Bobby to get this Anderson to come and see me, which he did. I told Anderson that I wanted rid of my husband, who was threatening to expose me and have me murdered. Anderson was a businessman, and I told him that my husband was worth over fifteen million pounds and that I'd pay him half of that if my husband was killed. I also offered to sleep with him any time he wanted to. Of course, he accepted my offer as he said it was more than the amount he'd been offered to kill me. As I said, Anderson was a businessman.

It is common knowledge that Lancelot was later murdered, and I believe that Anderson himself was responsible. But I then discovered that Lancelot had left all his money to a woman called Sally Warner, who lived in Farnham and with whom he'd had a child some years ago. As I was now without means, I was unable to pay Anderson the £7.5 million I'd promised him for killing my husband. At first, Anderson was very annoyed about me being unable to pay and made threats, but then he relented, saying that sleeping with me would be enough to settle the debt. But then my brother was murdered.

If I am murdered, and even if it looks like suicide, I hope this will give you some idea of who was responsible and why.

All the above is true.

'Well, that's it,' I said. 'The letter is signed Debra Foley, and she's written the name Corinne Black in brackets.'

'At least it gives us a motive, guv'nor,' said Dave, 'but it doesn't get us any nearer finding Anderson. He's not a colonel, anyway; he's a disgraced captain who got the chop from the army.'

'That's irrelevant,' said Kate, 'but are you going to let Henri Deshayes know, guv?'

'I suppose so,' I said. 'Not that it'll help him find Anderson. It's a pity that Debra didn't enclose a photograph of the elusive Anderson.'

'It might be useful if we were able to have sight of this list that was mentioned in the letter,' said Dave.

'I doubt that would help us to find Anderson,' I said, 'but, that apart, I somehow doubt that such a list actually existed. After all, I'm sure that Debra Foley would have been able to recall the important names without having first written them down.'

I telephoned Henri Deshayes and told him about the letter and promised that I'd email him a copy.

'At least we now have a motive, 'Arry,' said Henri. 'For what difference that will make.'

I finished my call with Henri Deshayes and asked Dave to get our car on the front. 'We're going to visit Dudley Phillips, Dave.'

'I've got a feeling that this day is never going to end, guv'nor,' said Dave.

'I know how you feel,' I said, which afforded Dave no comfort whatsoever.

EIGHTEEN

There was a sign on the door of a shop with blacked out windows that told us that Dudley Phillips carried out business there as a couturier.

I rang the bell, and moments later the door was opened by a middle-aged grey-haired woman in an overall. She had a pencil stuck in her hair.

'Yes?' The woman glared at us with the sort of hostile expression that I imagine she reserved for commercial travellers and other itinerant sales persons.

'Is Mr Phillips here?' I asked.

'Who wants to know?' She removed the pencil, scratched her scalp with it and replaced it in her hair.

'The police,' said Dave.

'Oh!' The woman's expression softened, but only a little. 'You'd better come in, then,' she said. She led us through a showroom that was crowded with dresses on racks and opened a door on the far side. 'The law's here to see you, Dud.'

We followed her into a workshop. There were about seven or eight women sitting at sewing machines busily working, and the entire place was a hubbub of noise and activity.

'It's a bloody sweatshop,' whispered Dave. 'I bet the Border Agency would have fun here.'

'I'm Phillips.' The man who crossed the floor had a toothbrush moustache, was probably in his mid-fifties and was wearing old flannel trousers and a green cardigan over a shirt that had definitely seen better days. He wasn't very tall, but was decidedly overweight. His plastic-framed spectacles had a piece of sticking plaster wrapped around the bridge, as though it had been broken at some time. He certainly didn't look like the sort of companion that Foley, Darke, Townsend and Anderson would have selected as a poker partner. But poker, or gambling of any sort, for that matter, begets strange bedfellows. 'You from the local nick?'

'No,' I said. 'I'm Detective Chief Inspector Brock from the Murder Investigation Team, and this is Detective Sergeant Poole.'

'Oh, right. You're here about Lancelot Foley getting topped, then. Come through to the office.'

The office was a tip: a desk laden with paperwork, ledgers, and a bolt of cloth. There were more bolts of cloth leaning against the walls, and several fashion sketches were propped against the side of the desk. Another sketch stood on an easel.

'We're getting ready for a show,' explained Phillips in a rich Cockney accent. 'Take a pew.' He cleared magazines and catalogues from a couple of straight-backed chairs, tossed them on the floor and flicked the seats with a dirty handkerchief. We decided to remain standing.

'I don't know anything about Foley getting topped, if that's what you were going to ask,' said Phillips. 'Don't surprise me it happened, though.'

'Why's that?' I asked.

Phillips perched on his desk, facing us. 'He was a nasty bastard, full of piss and importance. And he cheated at cards.'

'Why did you play with him, then?' asked Dave.

'Because I cheated an' all, only I was better at it than he was. And I took him for a couple of centuries over the months. Anyhow, he could afford it. Bloody loaded he was.'

'How did you come to meet him, then?' I couldn't imagine what, if anything, this East End Londoner had in common with Lancelot Foley, he of the airs and graces.

'He brought one of his tarts down here about a year ago. Wanted her kitted out with clobber that'd be suitable for when he took her on holiday down the South of France. Money no object, he said, stupid bugger. I quoted him five grand, and of course he haggled, as I knew he would. So I let him beat me down to four grand, which is the figure I had in mind in the first place. Even that was about a five hundred per cent mark-up. Anyway, while this tart of his was picking out the right cloth for the schmutter, we got talking, and he said as how he couldn't waste too much time on account of having a poker game spoiling that afternoon. I told him that I liked a hand of poker, and he invited me to join in. After that we met about once a week.'

'So you know Hubert Darke, Gavin Townsend and William Anderson.'

'Yeah, course I do. That was the regular little team. Sometimes there'd only be the four of us, on account of Foley being in some play. Other times Bill Anderson was away on business. Least that's what was said, but I reckon he was a bloody villain.'

'What makes you say that?' asked Dave.

Phillips gave Dave a crooked smile. 'Takes one to know one. All right, so I've had a run-in with the law a few times in me youth, but I'm as straight as a die now. But Anderson never let on where he was off to. Just disappeared for weeks on end and then come back as big as you like, usually with a suntan. Said something about being away on business, but never said exactly what this business was. Well, if you believe that load of old moody, you'll believe anything.' At this point the phone rang. Phillips picked up the receiver and dropped it back on the rest without answering. 'Only be some tart wanting a job as a model,' he said. 'As if I hire models all ready.'

'What about this argument that Foley had with Townsend?' I asked.

Phillips scoffed. 'Townsend accused Foley of cheating, daft bugger. I dunno why he never stayed shtum. He could've let it go and got it all back in a couple of hands. I'd've helped him if he'd asked. Like I said, I could have taken Foley over and over again, and he wouldn't know what had happened.'

'Was there a fight?' asked Dave.

'Nah. Mind you, that Townsend looks as though he could use his dukes. Professional yachtsman, I think he is. Some poofy job like that, any road.'

'Where were you on the night that Foley was murdered?' I asked. 'That was the fourth–fifth of February, a Monday into Tuesday.'

'Where I always am at night. Tucked up in bed with Miriam, of course. You can ask her, if you like. She's the one what answered the door.'

'I don't think that'll be necessary, Mr Phillips,' I said. I'd rapidly come to the conclusion that Dudley Phillips was one of that rare breed, an honest villain.

A few days later I received a report from Counter Terrorist Command giving the results of the fingerprint examination of Wisteria Cottage at Romford. It was no surprise that one set tallied with those we had taken from Jim Finch, now awaiting trial for attempted murder. The set of Robert Miles's prints taken from his body after his murder matched some that had been found at Wisteria Cottage and were also found at Debra Foley's Keycross Court apartment. But we knew from her letter that her brother had visited her there. None of the others found in the Romford house matched any held in the national fingerprint collection.

However, there was one significant revelation: one of the prints found at Wisteria Cottage matched those that Linda Mitchell, the senior forensic practitioner, told me had been found on Lancelot Foley's walking stick, abandoned in the roadworks excavation alongside his body. We didn't know who they belonged to, other than to say that they weren't Miles's or Finch's. But my guess was that they belonged to the elusive Colonel Anderson.

I passed a copy of the report, together with facsimiles of the actual prints, to Henri Deshayes in Paris.

Two hours later Henri called me back to say that one of the sets from Romford matched a set found in the room used by Anderson and Debra Foley at the Santa Barbara Hotel in the rue de Castiglione. But they weren't those of Debra Foley. Slowly, ever so slowly, the net was closing.

Despite having told Lee Jarvis, our resident computer expert, that we didn't need him any more, we called him back, as he was faster than Dave at interrogating Robert Miles's laptop, and he now came up with another piece of interesting information. It seemed that on widely spaced occasions Robert Miles had been paid substantial sums of money by Colonel William Anderson, presumably for mercenary operations or contract killings. The payments had been made from Anderson's bank in Newcastle, and Miles had saved the account details on his laptop. I presumed that having his account as far away as

Newcastle was another ploy on Anderson's part to spread details of his activities as widely as possible. But he hadn't counted on Miles doing a bit of self-preservation of his own.

I emailed this latest information to Henri Deshayes, just in case it might come in useful.

Minutes after receiving my email, Henri called me. 'These bank details could be very useful, 'Arry. I'm sure that Anderson will have to draw cash at some time. I've had one of my officers alert banks in the capital, and I've put half the Paris police force on standby in case he makes a withdrawal. If he does a withdrawal in Paris, I think we might just catch him.'

'I wish you luck, Henri.' I had grave doubts about the feasibility of that plan, having tried it myself in the past without any success. By the time that police arrived at the ATM, the suspect had long gone.

'I have also circulated to the press and television stations the computer generated likeness of Anderson prepared by the hotel staff,' said Henri, 'but whether it will do any good remains to be seen.'

I had no great faith in E-fit likenesses of a suspect. In my experience they created a vast number of telephone calls from helpful members of the public who'd seen the wanted individual everywhere between Land's End and John O'Groats. Each one had to be followed up, and usually all that they achieved was to waste police time when we could have been searching for a suspect using conventional methods. All we could really do now was to sit and wait.

And wait we did.

NINETEEN

B y the end of June, some four months after the killings, we were no further forward with our investigation into the murders of Lancelot Foley and Robert Miles. In the intervening period they had given way to other murders that had occurred and been solved, and the substantial paperwork that accompanies such enquiries had been consigned to the archives.

The coroner's inquest into those two deaths had been reopened on the eleventh of March, and the jury had concluded that both men had been murdered by 'person or persons unknown'. It was not a satisfactory outcome, but in the case of those two particular murders, it was the only verdict possible. However, the cases were still open; Scotland Yard never closes a murder enquiry until there is a conviction or the suspected murderer is dead.

A few days after Gail Sutton had left for Los Angeles, I'd received an email from her saying that she'd arrived safely and was having a great time. Another email had followed a month later, in which she said that her contract had been extended and she had put her Kingston town house on the market. So that, I concluded, was that.

In Paris, Commandant Henri Deshayes, in his shirtsleeves, sat in his office at the quai des Orfèvres dealing with the sort of administrative matters that are the lot of detectives worldwide. Although the murder of Debra Foley had faded from his mind, it was still the most important case remaining on the list of unsolved crimes. When it had occurred, back in February, the press had criticized the police and demanded action. Their strident headlines had screamed that it was nothing short of a national scandal that an English actress on holiday in Paris should have been brutally murdered. And they'd predicted that it would have a dire effect on the tourist trade.

But it had had no effect whatsoever, and other more vital
events had occurred to occupy the time and the computers of
the capital's newspaper reporters.

While Henri Deshayes was stuck in his office, in the tree-lined
avenue des Champs-Elysées the sun was shining, the cafes
were busy and harassed waiters struggled to keep up with the
demands of their international clientele.

At one of these cafes, within sight of the Arc de Triomphe,
a middle-aged man was sitting at an outside table enjoying
his mid-morning pastis and reading that day's edition of *Le
Figaro*. Occasionally, he would glance up to admire some of
the pretty young women who were strolling casually along
the crowded pavements. Little groups of tourists stopped to
read the menus displayed in frames outside, wondering what
the dishes were, and busily consulting pocket dictionaries and
currency converters. The man's name was Lucien Josse. Until
his recent retirement, he had been an officer of the *Police
Judiciare*, and had last reported for duty at *le trente-six* four
months ago, just after the murder of Debra Foley. Although
he was now a little fatter, his flowing moustaches perhaps a
little longer and spectacles had become a necessity, he had
lost none of his detective's acumen.

His attention was drawn to a man seated at a nearby table.
The man was about forty, well-built, clean-shaven and attired
in chinos, a white open-necked shirt and a blazer. Speaking
in English, he was engaged in an animated conversation on
his mobile phone. Not that that was unusual; at this time of
year, there were many English tourists in the capital.

Nevertheless, there was something about the man that interested Josse. It is never easy to quantify the instincts of a
detective. It is perhaps a skill honed over many years of dealing
with the criminal underclass, but it is not something that can
be taught because a detective would be unable to define it,
much less set it down in the form of a textbook. Suffice it to
say that Lucien Josse possessed it.

Wanting to study the man more closely, but without arousing
his suspicion, Josse turned in the man's direction, but signalled
to a waiter who was standing behind the Englishman. '*La*

même, m'sieur,' he said, holding up his empty pastis glass, but casting a covert glance at his suspect.

'*Oui, m'sieur,*' muttered the waiter, and went back into the cafe to fulfil Josse's order.

When Josse was still working at the quai des Orfèvres, he had studied and remembered the computer-generated likeness of the man suspected of Debra Foley's murder that had been prepared by the staff of the Santa Barbara Hotel in the rue de Castiglione. The original E-fit had shown the suspect with a beard and spectacles, but a computer artist at *le trente-six* had produced another version that took away the beard and glasses. Although by no means certain that this was the man seated at the next table, Josse was now sufficiently confident to warrant calling the police. He took out his mobile phone, dialled one-seven and waited for a reply. Turning his back to the man he suspected, he quietly explained who he was and that it was possible that Debra Foley's murderer was sitting at the next table to him.

Despite Josse having suggested that the police arrive discreetly, five minutes after he had made his call, two police cars arrived from the direction of the place de la Concorde, and another from the Arc de Triomphe. All three had sped to the scene with blue lights flashing and two-tone horns screaming. In the event, it merely served to alert Josse's suspect.

As the police alighted and moved rapidly towards the cafe where Josse was seated, the retired detective covertly indicated the suspect. The suspect, displaying some innate sense of danger and a degree of physical fitness, leaped from his seat and vaulted over the screen into the next cafe. Knocking over chairs and tables as he ran, he spilt wine and food over furious customers. Ignoring their protests, he vaulted a second screen into a third cafe and out into the street.

Continuing to run very fast, the suspect turned into the rue Washington. As he ran he pulled a key fob from his pocket and released the locks of a Jaguar car. Almost throwing himself behind the wheel, he started the engine, drove off at high speed and back into the avenue des Champs-Elysées.

The police, who had spent too long sitting in cars to be a

physical match for the fleeing suspect, had seen the man escape and immediately ran back to their cars.

Within minutes they were in pursuit, the radio operators in each of the cars sending somewhat garbled messages to the control room. Very soon other nearby police units were driving fast towards the avenue des Champs-Elysées. It seemed to the casual onlooker that suddenly the avenue was filled with blue lights and the air rent with screaming two-tones. One cynical bystander suggested to his girlfriend that yet another police drama was being filmed.

The Jaguar, by now doing sixty miles an hour, drove into the place de la Concorde, its tyres screeching, and narrowly avoided a Parisian taxi, the driver of which firmly believed he had a divine right of way, regardless of other road users, density of traffic or street signs.

By now some ten police cars were following, but others were waiting in side turnings across the capital, listening to directions from the leading police car, the officer in which was now in a position to give a lucid commentary on what was happening.

The suspect drove into the rue de Rivoli but took the turning too wide and scraped the side of a postal service van, leaving the driver screaming volubly at the departing Jaguar, now lacking one of its wing mirrors.

From there the suspect threw a sudden sharp left turn into the rue de Louvre, the wheels on one side of his car almost leaving the ground and forcing a cyclist to throw himself and his machine on to the pavement to avoid certain death. Weaving in and out of the traffic in his desperate attempt to escape, the fugitive was paying no heed to the danger either to himself or others using the road. Another screaming left turn took him into the rue Etienne Marcel, scaring the life out of a woman pushing a pram, until finally the speeding Jaguar entered the place des Victoires. But it was here that his luck finally ran out.

By now police cars marshalled from all over Paris had been joined by units of the national gendarmerie and were homing in on the suspect's vehicle. By some stroke of good fortune – the police subsequently claimed it was good tactical planning – police cars simultaneously entered the place des Victoires from each one of the several streets leading off it.

In his attempt to avoid one such car coming straight at him, intent on ramming him, the suspect veered sharply and collided with the ornate railings surrounding the statue of Louis XIV mounted on a horse.

Still unwilling to surrender, the suspect leaped from his car with a machine pistol in his hand and opened fire at the nearest policeman. The policeman fell to the ground, dead from a bullet in his heart. Two other officers were wounded before another police officer opened fire with his automatic SIG-Sauer Pro SP pistol, killing the suspect instantly.

TWENTY

Commandant Henri Deshayes was scratching his head through his thinning hair as he wondered at which of the nearby cafes he would have his lunch when the door of his office burst open.

'What is it, Lieppe?' asked Deshayes, irritated at the unheralded entry of one of his lieutenants. Here, at *le trente-six* his mood was entirely different from that which he had displayed when in the company of Kate Ebdon, the charming young London detective, or when he was talking to his friend Harry Brock. Deshayes was renowned at headquarters for the shortness of his temper and the sharpness of his tongue. 'Don't you ever knock, damn you?'

'I think we have Anderson, *Patron*,' said Marcel Lieppe, ignoring his chief's reproof. A brash, blond young detective, Lieppe regarded Deshayes and the commandant's contemporaries as dinosaurs. His attire was far too modern to be in keeping with what his superiors at *le trente-six* thought was suitable for an officer of the esteemed *Police Judiciare*. 'The uniformed police have shot a man in the place des Victoires, *Patron*. Apparently, Lucien Josse was sitting in a cafe in the avenue des Champs-Elysées enjoying a pastis and thought the man at the next table was Anderson. He said he recognized him from the E-fit likeness.'

'Josse was always a good detective,' said Deshayes, his irritability lessening slightly.

'He alerted the police and they gave chase,' continued Lieppe, 'but when the suspect was forced to stop in the place des Victoires he opened fire. It is unfortunate that one officer was killed and two wounded.'

'But is the *suspect* badly wounded?' demanded Deshayes, dismissing the death of the policeman as one of the misfortunes of the war against crime. 'And do up your tie properly, Lieppe!

As a matter of passing interest, do you happen to have discovered the man's name?' he asked sarcastically.

'He had an American passport in the name of Geoffrey Crawford.'

'Scotland Yard suggested that Anderson might be using another name. Have you spoken to him yet?'

'Unfortunately, he is dead, *Patron*.'

'It would have been useful had you told me that in the first place, Lieppe.'

'My apologies, *Patron*. But if it is Anderson, I don't understand why he was in a cafe and talking in English on his mobile phone. He must've known that all the Paris police were hunting for him. At the time of the murder there was enough about it in the papers, and his image was published everywhere, including on the television. And there was a "wanted" notice on the board outside this headquarters.'

'There is an English expression that seems to cover it, Lieppe,' said Deshayes. 'They call it "hiding in plain sight". You see,' he continued, 'contrary to what you may think, all the Paris police were *not* looking for him. They thought that a man who had committed a murder in the city would be absolutely mad to stay here. But that is what makes a clever criminal; one who does what the police are not expecting him to do. You would do well to study the criminal mind instead of worrying about what colour shirt you were going to wear. But if it is Anderson, his death will save the Republic the cost of a trial and the expense of keeping him in La Santé for the rest of his life.'

'But surely, *Patron*, he would have been sent to Clairvaux prison, not La Santé?'

Deshayes waved an impatient hand of dismissal. 'If it is Anderson who has been shot to death, the question won't arise, Lieppe. Where have they taken the body?'

'To the Georges-Pompidou Hospital.'

'Why did they take him there?'

Lieppe shrugged. 'I don't know, *Patron*.'

'Well, you should know,' snapped Deshayes. 'We shall go and take a look at him,' he added, putting on his jacket.

*   *   *

'I don't know him, Lieppe.' In the mortuary at the Georges-Pompidou Hospital in rue Leblanc, Deshayes stared down at the body of the man who had killed a Paris policeman and wounded two others. 'But I admit he looks like the image the staff at the hotel manufactured. I will telephone my good friend Chief Inspector Brock. Maybe he will know him. I shall ask him to come and take a look.'

I was sitting in my office, struggling to compose a report for the Crown Prosecution Service, when Henri's call came through. He described all that had happened that morning in the heart of the French capital and sounded very excited at the possibility that he may, at last, have found Debra Foley's killer. Already, the French police had compared the dead man's fingerprints with those found in the hotel room where Debra Foley had been killed, and they matched. Henri did seem a little disappointed though that the suspect was dead. I got the impression that he would've liked to obtain a confession from him, just to tie up the loose ends of the case.

'I will send you an email with all the details, 'Arry. And perhaps you will come over and take a look.'

'Thanks, Henri, I'll certainly do that, but may I ask a favour?'

'Anything, 'Arry, just name it.'

'Would you avoid mentioning in your email that the man is dead? Perhaps you would just say that you need my assistance in identifying him. Otherwise my boss will kick up a fuss about the cost of my going to Paris again.'

Deshayes emitted a bellow of laughter. 'OK, 'Arry, I know what you mean. I once had a boss like that. Expense claims were always a problem, and he would count the francs as if they were his own.' He paused. 'That's when we had francs, of course,' he added, a note of regret in his voice.

It was just after two o'clock when the email came through. I took a copy into the commander's office.

'I'd like permission for Sergeant Poole and I to go to Paris, sir. The *Police Judiciaire* has a man in custody who Commandant Deshayes believes is the killer of Debra Foley.'

'But why should that concern the Metropolitan Police?' The

commander looked up sharply. 'I can't really see that it's
necessary for you to go over there again. Surely you did
everything that was required the last time you were there back
in February.'

'I think that in the interests of international cooperation it's
vital, sir. It's also possible that the man has already confessed
to the murders of Lancelot Foley and Robert Miles. The
evidence certainly seems to indicate that he's the murderer.' I
laid the email on the commander's desk, but didn't mention
that the suspect was dead. Nor did I mention that fingerprint
comparison made the identification almost certain. 'That would
clear up a crime that's been on our books for far too long.'

'We shall see.' The commander took some time to read the
email, and then he read it again. 'Yes, I think you must go,
Mr Brock,' he said, making a rare decision without referring
to the DAC. 'When were you thinking of going?'

'Today, sir.'

It was about half-past six French time when we touched down
at Charles de Gaulle Airport. Henri Deshayes was waiting to
meet us.

'You have not brought the charming Kate with you, 'Arry.'
The tone of Deshayes' voice managed a combination of
disappointment and censure, all at once.

'She is very busy, Henri, but she sends you her love.' I wasn't
going to bring Kate Ebdon with me; not after the last time.

With the usual blue light and two-tones, Henri's car carved
its way through the evening traffic without delay.

Once at the Georges-Pompidou Hospital, Henri waved aside
the receptionist's objections about the lateness of the hour and
made straight for the mortuary.

'Ah, *M'sieur le Commandant.*' The mortuary attendant, an
effeminate middle-aged man, almost bowed when Deshayes
appeared. 'You wish to see the body again?'

'Yes,' said Deshayes. 'I want my friend from Scotland Yard
to examine it.'

'Examine it?' The attendant sounded surprised at Deshayes'
request. 'But already the post-mortem has been conducted,
M'sieur.'

'I know that,' said Deshayes sharply. 'I mean that he merely wishes to see the man's face.'

'Oh, I see.' With a flourish born of years of practice, the attendant flicked aside the shroud sufficient for me to see the face of the deceased gunman who had killed a French policeman and wounded two others before being killed himself.

'Do you know this man, 'Arry?'

I looked closely at the face, noting the cleft chin and the two-inch scar on the right-hand side. 'Well, I'll be damned,' I said, recognizing the man instantly, and turned to Dave Poole. 'D'you know him, Dave?'

'Well, of all the crafty conniving double-dealing deceiving bastards,' said Dave, shaking his head.

Deshayes looked at me, a puzzled expression on his face.

'I think Dave means that he recognizes him, Henri,' I said.

Dave and I had stayed overnight in Paris. That evening, Henri took us to dinner at a small restaurant patronized by the detectives of the *Police Judiciaire*. We swapped stories about various cases, and Henri regaled us with tales of how hard a life it was to be a detective in Paris. Dave had pulled out his handkerchief and dabbed at his eyes.

Before we left Charles de Gaulle airport the next day, Henri had given me a copy of the fingerprints taken from the dead man. When we arrived at Belgravia police station, I immediately sent them to Linda Mitchell by hand.

At two o'clock she came back with the answer I'd been hoping for. They were a match with the prints found on Lancelot Foley's walking stick.

'Got him,' I said. 'They always make at least one mistake, Dave.'

'Careless bastard,' said Dave. 'He deserved to be captured.'

The young woman ushered us into the sitting room and went in search of the lady of the house. A minute or two later she joined us.

'I'm Detective Chief Inspector Brock, and this is Detective Sergeant Poole, Mrs Tate.'

'You've been here before,' said the woman in the husky

voice I'd noticed the last time we were here. 'Have you come about my husband?'

'Yes, Mrs Tate, I have.' The occasion to which she referred was after businessman Charles Tate's Mercedes had been seen outside Keycross Court. When we'd interviewed him, he'd admitted visiting Debra Foley, alias Corinne Black, for sex. However, I now had good reason to believe that he was lying about it being a sexual encounter on that occasion. In fact, as it turned out, his entire life was a lie.

'But when you came to see him back in February I think it was, you said he had nothing to do with the enquiries you were making about . . .' Elizabeth Tate paused. 'Was it Keycross Court?' The woman obviously had keen recall.

'Yes, it was.'

'Please take a seat. I suppose you've come about the missing person report, then.'

'Missing person report?' I have to admit that her question caught me on the hop. 'I'm afraid I know nothing about any such report. Where did you file it and when?'

'At Kensington police station on Sunday the seventeenth of February.'

'You seem very sure of the date, Mrs Tate.' I wondered briefly why we'd not picked that up. Missing person reports are filed on the police national computer, but as we had not entered Charles Tate's name as a person of interest to us the report hadn't come to our notice. If only we'd been more suspicious of Tate when we'd interviewed him, we might have made an arrest much earlier and prevented the death of Debra Foley. But Tate had presented a convincingly plausible and confident character.

'One tends to remember the date when one's husband disappears, which was two days before that,' she said quite firmly. 'As a matter of interest, I also remember quite clearly the date that my first husband died.'

I was obviously wrong when, on the occasion of my last visit, I'd formed the opinion that Elizabeth Tate was a fragile and not very intelligent woman. But then I remembered the sharp way in which she'd upbraided her maid Hannah for making a mistake about the plural of "gentleman" and her failure to address her mistress correctly.

'I'm sorry to have to tell you that your husband is dead, Mrs Tate.'

'Oh! When did this happen?' Elizabeth Tate remained dry-eyed and showed no emotion at the news.

'Yesterday morning in Paris.'

'In Paris? What on earth was he doing there?'

It was difficult to know where to start. I was beginning to realize that this woman knew nothing of her husband's alter ego.

'Did you know that your husband had been in the army, Mrs Tate?' I said, easing my way into an explanation that wasn't easy, no matter how I tackled it.

'No, I didn't. I think you must be making a mistake, Mr Brock. He would have told me, surely?'

'His real name is William Anderson, and he was a captain in an infantry regiment, but was cashiered for striking a non-commissioned officer who was having an affair with Captain Anderson's wife. His first wife, of course.'

'You must have got this all wrong, Mr Brock,' said Elizabeth, but the shocked look on her face belied that statement. 'His name's Charles Tate, and he told me he'd never been married before.'

'I've no idea what happened to his first wife, I'm afraid,' I said, 'but I can assure you that he was William Anderson. We have made checks with the register of births, deaths and marriages, and his fingerprints bear out his true identity. There can be no mistake.'

Elizabeth Tate rose unsteadily to her feet. 'I think I need a drink,' she said. 'Can I get you gentlemen one?'

'No, thank you,' I said.

She crossed to a cabinet on the far side of her living room and poured herself a stiff neat whisky before sitting down again. 'Something tells me that there's worse to come.'

'Your husband was a mercenary, Mrs Tate, hiring himself out to fight other people's wars for them,' said Dave. 'From our enquiries, we've learned that he went to Africa and to the Middle East on several occasions and in one instance master-minded a coup d'état during which the then head of state was assassinated.'

'That would account for it,' said Elizabeth mildly.

'Account for what?' queried Dave.

'His absences abroad. But he told me that he was away on business conducting some complicated deals that sometimes took several weeks.'

'That was partly true, Mrs Tate,' said Dave. 'We know from our enquiries that your husband was running a successful import and export business. In fact, from our examination of his company's accounts, he was very successful. Did you know he also owned a house in Romford?'

'In Romford? He never mentioned it.'

'It was the centre of his mercenary operations,' Dave said.

'You see, Mrs Tate,' I continued, 'when I said that your husband died in Paris yesterday, I wasn't telling you the whole story. The fact of the matter is that he was shot dead by police, upon whom he had opened fire. As a result one policeman was killed and two others wounded.'

'I don't believe it.' Elizabeth Tate crossed to the cabinet a second time and poured herself another whisky. 'But why should he have shot at policemen in Paris? None of this is making any sense.'

'There is little doubt that he murdered three people: two in London and another in Paris. The police, both here and in France, had been searching for him for almost four months.'

Elizabeth drained her glass, but seemed remarkably tolerant to the effects of the alcohol she had just consumed. I could only assume that the shock she had experienced had prevented the onset of insobriety.

'But who were these people?'

'Lancelot Foley, the actor, was the first, Mrs Tate,' said Dave.

'I read about that, and there was quite a lot about it on television,' said Mrs Tate. 'I can't believe that Charles would have murdered him.'

'And then we believe him to have murdered a Robert Miles, one of his fellow mercenaries,' continued Dave, 'who coincidentally was Lancelot Foley's brother-in-law. The French police have positive evidence that he also murdered Debra Foley in a Paris hotel. She was the wife – or widow, I should say – of the actor Lancelot Foley and was herself an actress, but also a prostitute.'

'Your husband had first visited her under her other name of Corinne Black,' I said, taking up the story, 'who kept an apartment at Keycross Court for the express purpose of having sexual intercourse with her clients. Although your husband claimed to have met her there for sex, I now have doubts about the veracity of that statement.'

'So that's why you came here that day.' Elizabeth levelled an accusing glare in my direction. 'You thought he'd been having sex with this woman. But why did he have to murder these people?'

'Debra Foley had asked him to murder her husband, because she was afraid that her husband would tell people that she was a prostitute and thus ruin her acting career. But when she couldn't pay him for the hit, Lancelot Foley having left all his money to another woman, your husband took her to Paris and murdered her.'

'I'm finding it very difficult to take all this in. How did that finish up with Charles being shot by the police in Paris?'

'The French police had positive evidence that your husband was the killer of Debra Foley. As I said just now, your husband and Mrs Foley had been sharing a room at a hotel there, and that's where he murdered her. But months later he was recognized in the avenue des Champs Elysées by a retired French detective who alerted the police. A chase through Paris took place, but when your husband was cornered he attempted to shoot his way out.'

Elizabeth Tate leaned back against the cushions of the settee in which she was sitting and stared absently into her empty whisky glass. 'What am I going to tell my son?' she asked eventually.

'Was your husband the boy's father?' I asked.

'No,' she said. 'He was the son of my first marriage, but shortly after my first husband died I met and married Charles, or whatever his name is. It was more for the security than anything else.'

'Did your husband make a will?' asked Dave.

She stared blankly at Dave. 'I suppose so. I don't really know.'

'I should see a solicitor if I were you,' said Dave. 'We believe that your husband had a substantial bank account. If your solicitor gets in touch with the legal department at

Scotland Yard, someone there should be able to provide you
with the details.' Dave knew better than to give Elizabeth Tate
those details himself; the Commissioner took a poor view of
police officers becoming involved in civil matters.

I hadn't had an opportunity to see the commander when Dave
and I got back from Paris. Or to put it another way, I'd skilfully avoided seeing him. But now there was no alternative.

'Ah, you're back, Mr Brock. What have you to report?'

I started to give the commander a precis of all that had
taken place both here and in Paris, but he stopped me once it
became clear that I had succeeded in confusing him with the
complexities of the entire investigation.

'I think it would be better if you wrote your report, Mr
Brock, and then I'll be able to study it at length and be in a
position to make recommendations.'

'Good idea, sir,' I said. But I did wonder what sort of
recommendations he had in mind. Frankly, I couldn't see that
he could add anything to all that had happened. Unless he had
it in mind to put my name forward for a commendation. But
I somehow doubted that.

It was now six o'clock, which was the commander's going-
home time, and that was the most likely reason for him to
have curtailed my explanation.

I put my head round the door of the office occupied by Kate
Ebdon and Len Driscoll. Only Kate was there. I sat down in
the armchair adjacent to her desk.

'Everything turned out ripper, then, guv,' she said.

'Yes, it did.' And then, without a thought for the long-term
ramifications, I said, 'D'you fancy having dinner with me
tonight, Kate?'

'Is it the whole team, guv?' she asked, aware that celebra-
tions of that sort were often held after the successful conclusion
of a case.

'No, just you and me.'

Kate flashed me another of her conspiratorial smiles and
reached out to touch my hand. 'I'd like that very much . . .
Harry.'

9 MAR 2016

Lightning Source UK Ltd.
Milton Keynes UK
UKOW04f2218201115

263168UK00001B/5/P